D0627744

THE
LEGACY
OF
NOBODY
SMITH

a novel based on true events

FOREWORD BY
DR. TONY EVANS

THE
LEGACY
OF
NOBODY
SMITH

a novel based on true events

LESLIE BASIL PAYNE

THE LEGACY OF NOBODY SMITH
© 2016 by Leslie Basil Payne

All rights reserved. No part of this publication may be reproduced, stored in a retrieval system, or transmitted in any form or by any means – for example, electronic, photocopy, recording, film – without the prior written permission of the publisher. The only exception is brief quotations in printed reviews in a magazine, newspaper or on the Web.

Print ISBN: 978-0-692-63693-0
Kindle ISBN: 978-0-692-63475-2
Edited by Robin Patchen

Cover and Interior Design by Roseanna White Designs
Cover photo from www.iStockPhoto.com

Lyrics for the hymn "Come, Thou Fount of Every Blessing" are by Robert Robinson (1735-1790) and are found in the public domain.

Scripture quotations taken from the New American Standard Bible®, Copyright © 1960, 1962, 1963, 1968, 1971, 1972, 1973, 1975, 1977, 1995 by The Lockman Foundation Used by permission." (www.Lockman. org)

This novel is based, in part, upon actual persons and events. However, numerous characters and events portrayed and the names used herein are fictitious. Any similarity of those fictitious characters to the name, attributes, or actual background of any factual person, living or dead, or to any actual event or product is entirely coincidental and unintentional.

Printed in the United States of America
Published by Leslie Basil Payne

For anybody

who ever felt like

a nobody

FOREWORD
By Dr. Tony Evans

Nothing is more important than family. Family is the foundation of civilization. The saga of a nation is truly the saga of its families written large.

I am the beneficiary of a strong family legacy as I stand on the shoulders of a mother and father who passed on faith, virtue and values that I have had the privilege of passing on to my own children.

In addition, I, like many others, share the legacy of having been impacted by members of my extended family, like my Uncle Smitty. Uncle Smitty was my special uncle who reinforced what I was receiving at home from my own parents.

My mind is full of fond memories of the many family gatherings when we would go over to my aunt and uncle's house, and we would experience the joy of extended family fellowship. Uncle Smitty seems to have had a special connection with me. Maybe that was because he only had daughters, and I represented the son he never had, or maybe he saw something in me worth investing in, or maybe it was the premonition that God would call me into the ministry; and since he himself was a minister, I became an informal mentee. Whatever the case, Rev. Smitty Smith was a major part of my life and a major influence and model during my formative years.

Uncle Smitty's impact was not limited just to my early years however. Whenever I would go back to Baltimore to visit my parents, I would inevitably find myself visiting my aunt and uncle, or having them visit my home. Uncle Smitty would always be full of encouragement. He had either read one of my books or heard one of my messages on the radio, and this would lead to spiritual and theological discussions, always ending with an encouraging word.

When we boil life down to its core, we are ultimately left with what matters most, and what matters most are our relationships. It starts of course with our relationship with God through faith in Jesus Christ, and then extends to our relationship with family.

I am grateful to God for the life, love and ministry of Rev. Smitty Smith. He has left behind a legacy to be proud of. As you read this wonderful story based on the life of a great man, you will discover that God has indeed made and molded a quality man who not only lived His will, but who also transferred his God given strengths to those coming behind him, of which I am but one example.

Dr. Tony Evans

Dear Reader,

The book you hold is the result of an honor and a promise. One of the greatest honors of my life was when Smitty asked if he could tell me his story. Smitty, an older man of exceptional regard in his community, shared his life stories with me, the daughter of his best friend Irving.

Occasionally I'd ask him, "Do your grandchildren know this about you?"

He'd shake his head, "Naw, don't think so."

Together we set out to get his story on paper for his family. What unfolded was a story for a much wider audience. The basic facts are all true. The details surrounding the facts are the result of research and my imagination creating a fictional account of a real man's life.

Smitty's words deeply touched me and changed how I see the world. As he lay on his deathbed, I promised him I'd do everything I could to get his story told to others — to you. It's been an honor to craft his life into a novel, I only wish he saw the end result. Smitty's funeral was by far the largest memorial gathering I've ever witnessed. I sat there and wondered why out of all those many hundreds of people he chose me. The only answer I have is I'm "Irv's girl."

Another honor in this writing journey was receiving a foreword by Smitty's nephew Dr. Tony Evans. He graciously gifted me with words not because of anything I'd done, but because his mother and his aunt requested something for "Uncle Smitty's story."

Any attention this book receives is thanks to Dr. Evans' name. Any impact this book has is to God's glory.

Leslie Basil Payne

CHAPTER ONE

1939

Smitty, 15-years old

The movie Gone With the Wind *premiers in Atlanta*

Hitler announces plans to regulate
"the Jewish problem" in Europe

A gallon of gasoline costs 10¢

I became a nobody when I was fifteen years old.

It happened as fast as my cousin Reggie could talk.

"Your brothers and sisters aren't your blood. They weren't born to your parents."

I knew that.

"Smitty, you weren't born to your parents either," Reggie said with a sneer. "They're not really your mama and daddy."

My hands curled into tense fists ready to punch that fool in the gut. Reggie was my best friend, but I wanted to leave him doubled-over, gasping for air. The problem was, Reggie was built like an oak tree. I was a skinny sapling he could snap in two. And anyway, much as I wanted to pound him with my fists, my legs were suddenly too weak to stand. How could I make him pay for what he'd said?

Reggie shrugged. "It's the absolute truth, Smitty. I swear."

"You're talking like a fool." My heart pounded blood into my ears until they buzzed.

"I've never lied to you before, and I'm not lying now."

I turned and looked away from Reggie. Both sides of the street were lined with narrow row houses built side-by-side, sharing common walls. White marble steps, making a long row of oversized teeth, met each front door. To an outsider Sandtown was one of the poorest neighborhoods in Baltimore. For Reggie and me, it was home. Each house lived in by colored families like our own, poor but proud people. Just like the shared walls supported the house next door, folks in Sandtown leaned on and cared for each other.

Though the sun had set hours before, the day's heat lingered inside my family's house. As stars dotted the night sky, Reggie and I rested on the front steps and hoped for a breeze. People'd be lounging like this all over Baltimore tonight, the whites in their neighborhoods, and us in ours. I don't know what the whites discussed, but in Sandtown, folks caught up on the latest family news and shared neighborhood gossip. Parents and grandparents discussed how President Roosevelt was handling the hard times. But tonight none of that stuff mattered to me, not after what Reggie had said.

We sat, saying nothing. Had any of the neighbors overheard what Reggie blurted out? I forced open my fists and rubbed my palms back and forth on my pant legs. Then I traced the steps' edge with one of my hands. The marble felt solid and cool under my fingertips until my fingers tripped on a crack in the marble. Stupid steps. My sisters and I scrubbed them over and over again, because Daddy liked it that way. And the dumb things were falling apart.

Reggie glanced in my direction with a smug expression. At nineteen, looking smug came easy to him. I was fifteen, struggling to breathe, fighting back tears.

"Well, say something, man. You'll get used to it all."

I stood and shoved my hands deep into my pants' pockets. "Not going to get used to it. You're lying."

The meaning behind Reggie's words smothered me more than the heavy August humidity. I couldn't move, so I stood there like a fool. A sour taste burned the back of my throat. If I didn't escape soon, I'd probably puke all over the steps my sisters had scrubbed that morning. So I gathered my strength, turned my back on Reggie and walked down the street.

All my life I'd been happy, like my daddy. Seems neither of us ever met a stranger, always made friends with folks, and everyone liked us back. When I was a boy, people in the neighborhood smiled at how I followed my daddy around like a shadow. Even now, every Saturday the two of us walked to Druid Hill Park for the neighborhood baseball games.

But this news from Reggie changed everything. Now, I wasn't sure of anything. Mama and Daddy had to be my real parents, they just had to be. I wasn't like the other kids at home. Daddy always said he and I were blood. He wasn't related to all the other kids—that was no secret—but he was to me.

He was my father.

Mama was my mother.

Could Reggie's words be true? They whispered of possibilities and shameful secrets, things folks didn't talk about in mixed company. The mere suggestion made my soul want to crawl down deep into my pockets and hide inside my fists. It could not be.

"Hey Smitty."

A friend sitting on his front step waved at me. I ignored him and walked faster to avoid conversation. I turned the corner and ducked into an alley.

A rusty tin can lay on the ground next to some crumpled up newspaper. I stopped and stared for a long time at that worthless can. Then I kicked it, followed it for a few steps, and kicked it again. Each time my shoe hit that can, it bounced down the street and filled the night air with an echoing sound.

A train whistle blew its haunting cry. The night seemed so full of empty sounds. Hollow cans and lonely trains.

I kicked the tin can again, harder this time.

I was that old tin can. And Reggie had pried me open, forced his way into the deepest part of me, and threatened to rip out everything that filled me up. I was only worth kicking.

How could I return home, see my parents, and pretend like everything was the same? Instead, I dodged neighbors all night and wandered vacant streets and alleyways.

I kicked that worthless can as I walked.

With every step, Reggie's words bounced around inside my head.

That was the night I became a nobody.

CHAPTER TWO

1930

Smitty, six-years old

First red & green traffic lights installed in Manhattan

Average cost to rent a house: $15 per month

As the last spoonful of oatmeal slid down my throat, I knew what I had to do.

"Mama, I'm too sick to go to the doctor." I felt a drop of milk on the corner of my mouth and wiped it with the back of my sleeve. "My stomach hurts."

"Use your napkin, Smitty." Mama slid the square piece of cloth closer to me. She didn't look worried about me being sick.

"Did you hear me, Mama?"

"I heard you, son. Now take your bowl into the kitchen. We need to catch the next streetcar."

"The streetcar? We're taking the streetcar to the doctor's?" The streetcar cost money, so we never rode it.

"Mmm-hmm." Mama nodded as I followed her into the kitchen, carrying my empty bowl and spoon.

I stood on my toes and used my right hand to place the

bowl on the counter beside the sink. My left arm, the lame, bent one, hung by my side and waited for a job it could do. It ached bad this morning, reminding me of what Daddy had told me last night, that a special doctor was going to look at my arm. He said the doctor might operate, and my arm would hurt a lot more than usual, but later it would feel better and be able to straighten out. I liked the *straighten out* part of what Daddy said. I didn't like the *hurt more* part. As I remembered the conversation with Daddy, my stomach started to hurt again.

Mama pulled her apron over her head, folded it neatly, and placed it on the kitchen counter. "You go get your jacket now, son. I was thinking maybe you could carry the coins to pay for the streetcar."

Last night, when I told Daddy I didn't want to see the doctor, he asked me to be brave. He forgot to mention about the streetcar. If I got to carry the coins and ride the streetcar, I thought maybe my stomach and I could be brave. I could at least try.

I'd do anything for my daddy.

◆

The tall, white doctor wore a white jacket and patted the top of a wooden table. "Sit yourself up here, young man."

I glanced up at Mama, because if I perched myself on a table at home, I'd have my bottom walloped.

Mama bobbed her head up and down. "It's all right, son. Do what the doctor tells you to do." She reached for my hand and helped me step on a stepstool. I climbed atop the table.

The doctor talked for a while as I waited, swinging my legs back and forth, back and forth. So far I hadn't had an operation, and my arm hurt about the same as it had that morning. So far, so good.

I looked down and admired my new Sunday shoes. Before I got them, they were Reggie's. He was ten years old. Before the shoes belonged to Reggie, they were his older brother's. Even though I was six, I felt older with shoes that used to be worn by a twelve-year-old and a ten-year-old. They were too big and had a hole in one sole, but I didn't care. They were better than my old Sunday shoes, which we gave to a boy at church.

The night before during dinner, when Daddy told me about going to see the doctor, he said I had to dress proper for the occasion. "The Smith family does not accept charity." He nodded at me from where he sat at the head of the table. "You wear your best clothes, so the doctor can see he'll be paid soon as we have the money."

Even though my new shoes were really for Sunday school and church, here I was wearing them on a Thursday. It made me feel important. I sat and watched the shoelace on my right foot flop forward and flip back with each swing of my leg. The lace on my left shoe was stubby, tied in a knot long before it got near the top lace holes. There wasn't enough lace on that shoe to flip or to flop. That's why I concentrated on my right shoelace.

"Smitty, stop your swinging now." Mama gave me *the look*. My legs stopped before she finished her sentence. "You do what Dr. Kidlowski tells you to do."

It seemed risky, but I did what the doctor instructed. And that's how I ended up sticking my tongue out at a white man. If I'd done that in public, they would've arrested me and thrown me in jail 'til I rotted and died. After I stowed my tongue back where it belonged, the doctor pulled a small hammer with rubber on the top from his pocket and tapped on my knee. My leg kicked out in front of me like it had a mind of its own. He did the same thing to my other knee, and I almost kicked him. If I kicked him, I was sure I'd *really* end up in jail, even though I didn't mean to and he started the whole thing. But each time, thank you sweet Jesus, my leg missed the doctor by an inch. I wondered if I went to jail, would I still have an operation on my arm? My stomach started to hurt again.

I didn't know what all this kicking and looking down my throat had to do with my lame arm. Finally, after he poked around some more, the doctor examined both my arms. He didn't look too long at my right arm, but the left one he kept in his hands. He stroked and pressed the soft, brown cauliflower-looking things that grew along the inside of my elbow. They'd been there as long as I could remember.

He studied my arm for a long time and touched it all over. It didn't hurt any worse until he pulled up on my wrist and tried to straighten it. I shrieked! And then I started to cry. I swiped my right sleeve across my wet face and glared at the stupid doctor. He should have known better. The whole reason we were there was because my arm couldn't straighten out.

And then I realized the pain in my bad arm was nothing compared to what I feared might happen. Here I had hollered at the white doctor after I'd stuck out my tongue and almost kicked him. I was doomed. Mama wiped my nose with her handkerchief and smiled at me. That made me feel better, even though I was still scared about being thrown in jail. Maybe she'd visit.

The doctor scribbled something on a piece of paper, his brow all wrinkled up like my big brother Clifton's did when he tried to write his letters.

The doctor looked up from his paper. "Mrs. Smith, your

son's arm..."

Mama stood there barely moving, her gloved hands tightly holding her purse. She nodded her head and looked down at the floor as the doctor talked.

"Yes, sir," she said softly. She looked so pretty all dressed up in her Sunday dress. My mama was beautiful, that's what Daddy and I always said.

"No sir." She shook her head and bit her bottom lip. I didn't understand the words the doctor used. Maybe she didn't either.

"Of course not, sir." Mama said after the doctor said a whole lot of things.

How would I pass my time in jail? Maybe Mama would bring me some of her buttermilk biscuits and a bit of jelly. But what if part of the punishment of jail is, you have to eat dry biscuits? My stomach growled. I folded my arms over my belt.

I looked up at Mama, who was still listening to the doctor. Even though I didn't like how the doctor made my arm hurt, I liked being with Mama and not having to share her with my brothers and sisters. I was special from the others. None of them were born to Mama and Daddy, but I was. "Blood born," Daddy called it. I was their very own son. I didn't mind sharing my parents with the others. We were a family, but today, it was nice to have Mama all to myself.

She reached out and wrapped her plump fingers around my little ones. She gently tugged on my arm. Worries about jail and operations melted away when I looked up at her round face, the color of dark, rich coffee.

She smiled, glanced in the doctor's direction, and then back at me. "Thank you so much, Dr. Kidlowski. We really do thank you, sir."

Mama tugged on my arm again and nodded her head

for me to get down off the table. I pulled my hand away from hers. I jumped off the table all the way to the floor and landed on two feet with hardly a wobble.

"Smitty, tell the good doctor thank you."

My head and neck bent way back as I gazed up into the soft blue eyes of the white doctor with yellow hair. I figured he was the smartest man in the world, being a doctor and all. Maybe even as smart as Frederick Douglas.

"Thank you, Dr. Kidlowski." My collar choked me. Suddenly, I realized I probably wasn't supposed to look directly into the eyes of the doctor, so I looked down at my shoes and could breathe again.

When we stepped out of the doctor's office and into the hallway, Mama leaned against the wall and let out a big, long sigh. She adjusted her white gloves and switched her purse from one hand to the other before looking up and down the hallway. "Now, which way was out?"

We stood there and thought about it. I hoped Mama was thinking about it more than me. I had started thinking again about my operation, wondering when it was going to happen. After a few minutes, a tall, white lady in a nurse's uniform came down the hall. Shiny, soft curls of silky brown hair framed her face. Her long lashes fluttered over deep brown eyes. She had perfect red lips, like a movie star I saw once in a magazine. She was the prettiest white lady I had ever seen in real life. I tried not to stare, but somehow her prettiness made me look more.

"Excuse me, miss." Mama spoke gently and smiled as the woman approached.

The lady stopped. Her perfect red lips twisted and puckered. Maybe she was sucking on a lemon drop candy and that's why she couldn't say anything. Her nose went up in the air and she made a face like something smelled.

Mama cleared her throat and looked down at her purse. "Sorry to be trouble, miss, but which way to leave the building?"

The lady looked cross and muttered about something being dirty.

"That way." She pointed and walked away fast as she could until she turned the corner at the end of the hall.

"Thank you, so kindly," my mama called after her.

Mama pressed her lips together, pulled her shoulders back, and tilted her chin toward the ceiling. "Come on, Smitty. We're done here."

"Why was she so cross, Mama? Did we do something wrong?"

"Not a thing, son. She's got the ugliness. Nothing for you to be concerned about."

How could such a pretty lady be ugly? Mama and Daddy talked about the ugliness sometimes, but I didn't really understand what it meant. One time I asked Daddy, and he said it wasn't something for little boys to worry about, that I'd learn soon enough. I guess I was late in learning, because I still didn't know.

Mama and I didn't talk as we walked the long hallway of the Harriet Lane Home for Invalid Children. The floor was a checkerboard of faded black and white tiles that seemed worn and weary from being walked on. If I were a floor tile, I'd get tired of people walking on me. The hallways smelled tangy. Mama had told me it was antiseptic. Whatever it was, when we'd first come in the building, I'd held my nose, and I sort of wanted to do it again. But I didn't, because I remembered Mama's scolding.

"James Henry Smith, you take your fingers off your nose. That's impolite."

"But it stinks." I shouldn't have argued. When she used

my full name, she meant business.

My skinny six-year-old legs worked to keep up with Mama's quick pace. She sure could move when she wanted to, even though she was short and round, especially next to Daddy. Together, we pushed our weight against the heavy glass doors and stepped out from the invisible antiseptic smells into Baltimore's clear summer sunshine. My eyes squinted, and I let the sun kiss my eyelids as the fresh air cleaned out my nose. I rubbed it to help the process.

Across the manicured lawn stood the building that looked like a castle but was really the Johns Hopkins Hospital. Folks bragged that it was one of the best hospitals that ever was, but it wasn't a place for colored boys like me. Mama had told me on the way in that Harriet Lane's Home for Invalid Children was part of Johns Hopkins, even though it was a different building. Kids who were seriously ill stayed at Harriet Lane's, and even colored kids like me were sometimes helped there. Whoever Harriet Lane was, she must have been very kind, just like my mother.

At the top of the steps, I slid my hand into Mama's. I jumped down a step and waited for her as she took her time. I jumped. She stepped. I jumped. She stepped.

"Mama, does that doctor play music?"

"Well, I don't know."

I jumped two steps at the same time. I was getting good at this. When Mama got to where I was, I asked, "Why'd he keep talking about banjos?"

Mama laughed long and loud. Daddy said her laugh sounded like a waterfall of liquid sunshine. "Not banjos, Smitty, hemangiomas. That's a big name for the tumors on your arm. He-man-gi-o-ma." She pronounced the word again slowly and had me mimic her. Mama and Daddy were always having me repeat words after them. They told me I was so bright, I needed to learn lots of words, but sometimes I got tired of it.

One time I told Daddy, "When you make me repeat words after you, I feel like a parrot."

Daddy's deep voice boomed, "At least you'll be an intelligent parrot and not a fool-headed one."

After that, I didn't grumble anymore. Instead, I decided that one day, I'd be as brilliant as Frederick Douglass. So I repeated the big word that sounded like banjos and jumped down the last two steps.

Mama continued. "Hemangiomas mostly shrivel up and disappear as a child matures. For some reason, yours are doing the exact opposite."

My left arm, deep brown in color, was always bent at the elbow where the spongy masses grew. When I stood still and looked at it, it ached more than usual. Sometimes it got real bad. Mostly, I ignored it.

"When you're older, Smitty, the doctor might operate, make those hemangiomas go away. Right now, you're too young. We'll wait awhile."

"When is older, Mama? How old will I be?"

Mama didn't hear me because she was busy talking to Jesus. When she finished she tugged on her dress, got things arranged the way she liked, and softly exhaled, "Thank you, sweet Jesus."

Mama had conversations with Jesus like she could see him. She said he was always beside us, so we might as well talk to him.

On Sundays we had devotions during Sunday school and prayed to Jesus as a congregation in church on Sunday mornings and Sunday nights. We were back at it again on Wednesday evenings. And I knelt and prayed every night before I crawled into bed. I didn't mind praying to Jesus, because I liked to talk. In fact, I ran my mouth so much at school, it got me in trouble almost every day. But for all the talking to Jesus I did, I didn't hear much back from him. Maybe he was busy listening to everybody else, or maybe he was the quiet sort. Whatever the case, Mama talked out loud to him a lot.

A streetcar rang its bell from the next block over.

"Are we getting on the streetcar now?"

"First, let's walk a ways, and if I have my directions right, you'll see your hard-working hero."

"Daddy!" My heart about exploded with excitement as I bounced up and down on my toes. Daddy left for his job so early, the sun wasn't awake. Most days, I didn't see him until dinnertime. This was a big event.

"That's right, son. We'll mosey on past the construction site. If we get the opportunity, we'll wave and holler hello, tell Daddy you'll have the operation when you're older. Then we'll ride the streetcar on home."

"When is older, Mama?" I slipped my hand back in hers. "When will I have the operation?"

"Not this year."

"Next year?"

"Maybe."

My stomach felt funny again.

"Or maybe the year after next." Mama looked at me and smiled. "So long as you don't grow too fast, Smitty, we'll have plenty of time to save money to pay the doctor."

I nodded my head wisely like Daddy sometimes did. "Mama, I'll grow as slow as I can."

<hr />

Daddy sat at the head of the dining room table for all our meals. The kitchen was too small for the whole family and a table, so Mama did the cooking in the kitchen. We did the eating in the dining room.

My older brother Richard sat to Daddy's left. Clifton, the oldest in the family, was on Daddy's right, and I perched next to Clifton. When Ruby, Mary, and Mama came in, we would all be at the table. So would the food.

"Daddy, is something wrong?" Richard asked.

I looked at our father. He held an envelope in one of his big calloused hands and a letter in the other. He didn't answer Richard, just gazed off toward the kitchen. I looked at Richard, who stared at Daddy.

The door swung open. Mama came in smiling, carrying a big platter of steaming hot fried chicken.

She looked up, met Daddy's gaze, and stopped. For a moment, she simply stood there. "Well?"

Daddy nodded. "It's as I thought."

"Oh, Charlie." Mama sighed. Without the smile on her face, she looked tired.

"Mmm-hmm." Daddy replied. They loved each other so much and knew each other so well, sometimes it was like they had their own secret language.

When Mama saw me already seated at the table, she brightened. "Smitty, your favorite dinner tonight, fried chicken." She placed the platter edged with little flowers and heavy with chicken on the table. This platter had only one chip. It was Mama's special occasion plate. We were still celebrating my not having an operation. At least not this year.

Mary came in with a bowl of greens, put it on the table, and took her seat next to Richard. Mary was eight years old and thought she was in charge of everything and everybody.

The scent of Mama's fried chicken set my mouth to watering. My tongue slowly circled around on my lips. It knew what was coming, and it couldn't keep still. I tilted my chair forward and stretched out my arm. Like an eagle on the hunt, my hand hovered in the air above the platter. My fingers flexed, anxious to swoop down and grab a juicy chicken leg.

"Smitty, you know better than that." Daddy's deep voice shattered my concentration.

I panicked.

He was right, I knew the rules, and there was my hand, in flight above the fried chicken before Mama sat down or Daddy said the blessing. I had to think fast, so I fanned the air over the chicken.

"I'm keeping the flies off it, Daddy." I used my most convincing tone of voice. "Can't have flies landing on Mama's delicious fried chicken."

Daddy wrinkled his forehead. His eyebrows crept closer together and he shook his head.

I fanned faster to prove my point.

"There aren't any flies in here, Smitty." Mary said. My blabbermouth sister. My other sister, Ruby, would have smiled and said I was doing something nice. She was thirteen and really Mama's niece, but to me, she was my oldest sister. Ruby was as gentle as Mary was bossy.

I stopped fanning long enough to look Mary in the eye. "There sure are flies around here. And I hope a big, fat fly lands on your chicken as you take a bite. Yum-yum! You'll be eating flies!" I laughed, imagining Mary as she picked a fly wing out from between her front teeth.

"Sit down and hush, Smitty," Daddy warned from the head of the table.

I glared at Mary then sat and studied the nicks in the

wooden tabletop. Heat crept up the back of my neck. I hoped a whole Egyptian-style-curse swarm of flies would whir their way into the dining room and land on Mary's plate. Even one or two would do.

Ruby came into the dining room carrying a pitcher of water. Mama followed with a bowl of mashed potatoes. As she approached the table, she tripped and caught her step. Her lips pressed together tightly as she placed the bowl on the table.

"That ol' piece of linoleum has gotten so ragged, and I keep forgetting to step up over it."

Each year at Christmas and Easter, if we had the money, Daddy bought Mama two big square pieces of linoleum flooring, one piece for the center of the dining room floor, and one for the kitchen. We didn't have money to buy rugs like Daddy wanted to, but Mama said linoleum squares were the next best thing. She said they were easier to keep clean than the wood floor, plus they looked special.

Daddy looked down at the table and cleared his throat. "We need to save a little more money, Ola, then I'll buy you new floor pieces."

"Oh Charlie, I'm only complaining because I'm tired after a long day. We don't need new linoleum, especially after that letter." She looked sad for a moment, then smiled at Daddy like he was the greatest man in the world. "You, the Good Lord, and our kids provide everything we need for this family. We're getting by fine."

"Just the same, one day I'm going to buy you new floor pieces." Daddy unfolded a linen napkin and smoothed it across his lap. He always insisted on fine napkins. "Let us pray."

We took each other's hands and bowed our heads as the fried chicken teased us with its glorious scent.

"Lord, these are some perilous days we're living in, so I'm asking you to bless the Army, the Navy..."

Here we go again. Daddy fancied himself a man of prayer. He would pray for us, for all the neighbors on our street, for folks on the next block, across the country, and around the world. I didn't know if I could make it through another one of Daddy's prayers without dying of starvation, right there with a platter of fried chicken within arm's reach. I sighed like a six-year old bearing a heavy burden. Would sighing during the blessing get me in trouble?

I opened my eyes and looked around the table. Mama stared at me with the one-eyed version of *the look.* Mary kicked my leg under the table. She was the daughter of one of Mama's relatives, but we'd been together my entire life, raised as brother and sister.

Across the table, Richard looked up, smiled, and winked at me. In his early twenties, he wasn't scared of Mary or anyone else in the whole wide world. He'd taught me my ABC's and how to write my name by the time I was five-years old. Richard thought I was smart, and the way he said it made me want to be smart. He motioned for me to bow my head again. I squeezed my eyes shut and bowed my head so low, it almost touched the table.

Daddy prayed on, despite Mary and me squirming in our chairs until they squeaked. Even though he had recited a long list of people who needed God's blessing, he kept on going.

"We ask you to bless those who keep us safe here at home, the police department and the fire department. Be with our beloved preacher, church family, and all people everywhere going through these hard times..."

My mind wandered until I finally heard, "In your Son's powerful and holy name we pray, Amen."

"Amen," the family echoed.

I held my breath as I slowly opened my eyes, afraid of what I'd find. Sure enough, the fried chicken was no longer steaming. It looked as cold as the mashed potatoes and greens. We all knew better than to complain. But I decided when I was grown up and had a wife and children sitting at my table, I'd pray fast. *Thank you, Jesus, Amen!* Get right to the point, that's what I would do.

Daddy motioned for Mama to begin. She always dished up first, followed by Daddy. Next, the plates were passed from oldest to youngest, which meant I was always last.

"Pop?" Clifton was older than Richard, but he was shy on account of not being smart.

"Yes, son."

"Usually, we get a letter, and you read it to us. Are you going to read us that letter?" Clifton pointed to the letter, which dangled dangerously over the edge of the table, like it was ready to jump to the floor.

Daddy's shoulders sunk. He was quiet for a moment, studying his plate of untouched food. No one said a word.

Richard stopped dishing out his greens. "Dad?"

Daddy looked up, cleared his throat, and sat up straighter. He looked at Mama. "The children need to know, Ola. They're in this, too."

Mama bit her bottom lip and looked away.

"This letter," Daddy began "is about our home. The landlord has decided to raise our rent, again."

Richard groaned and put down the bowl of greens. Clifton shook his head, pushed back his chair, and crossed his arms over his chest.

"I'm sorry to have to share this with you, especially you two, Clifton and Richard. I know you're working hard, same as me, and we barely make rent as it is."

"I'll get a job cleaning house," Mama announced.

"Now Ola, you already spend much of your day ironing all the pieces brought in for you to press."

"I'll be a maid during the day and iron during the night while everyone's asleep. Simple as that."

Daddy smiled. "You will not, darling. I need you in bed to keep me warm."

Clifton and Richard laughed.

Mama giggled and looked away. "Oh, Charlie."

I didn't know what was funny but laughed, anyway.

Daddy smiled at Mama. "I'll see about hustling up more work on Saturdays. Ruby and Mary, you need to pick up some work after school. It's been a while since you all added to the pot."

Ruby perked up. "I know, Daddy. Mary and I can get work erasing books when school starts again."

Clifton turned toward Ruby. "What's erasing?"

As Ruby took a breath to answer, Mary jumped in. "We erase the pencil marks in the schoolbooks from the white schools. When a book is erased clean, it's used in the colored schools. Last time, we got paid three cents a page. It might even be more by now."

"I can do that, too, Daddy." I was eager to do my part. "I can erase."

"No, you can't." Mary declared. "You're too little. Anyway, the teacher likes girls to erase, because they're more careful. The boys tear the pages."

I slumped in my chair.

Clifton spoke up. "What happens if we don't make the rent?"

Daddy looked at Mama, so I did too. Her eyes looked moist.

"If we are more than three months behind in our rent,

we have to move out. Simple as that. We're already behind one month." Through the open window in the living room, I heard familiar voices. An evening game of "Kick the Can" had started without me.

I remembered my friend Enoch. He was really good at playing "Kick the Can," until his family moved away from our neighborhood. "Did Enoch's family leave Sandtown because they couldn't pay rent?"

Mama nodded. "Yes. Saddest thing I ever did see when the Tucker family left Sandtown pulling their belongings in the children's wagons and a wheelbarrow."

We didn't have a wagon or a wheelbarrow.

"Where'd they go, Mama?" Ruby asked. "Lucy said she'd write to me, but I've never gotten a letter from her."

"They were headed to family living north of Baltimore. Don't know if they settled there or not." Mama looked up at Daddy, her eyebrows raised.

"Listen you all, we will be fine. We simply need to pull together as a family and work hard. A little hard work never hurt nobody, and you all have been working since you could walk." Daddy gave a big smile. "You hear me, Clifton?"

"Yes, sir." Clifton unfolded his arms and pulled his chair closer to the table.

"We can't do anything about the rent right now. And we need to eat up, since your Mama did all this beautiful cooking." He clapped his hands together and rubbed them back and forth with enthusiasm. "Let's get to it."

We all agreed and I waited for the food to get to me.

Our dining room was the same size and shape as all the other dining rooms in the row houses that lined Mount Street. I knew that because I'd been in many of the other houses when I did church visitation with Daddy. The kitchens were at the back of the houses, closest to the alley.

The dining rooms led into the living rooms, where there were windows that faced the street. The bedrooms were all upstairs, and wood stoves in the kitchens and dining rooms provided heat.

Our furniture was sparse, well-worn, and mismatched, but like Daddy and Mama said, it did the job. The centerpiece of pride in the living room was the old upright player piano. Daddy did some work for a man who couldn't pay with cash, but gave him a piano instead. My parents were proud of our home and took good care of it. Every day, Mama swept the wooden floors. And every day except Sundays, Daddy made sure we kids scrubbed the front marble steps with pumice, sand, and water. The rest of Baltimore scrubbed their marble steps once a week on Saturdays, but that wasn't good enough for Daddy 'cause Mama called the steps *elegant*, which I figured meant really pretty.

One time when Daddy was reminding me the right way to scrub the steps, I asked, "Why do we even scrub our steps? We're just going to walk on them again soon as they're dry."

"Son, you ever hear of a town called Cockeysville?"

"No sir." I sprinkled sand on the bottom step.

"Cockeysville is a fair distance from Sandtown, about twenty miles, I'd say. Out there's a big quarry where workers dug out this marble to build the steps of Baltimore's homes." Daddy worked the pumice in circles on the top step. "And do you know what else they built with this very same marble?"

"No."

"No, what?" Daddy prompted.

"No, *sir*."

"The marble used to build our front steps was the same marble used to build the Washington Monument in Washington, D.C."

"Oh." I wasn't exactly sure what a monument was, but

I knew Washington D.C. was a mighty important place.

"It was also used to construct sections of the United States Capitol Building. That's where the leaders of our country work."

I wondered if those leaders had to scrub the steps of the Capitol Building like I had to clean the steps to our house.

"So Smitty, if this same stone was used for our nation's capitol, seems to me we should make extra effort to scrub off the soot and keep our steps clean."

"Yes sir." I saw his point, but I'd agree even more when it was my sisters' turn to scrub.

The sound of Mama using the big spoon to scrape out the last of the mashed potatoes from the bowl and onto my plate brought my concentration back to dinner. I'd never again complain about having to scrub the steps so long as we didn't have to leave our home.

"We also have some new family goals," Daddy explained. It looked like everyone but me had been listening. "Going to have a new coffee can labeled 'Operation.'"

"What for?" Ruby asked.

"Smitty and I went to the doctor today. Real nice man, wasn't he?" Mama glanced my way. "He's going to operate on Smitty's arms when he gets older. Between the rent and an operation in our future, we need to save every nickel we can."

"We will, Mama." My brothers and sisters murmured their approval. Clifton smiled, reached over, and messed with my hair. Maybe an operation wouldn't be so bad.

Mama glanced over at Richard. "How's your job at Stewart's coming along, son?"

"Still going good." Richard was the first colored elevator operator at Stewart's Department Store. Part of the reason he got the job was because of his light skin color and good hair. "Yesterday Missus Feldman—she's married to the store manager—she left with so many shopping bags of clothing, she could barely carry them. Lord have mercy, some of those white women spend money like they have more than they know what to do with."

Mama finally passed me the chicken. "Here you go, Smitty."

"Don't mind if I do."

Mama chuckled at my pet phrase as she helped me dish up a juicy drumstick onto my plate.

"Don't you bellyache about those white folks." Mama put the empty platter on the table. "All their shopping is what gives you a job."

"That's right, son," Daddy agreed. "Are you keeping your uniform hat on? You can't afford any more reprimands. Lord knows, we need your job now more than ever."

"Yes sir." Richard's eyes danced around like Mary's did when she was lying, but nobody else seemed to notice. Richard saw me watching him and winked. I liked it when he trusted me with his secrets.

Richard was tall, handsome and my brother in all the ways that mattered. His father was a white doctor over on the other side of Baltimore. And Richard's mother was the colored housekeeper who worked in the doctor's house. Even though she wanted to, she couldn't keep Richard once he was born. That's how Daddy and Mama got him. They promised they would love him as their own, and they did. Richard had buttermilk-colored skin. His hair was soft, silky, and curled around his face. If I had good hair like my big brother, I wouldn't wear my hat, either.

"Richard's vain about his hair." Mary piped up, her voice going up and down the scale. "Isn't vanity a sin, Mama?"

Mama shook her head. "Hush up and mind your own

business, Mary."

I smiled. Mary stuck her tongue out at me when no one was looking.

"It's true, Richard, you could pass," Ruby added in her soft, tender voice.

"Nobody here needs to be pretending they're someone they're not," Daddy said. "No one needs to pass for white."

Richard gulped down his mouthful of food. "But it sure is a tough world for a colored man, Daddy."

Clifton nodded in silent agreement. Clifton was somehow related to Mama, but I forgot the details. When Richard taught me my ABC's, he showed Clifton at the same time, but he had trouble learning. Clifton never could write much more than his name and his numbers. When he was studying a newspaper, I knew he was only looking at the pictures, but I never let on. I loved Clifton, and he loved me back.

Daddy cleared his throat and set down his fork. "Now you all listen to me." He seemed to stare each of us in the eye, all at the same time. "True enough, sometimes this world isn't so friendly for us coloreds. At times, it can be downright ugly. But the Lord has never made a mistake, and it was no slip-up that you were born colored." He was silent for a moment then continued as he pointed at each of his children. "Every one of you has dignity and a purpose, simply because you are a child of God. Your job is to work hard and reach for opportunities to improve yourselves, so you can do your best for God's glory. It's not always going to be so difficult for colored folks."

Clifton squinted and shook his head. "How do you know, Daddy?"

"We've come a long way even in my lifetime, Clifton." Daddy leaned forward. "You all hear me on this, and don't you forget it. Things will improve for us coloreds, and I want you ready. You need to be ready."

A few beats passed until I finally spoke. "How can I do better, Daddy, when I can't even erase books to help you pay the rent?"

Daddy leaned down further and looked me straight in the eyes. "We'll think of something, little man. We'll think of something."

CHAPTER THREE

1930

Smitty, six-years old

*Excavation work begins for the construction of
The Empire State Building*

*Clarence Birdseye invents frozen food with his process
of quick freezing*

Average cost of a car: $600

"I'm almost finished, Dad. Did I do good?"

I stood in the small space between our house and the alley. The yard used to seem a whole lot bigger when I was a little kid. But I was six going on seven. And I wasn't playing, I was working, building a wagon. Yes sir, I labored under sunshine and blue skies like a grown man.

The large hammer hung in my hands while I took a breather. Daddy came around from the alley into the yard and in two strides stood beside me. I wanted to show him how much better I'd gotten at hammering since earlier that morning.

"How's it coming along, Smitty?" Daddy slipped his

hands deep in the pockets of his coveralls.

"Real good, Daddy, three more nails, and I'm done—watch!"

With my left hand, I positioned a nail. That was something my lame arm could do real good. With the hammer in my right hand, I beat those nails down. My tongue peeked out from the corner of my mouth. I hammered better when my tongue helped. After a few more poundings, the last board was in place. I stepped back to admire my work. A few of the nails were bent, but they still did the job.

"My, my, Smitty, that was a lot of work to fill in that wagon frame. You hammered in all those boards exactly like I taught you."

He smiled at me and hummed a tune as he glanced around the yard. There was a baby doll carriage lying in a corner of the yard by the house. It belonged to my sisters, but they hadn't used it in a hundred years.

"Now bring that old doll buggy over here, son. Those wheels look like the right fit for your new wagon."

I watched, amazed as Daddy quickly figured how to put wheels on my wagon. In a matter of minutes, the job was done. My Daddy could do anything. After the wheels, he added a length of rope for a handle. It was complete, I had a brand new wagon all my own.

"What do you think, son?"

I felt a silly smile creep across my face. My chest puffed out like I was a proud-strutting-rooster, but I couldn't help myself.

I darted across the yard to the back door of our house and threw open the kitchen screen door. "Mama, Mama! Come quick! Come see what Daddy and me built!"

I spun away from the door as Daddy corrected me. "Daddy and *I*, son, say 'Daddy and I.'"

Small puffs of dirt surrounded my play shoes as I skidded to a halt. I turned around, ran back to the door, yanked it open and yelled, "Daddy and I."

While I leaned inside the kitchen door (and Daddy couldn't see me), I rolled back my eyes, dropped open my mouth, and shook my head till it rattled. *This is no time for an English lesson, Daddy,* but I didn't dare let my thoughts slip out. Lucky for me my eyes didn't get stuck back in my forehead like Mama promised would happen one day.

I skipped back to the wagon, knelt by it, and stroked its wooden planks.

The screen door squeaked open and softly bounced shut behind Mama. "What's all the fuss about?" She wiped her hands on her apron.

I jumped up, skipped to Mama, and tugged on her damp hand to pull her closer to my prize. But before I could soak up all the praise Mama was sure to give, the screen door swung open, and Mary came out, talking like she always did.

"Where are you going, Mama? I haven't finished telling you about what happened last night, and then I was going to ask you if I could go over to Betty's house. Do you think I could, Mama? Please." Mary hardly ever took a breath. She narrowed her eyes at me. "What are you and Daddy doing out here?"

"Look!" I pointed at my wagon and puffed out my chest.

Mama didn't disappoint me. With both hands on her broad hips, she slowly ambled her way around my wagon. She shook her head in pure amazement and made soft clucking sounds like the hens down at the market. Not wanting to be left out of things, Mary imitated Mama complete with her hands on her hips and a few clucks of her own.

"Smitty worked hard on his wagon, ladies," Daddy said.

Mama hummed in her sing-song way, "That sure is somethin' to behold." As she smiled, her teeth shined in the sunshine against her dark coffee skin.

"Sure is." Mary echoed. "Something to behold."

"Smitty"—Daddy rubbed the whiskers on his chin—"I think I'll call you 'The Wagon Master.' What do you think?"

The Wagon Master. That sounded real nice. I stood a little taller and looked at Mary to make sure she'd heard. I was The Wagon Master.

Daddy kept talking as I gazed up into his golden brown face. "Now little Wagon Master, can you think of how you and your wagon could earn money to help pay rent?"

I scratched my head and tried to concentrate.

"Oh I know, Daddy." Mary stepped beside me. "He could build more wagons and sell them. I'm sure there's someone who'd like to buy a fine wagon like this one. He could sell them for a whole lot of money." With each word, she inched a little closer to Daddy. I bumped her with my shoulder. Accidentally. Sort of.

"Mary, I'm talking to Smitty right now." He placed his hands on her shoulders and steered her back toward Mama. "And no, he can't build more wagons, because we don't have any more wood." Daddy turned back to me. "Now, have you thought of a way to use this wagon to earn money?"

I squinted, because sometimes at school that helped me come up with the right answer in arithmetic. Then, I wrinkled my nose while I squinted. That was my most powerful thinking expression. Still, I couldn't figure how my wagon could help bring in money for the family. I shook my head in defeat.

Daddy knelt down and balanced on his haunches so he could look at me in the eye. Sometimes he helped me think that way.

"Okay then, where is it you like to go with Mama? And you help her carry bags home?"

"The market?"

"That's right. Now think about the women who don't have a boy to go to market with them." He paused so I could think. "Could you use your wagon to help them?"

"Yes!" I hopped on one foot like I did sometimes when I was excited. I remembered seeing boys with wagons stand on the corner by the market. They pulled customer's bundles to their homes. "I could pull their marketing."

"And what do you think a woman would do after you hauled her marketing to her home?"

"She'd say thank you." I grinned.

Mama and Daddy laughed softly and looked at each other.

Mama nodded her head. "I'm sure they'd thank you. But some ladies would be happy to tip you for hauling their bundles. They'd pay you."

My heart beat faster as I imagined the feel of a coin in my hand. "Let's do it!"

"I've hustled up other work for myself this afternoon. I can't go with you." Daddy stood up tall and blocked the sunshine. I stood in his shadow and bent my neck back to look up at him.

He continued, "You're old enough to do this on your own. Remember now, you're The Wagon Master."

Mama's smile melted. "I'm not sure about that. Going alone?"

"He'll be fine."

I didn't want to walk to market by myself. "Can Ruby come with me?"

"No." Mama answered. "I wish she could, but Ruby woke up sick this morning. She's in bed, a cold cloth on her head.

Daddy's going to give her a spoonful from the medicine bottle soon as we get back in the house."

I shuddered. Memories of Daddy's bitter tonic scared my taste buds and made me want to gag. His medicine might heal like he claimed, but it tasted terrible. Poor Ruby. Maybe walking to market alone was better than taking the tonic.

Mama whispered to Daddy, who leaned in closer. She squinted her eyes slightly as she looked up into his face. She must have been worried, because she bit her bottom lip.

Daddy shook his head, kissed her forehead, and pulled her close.

Mama whispered again. This time, I could hear her, even though I pretended not to. "But he's just a baby."

"He's old enough. We can't protect him forever."

Daddy took a deep breath and bent down to talk to me. "Mama's afraid you're too young to walk to market by yourself, but soon you'll be seven years old. You know your way around."

"I sure do." I looked at Mama and stood as tall as I could. "Don't you worry." Then I remembered about the white neighborhood. "Maybe Mary could go with me." I glanced in her direction. She'd lost interest in my wagon and had wandered to the back alley.

"No." Daddy answered. "Mama's ironing today, so Mary's going to do the house chores and cooking. We're all doing our part to pay the rent, son. Time to do your share."

I bit my lip. I worried like Mama.

Mama sighed. "Smitty, you do know your way to the market, like Daddy says. You've known it for years." She leaned over and brushed some dirt off my britches. Mama always wanted my clothes to be clean. I never knew exactly how I got dirty—it happened when I wasn't looking. She brushed off my knees, thighs, and bottom. It felt like some kind of Mother Blessing for my new job.

"And your Daddy's right, you'll be fine. The Lord's with you even when we can't be." She took my chin in her hand and looked directly at me with sad eyes. "When you have to walk through the neighborhood that belongs to the whites, *don't dawdle*." She spit on her fingertips and rubbed something off my chin. "Keep your head down and mind your own business. You know the rules. You walk through the white section every day going to school with your sisters."

"You ready?" Daddy looked so proud, I was determined not to disappoint him. He needed my help to pay the rent, so we could stay in our home.

I swallowed, though it was harder to do than normal.

"Yes, sir."

Daddy picked up the rope handle and carefully placed it in my hands. It was like he was a king handing a sword to his knight.

I felt like I could do anything, even walk to the market alone.

———◆———

"Out on your own today, Smitty?"

One of Mama's friends knelt on the sidewalk and scrubbed her bottom marble step. Underneath her apron and housedress, her big bosoms swung to the rhythm of her scrubbing. The faded fabric went this way and that.

"Yes ma'am, headed to market. Daddy and I built my wagon." I lifted the rope handle as she sat back on her heels. "And I'm looking for the bloody sand piles Mr. Mosley talks about. My sisters never want to look for them when we walk to school."

She laughed as she wiped her forehead with the back of her hand. "Let me know if you find them. I been looking my whole life." Her ebony skin glistened with beads of perspiration. A few clumps of hair puffed out from beneath her kerchief.

She began to scrub again, and I hurried along, grateful to escape without a hug. The women of Sandtown looked out for their own children and everybody else's. It was like having a mama every couple of houses. Mostly this was good, but it was a bad thing if I was in trouble. First, I'd be in a mess with the Neighbor-Mama and then all over again with my own Mama.

Another danger from all the Neighbor-Mamas was death by suffocation. Last Sunday, Sister Somebody-or-Another was eager to see me all dressed up in my church clothes. She dragged me close for a hug, pulled me to her, and squeezed. My face was buried deep in her chest as she rocked me back and forth. I could hardly get air. Thought I'd die. Death by hugging. That'd be a sad way to go.

Whenever I thought about walking through the white neighborhood by myself, I didn't feel brave like The Wagon Master. So instead, every time I passed an alley or crossed a street, I looked for bloody sand piles.

Mr. Mosley was the oldest old-timer in Sandtown, about as old as Methuselah. His skin was wrinkled like an elderly raisin, and his black-brown eyes were covered with a haze of cloudy yellow. During the summer, Mr. Mosley's family would set out a kitchen chair by their marble steps for him to sit and take in the night air. On special evenings, neighbors gathered around to hear him tell stories, and that's when he'd tell us how Sandtown got its name.

In the 1800's when he had been a small boy, two drunk

workers from the Mount Winans distillery got into a fight. First, it was words and fists. Then one pulled out a knife, and so did the other. In the end, the victor lay panting next to the dead man, both of them lying in a pond of blood. People piled sand on the blood to clean up the street, but because there was so much blood, it required huge piles of sand. Time went by and folks had gotten to identifying the area by the piles of sand. And that's how Sandtown got its name. Scary, maybe, but nothing like what I was facing now.

Standing at the next corner, my mouth went dry, and I bit my bottom lip. The white section was just across the street. Except for skin color, it was hard to make sense about what was so different between our neighborhood and the white neighborhood. But skin color was enough. Our neighborhoods sat next to each other, worlds apart.

Keep your head down. Mama's voice echoed in my mind. I took a deep breath, stepped into the street, and walked on. Obediently, my wagon followed. My fingers tightened around the rope handle.

I whispered Mama's instructions to help me remember. "Mind your own business. Don't dawdle." I looked down and watched my shoes step along the walkway.

When my shoes come toe to toe with a pair of girls shiny black ones, I stopped and held my breath. A pair of pale-skinned shins and ankles wearing white socks with lacy trim stood still inside the shiny black shoes. I didn't move. Peals of high pitched giggles assaulted my ears. Not knowing what to do, I stayed still staring at my own worn out, dirty play shoes.

The white girl stepped back away from me. I heard whispered words followed by the slap of running feet. The laughter faded to the distance. My right hand, tight and cramped, gripped the wagon rope. I switched and let my left hand take over even though it was weaker. The rest of me tried to breathe again.

The more I walked, the farther away the market seemed. When Ruby, Mary, and I walked to school, it didn't take this long to get through the white section. Sweat trickled down the center of my back. I wished my sisters were with me. Mary could even boss me around, and I wouldn't complain.

I paused to catch my breath, and the sweet smell of tobacco drifted past my nose. *A cigar.* Mr. Mosley and other men in Sandtown chewed tobacco, but smoking a cigar was a whole different story. The scent was dreamy, like faraway lands and foreign people with musical voices. My eyes didn't obey the rules. They looked up in search of the sweet smell, and that's when I saw the screen door. A painted screen. I'd seen other painted screen doors in the white neighborhood, but this one was new. Beautiful green mountains with flowing waterfalls and blue skies, about the most beautiful place I'd ever seen. It must have been a million miles away from Sandtown.

Painted screens were a thing of pride in Baltimore. Mama said it wasn't a sinful pride, it was a happy pride. The same way we felt about our marble steps. For those who could pay the dollar it cost, bright colored scenes were painted on the wire screen of their front door. The air could flow through the screen while the paint gave privacy because it reflected light. Someone on the street couldn't see through the screen into the house, they only saw the picture. But the folks inside could see out. And that's the part I forgot.

The screen door squeaked as it opened. The mountain scene vanished, and there stood a sweaty white man in a stained T-shirt. Hair poked out from under his armpits, and his belly hung over a worn-looking belt. He leaned against the door frame. One hand held up a cigar, the other held a bottle. It was too late to look down—I'd already stared directly at him.

He sucked on his cigar and blew the smoke in my direction, glaring at me through the polluted air.

"What you looking at, boy?" he snarled, showing off his yellow teeth.

The smoke made my eyes burn.

This was the first time I'd ever encountered a white grown up person by myself. This man must've been watching me as I'd admired his painted screen. How long had I looked at it? My heart began to thump wildly. My mouth opened. My dry tongue stuck to the roof.

I waited and hoped words would come. Nothing.

Only fear.

He looked mean. And drunk.

I wondered if he had a knife like the men in Mr. Mosley's story.

"I'm talking to you, nappy head! What you lookin' at, boy?"

Shame washed over me. I stared at the ground.

"I seen you and your two dark sisters walkin' to school every day."

I didn't move.

His gravelly voice grew angry. "Can't figure out why they have a school for the likes of you. You're all dumb as dirt. Never going to amount to anything."

I stared at my muddy play shoes and the tattered hem of my pants, frozen in the summer heat. There was nothing I could say. He caught me admiring his beautiful screen. I had no right to do that.

"Get a move on!" he barked. "Such a pitiful fool, standing there all dark and dumb."

He spit in my direction. "Get moving! And don't you stop!" The screen door banged shut. "*Go!* Before I call the police!"

I started running. Every fiber in my body wanted to escape. My feet tried. I ran two strides before my wagon pulled back on my lame arm. Tumbling forward, I sprawled on the ground. The palms of my hands and one of my knees burned. The man, hidden behind his screen, bellowed a sinister laugh. As I scrambled to stand, I felt a tug on my leg. My pants tore, and a piece of cloth flapped from the hole. Blood trickled down my knee.

I ignored the pain and ran faster than I'd ever run before. Ran until the sweat blended with my blood and tears. Ran until I gasped for breath, trying to suck air into my lungs. Ran to get away from the ugliness spit at me by a white man.

My treasured wagon bounced and tumbled behind me, the rope burning my scraped up hand. Minutes later I stood in front of the market. My heart pounded so loud I thought my ears might explode.

I pulled up my shirt tail, wiped my eyes and my nose, and tried to remember why I was at the market all by myself.

◆

Once when my arm had hurt real badly, Mama walked me through the market to look at things and sniff the good smells. Somehow, it helped my arm feel better. Maybe throbbing arms and scrapped knees were kind of the same, so I figured I'd walk through the market to feel better and braver, like The Wagon Master who helps his family pay the rent.

Slowly, I made my way up and down the aisles of fresh

produce, meats, and home goods. Most of the shoppers were women. Some had little children in tow the same way I pulled my wagon. The air hummed with conversation and greetings between buyers and sellers, neighbors and friends. I strolled past bins of oranges and grapefruits, then slowed to admire large, round cantaloupes displayed in wooden crates.

Tables were piled high with corn on the cob still in green husks with yellow tails of silk. Peppers, both green and red, decorated the next table, and after that, a wooden crate of green zucchinis. Collard greens, kale, beets, string beans, and peas were displayed in rounded piles, a mountain range of vegetables.

Around the corner stood a heap of onions: big yellows, small whites, and medium brown balls that were sure to get a woman crying soon as she cut into them.

Turkeys and chickens plucked naked hung over rows of wooden crates. A soft, brown feather drifted up from a crate, and inside, a plump hen lived out what were sure to be her final hours. She and the chickens in the other crates clucked and carried on, gossiping like the two women by the cantaloupes.

Fresh fish, oysters, and crabs from the Chesapeake Bay sat on solid blocks of ice. As I walked past, I took a deep breath. The air was scented with smells of the sea. Maybe when I grew up, I'd become a sailor, sail around the world and fight pirates.

Finally, my favorite aisle, lined with bins of brown sugar and white sugar, jars of molasses and honey, candy, and one of my favorite things in the whole world. I stopped in front of the counter that displayed big blocks of luscious chocolate. Mama bought chocolate twice a year at Christmas and Easter. But Mama taught me that we could enjoy the smell of chocolate without having to spend money to buy it. We always walked by so we could take a whiff. I liked the smell. But I liked eating it better.

The man with yellow hair behind the counter leaned forward. "Hello, young man. On your own today, yah?" He talked in a musical way. Mama said it was because he was Swedish. "You buy some chocolate for your mama?"

"I'm only smelling it today." I demonstrated with a deep breath. As my mouth began to water, I remembered I came to the market to help my Dad, and I couldn't let him down. So I left the chocolate behind and found a place on the street corner by the market.

Shoppers hurried across the street and greeted neighbors passing by. A few horse drawn wagons loaded with fresh produce were parked by the sidewalk. These Arabbers would lead their horses through the neighborhood streets and sell their goods to folks who heard their distinctive hollering. I used to pretend I was an Arabber and imitated their calls, part understandable, part gibberish. When Mama heard an Arabber call from the street, she ran outside with her change purse. When she heard me yell like an Arabber inside the house, she threatened to swat my bottom if I didn't pipe down.

"Who said you could stand on our corner?" A fat boy asked the question. His round face looked like one of those cantaloupes I'd just seen, only uglier.

"My daddy."

The three other wagon boys who stood at the market corner laughed at my answer, but not the fat boy. He stuck out his bottom lip, dropped his wagon handle, and stomped towards me.

He wasn't much taller than I was, but he was a lot rounder. He poked me on the shoulder with his sausage finger.

"Well…" Poke.

"…I say…" Poke.

"…you can't." Poke. *Push.*

I held my ground and stared at him. So far, I'd survived a group of giggling white girls, a cigar smoking, spitting white man, scraped hands, and a bloody knee. I hadn't come this far to be turned away by a boy with a melon for a head. I stared back at him, took a deep breath, and prayed he didn't know I had no idea what to do next.

"Leave him alone." A deep voice behind me. "Smitty's my neighbor. He can work here."

The boy with sausage fingers slunk away. "I was only playing."

My defender was Valentine, a tall ten-year-old who lived over on Carey Street. My sisters giggled and fought over who would marry him one day. Girls can be so dumb.

"Nice wagon." Valentine smiled. He stood straight, shoulders back, oozing self-assurance.

"Thanks." With his approval of my wagon, all the confidence of The Wagon Master returned. I was ready to work.

And then I waited. Waiting can be hard work. I hummed for a while until Cantaloupe Head glared at me. I smiled at him, hummed softer, turned to avoid his gaze, and bumped right into a lady from church.

"Smitty. How are you today?" Mrs. Bailey steadied herself as she shifted her armload of bags. "What do we have here?"

"Hello, Mrs. Bailey." I gave her my most charming smile. "Would you like me to pull your bundles home for you?"

"You know, that sounds real good."

I sighed with relief and helped her arrange her marketing into my wagon. As we walked to her house, it was as if my wagon's personality changed. The weight of the bundles seemed to put it off kilter, like it was in a bad mood. I did my best to make it follow me, but sometimes it zigged when it should have zagged. I experimented pulling it with my right arm, then my left. But it seemed to do best when I held the rope with both hands, which was fine until my lame arm started to ache.

Mrs. Bailey's husband was an elder at church, and I guess that made her important, too. She chattered about all sorts of things.

"Sure is lovely weather we're having lately."

"It's a shame about the Walker boy, don't you think Smitty?"

"Pastor preached a powerful sermon on Sunday."

"The women of the church are going to prepare the entire meal."

I answered "yes ma'am" and "no ma'am" when it seemed fitting, hoping I didn't say one when I should have said the other. She finally got quiet when we stopped in the alley near her kitchen door.

"Well here we are, home sweet home." She picked up some of her marketing, and I did the same. One trip in and out of her kitchen, and we were done. My heart thumped double time when she reached into her change purse, pulled out a nickel and a penny, and pressed the coins into the palm of my hand.

Energized, I skipped back to the market, with the sweet sound of coins jingling in my pocket. At this rate, I might earn enough to pay the whole rent. Then Daddy could buy Mama new floor pieces with his money.

Three customers later I had a white woman.

"Okay, boy." She dropped her bundles in my wagon. While I tried to make sure things were settled in, she started walking away. Fast. I trotted behind pulling my moody wagon. Next thing I knew, the rope tugged on my arm, and I heard a thump. Must have been a rut in the dirt or a rock under the wheel, but whatever the cause, my wagon was lying on its side, and so were the woman's bundles. A couple of onions rolled in the dirt. I scrambled to scoop things up before she saw, but it was too late.

"Boy! What the devil have you done!" She screeched worse than I'd ever heard before. My palms got sweaty, and I dropped the apple I'd just rescued from the street. Once I got everything back in the wagon, I tried to catch up closer to her. Somehow my shoe lace had come undone. I stepped forward but my shoe didn't, and I was on the ground again.

Same knee.

More burn.

More blood.

The world got blurry, and I wiped my eyes quick as I could before she saw. My hands were dirty, I felt the grit on my face.

Finally I stopped my wagon near the door where she stood tapping her foot.

"Don't bother." She scooped everything up in one sweep, stomped up her steps, and slammed the door shut.

The lock clicked.

She pulled the curtains closed tight.

I stood and stared at the locked door with the closed curtains.

My wagon sat beside me like a faithful friend. The way its rope handle was lying in the dirt made it look sad. I picked up the rope. Bristly rope fibers rubbed into my scrapped up palm while blood oozed down my aching knee. I couldn't keep from wondering if there was an easier way I could help pay the rent.

◆

"Ola! The Wagon Master's home!" Daddy's voice bellowed as he greeted me at the front step. He was just getting home from work. "Good to see you, son. Take your wagon around back. We'll settle up inside."

In the kitchen, Mama poured steaming hot water into a bowl, dropped in a cube of starch, and stirred. "Wipe your feet, Smitty. Mary swept the house today, and a lot of the dirt had your name on it." The room was hot and steamy. Mama's skin dripped with perspiration, and even Mary looked wilted as she peeled potatoes into a bowl. "How's my little working man?"

Tired as I was, I stood tall. "Got a heap of money in my pocket, Mama, listen." I jingled the coins with my fingers.

Mary rolled her eyes, but Mama laughed.

"Go meet your Daddy in the dining room. And don't touch a thing. Pressed clothes waiting to be picked up, don't want you messing them up."

Daddy stood beside me as I unloaded a fistful of coins onto the table. I looked up at him for approval.

He nodded "Well done, Wagon Master." He messed with my hair and made me laugh. We divided and stacked the silver and copper coins as he gave me a lesson in counting money.

"How much is it, Daddy?"

Mama came in from the kitchen mopping her brow with a kerchief.

"Our son did well, Ola. He brought in twenty-eight cents."

Mama murmured her approval.

"Is it enough to pay the rent, Daddy?"

"It's enough to be a big help, Smitty. We'll let you put it in the coffee can with the rest of the rent money."

Mama eased herself down onto a chair. "Smitty, what's this?" She took my hands in her softly calloused ones and examined the cuts and scrapes on both of my palms. "Charlie, look here. Did you fall, son?"

Heat crept up my neck. I chewed my bottom lip, unsure what to say.

"Boys fall all the time. Don't get all worked up," Daddy said, rescuing me.

"Maybe," Mama countered, "but your son tore his pants and bloodied his knee something awful. Look at this." Mama reached down to inspect my knee before I could stop her.

"Ow!" My bottom lip quivered. I pressed my eyelids shut and commanded my eyes not to cry. It worked. Mostly.

Daddy knelt on the floor to get a better look at my knee. "We need to clean that up. That's no little scrape." He looked at me with the big, brown pools of love that were his eyes. "What happened?"

My breath quickened. My ears buzzed. Inside my head, I heard the sinister laugh of the cigar smoking white man. Then I heard the white woman screaming, *What the devil have you done?* And the girls giggling. All the echoes in my head were wrapped in swirls of gray, smoky air. I wasn't sure if I could breathe.

"Tell us." Daddy whispered, his hand on my shoulder.

Part of me wanted to tell. Part of me wanted to hide.

"Smitty?" Mama's voice was soft and soothing. Her hand cupped the side of my face as her thumb expertly wiped away the tear trickling down my cheek.

And so I told them. About the group of giggling girls. About falling when I ran from the man behind the painted screen. And about how my wagon fell over, made the white woman shriek, and I fell again because of my stupid shoelaces. I told them because they were my parents. I could trust them. Yet inside I had a weighty feeling, like my soul was wearing an overcoat too big and too heavy for my size. I thought maybe by telling my parents what happened, they could help me get out from under the burden. But that invisible heavy overcoat stayed on and trapped me inside. Even my Daddy couldn't get it off me.

When I was done my telling, Mama looked at Daddy. "Oh, Charles."

"Not now."

Mama touched carefully near my knee but talked to Daddy. "Looks like he's going to have quite a scar here."

"Outside scars heal." Daddy sighed. "It's the inside ones I worry about."

CHAPTER FOUR

March 2008

Smitty, 84-years old

Average cost of a new car: $27, 958

"Sorry I'm late, ladies. Traffic was a mess." I place the plastic grocery bags on the kitchen counter and toss my keys in their spot, so I can find them next time. Out of habit, I reach into my pants' pockets, pull out some change, and drop it into the coin jar beside my keys.

My wife turns her beautiful face towards me and gives me a kiss. "Welcome home, darling. Leslie's here." She waves in the direction of our guest, who is getting up from a chair at the kitchen table.

Leslie wraps her young arms around me for a hug and a kiss. Being an old man has its advantages.

"So good to see you, Mr. Smith. How are you?"

"Handsome as ever." I use her father's favorite reply.

Leslie laughs, and her brown eyes sparkle. "Let me help you with the groceries, Mrs. Smith."

The two of them unpack the bags I bring in from my truck. I slip off my overcoat, hang it on a hook in the breezeway, and ease myself down onto a kitchen chair. My hips and knees ache today. The ladies admire my purchases, unpacking the bags with the same awe they would have opening gifts on Christmas morning. Chicken parts packaged in saran wrapped containers. Bunches of fresh greens. Containers of microwave mashed potatoes. Boxes of cereal and instant oatmeal. And a package of Dove's dark chocolates, my favorite.

"I got the dry cleaning, too. It's hanging up in the breezeway."

"Oh thank you, Smitty."

I like keeping my wife happy. She pours each of us a glass of water, and we walk into the sunroom. Leslie settles into a comfortable chair, and my bride and I sit across from her on the loveseat. After we paid off the mortgage on the house, we added this room. I love the warmth of the late winter sunshine and steal a glance outside to the yard. Soon the grass will turn green and the lawn will be bordered with flowers. First, the daffodils, beautiful hopeful bursts of yellow in early spring. Later in summer, the Black-Eyed Susans will show up, yellow rays of petals circling a dark-brown, spherical center. They stay bright and cheery even on the hottest, most humid days in Baltimore.

We chat a while, sip our water, and find reasons to laugh. Leslie looks so much like her father, it makes me ache inside. I miss him more than I can say.

Finally, I get to the reason we invited our young friend for a visit. "Leslie, would you help me get my stories down on paper?"

Her smile freezes then fades. "Oh, Mr. Smith—"

"The other day the phone rang. It was Tony's granddaughter. She had a paper to write for school. I hear her sweet, little voice over the line asking, 'Uncle Smitty, have you ever heard of the Great Depression?'"

After we share a laugh, I sip my water. "I said, 'As a matter of fact I have.' Went on to tell her about hauling marketing with my wagon and working as a shoeshine boy. Told her about my daddy being a hod carrier."

"A hod carrier?' Leslie asks. "What's that?"

"The lowest job on a construction site. A hod's a three-sided wooden box with a long handle." I draw a little picture on the back of an envelope to show her. "The box was packed full with ten or twelve bricks. Maybe cement. The hoddie then balanced all that weight on his shoulder, climbed up and down ladders without falling or breaking a brick, and made deliveries to bricklayers who might need as many as a thousand bricks a day." I shake my head in amazement. "The taller the building , the higher the climb in sweltering sun or frigid wind. It was menial labor, back-breaking work, and it's what my daddy did, day after day, without complaint."

My wife speaks up. "Didn't he wear long underwear all year round?"

"That's right." I laugh, picturing that. "During the winter, he wore two sets of long underwear to keep warm. He used a different set in the heat of summer. He claimed the cotton long underwear cooled him by absorbing his perspiration." Do young people today really know what it means to work that hard? "No matter the conditions, Daddy never complained. He was grateful for the work and took it seriously."

Leslie leans forward, listening with interest.

"As I told my great-great niece a little about my childhood, I realized there's so much my family doesn't know."

"It's true." My wife gently pats my knee. "You've got a

whole lot of history that needs to be told, darling. Folks have always told you to write it down."

"So now you're asking me to help?" Leslie asks.

I smile my most charming smile. "You're the only published author I know."

Leslie sits back in her chair and laughs. "I've only had a few short stories published. What about your nephews? Tony? And Bo? They're big writers."

"They live too far away. Besides, you're prettier to look at."

Leslie shakes her head and laughs but says nothing.

"You wouldn't deprive a dying man his last wish, would you?"

Her smile fades. She tilts her head to the side. "How are you feeling?"

"I feel fine, just fine."

The love of my life pipes up. "It's hard for us to believe the doctors gave Smitty such a grim cancer diagnosis. He's really doing quite well."

I nod my head. "Even so, I'm 84 years old. If I'm going to do something, I best be getting busy."

"I'm honored you've asked me, really I am." Leslie's words are hesitant. "But I don't know if I'm qualified for the job." Absentmindedly she rubs her hand along the side of her face, exactly like her daddy used to do. We all laugh at the implications.

"Think about it, will you? And come back to hear some of my stories. You don't have to write anything down, just listen."

She nods. "I can listen."

"And I can talk."

My wife's face tilts up slightly, and she laughs, the liquid sunshine kind of laugh. "You sure do know how to talk, darling. You sure do."

While we laugh, I pray I'll be able to say what needs to be said.

Chapter Five

1934

Smitty, 10-years old

First U.S. ski tow rope begins operation in Vermont

W.E.B. DuBois resigns position at NAACP

Construction worker's annual income: $907

"Are you sure we can afford it, Daddy?" I crossed my fingers, hoping and praying the answer was still yes. "Two weeks away means I miss a lot of shoeshine work."

My uncle was a shoe repairman. Recently, he'd helped me build a shoe shine box and filled it with tins of half used polish, rags, and a used shoe brush. These days my wagon sat neglected by our back steps. I made more money shining shoes after school and on Saturdays than I did hauling groceries. I'd made plenty of homely men look a lot better by polishing their shoes this summer. Even though I was the best shoeshine boy in Baltimore, I wanted to get away to Boy Scout camp something fierce. Camp was the greatest experience in the whole wide world. Yet there were two coffee cans I was concerned about. One was for rent, the other for the operation on my arm.

We'd never been more than one month behind on our rent, yet the threat of harder times always loomed over us. Ruby still hadn't gotten a letter from Enoch's sister. To me it seemed like the Tucker family fell off the face of the earth after they left Sandtown. I didn't want my family to fall off the earth. As for the operation on my arm, I wanted my arm to stop hurting so terribly, but my stomach still felt funny at the thought of surgery.

"We'll get by, Smitty. You can go." Daddy assured. " Now, go finish your packing. You leave in the morning."

Mama looked up from the couch, thimble on her thumb and needle and thread in her hand. "Got the last two missing buttons replaced on your uniform, Smitty. Take this upstairs to wear tomorrow."

"Thanks, Mama." I grabbed the uniform pants and shirt and ran up the stairs two at a time. My duffle bag lay balled up inside the travel trunk in my room. Someday I was going to travel the world, put stickers all over that trunk. I smoothed the duffle bag out on my bed, opened it up, and pulled clothing and necessary items out from my dresser.

Boy Scout uniform? Check.

Swiss army knife? Check.

Canteen? Check.

Mess kit? Where was my mess kit?

"Mama, I can't find my mess kit!" I thundered down the stairs. "Where's my mess kit? I bet Mary took it She's always taking my stuff." Mama wasn't in the living room. "Mama!"

She hollered back from the kitchen. "Quiet down! Your mess kit is in one of these cupboards. You need to find it yourself."

The next morning my mess kit was safely stowed in my duffle bag, which sat by the front door. I gobbled down oatmeal with raisins and brown sugar.

"Slow down." Daddy said. "You don't need to be at church for another hour." He leaned back and drank his coffee. I didn't understand how he could drink hot coffee on a steamy August morning. "Your Cousin Reggie's going to meet us here, then I'll walk you both to the church to meet up with your troop."

"Reggie's been all quiet and moody lately."

Daddy laughed. "Reggie's fourteen. Being quiet and moody is his job."

"He's not as much fun these days."

Mama lifted her eyebrows when I swiped my mouth with the back of my sleeve. "I sure hope you use your napkin and have better manners in front of Mr. Ames." Mama didn't know what camp was like. We Boy Scouts ate out of our mess kits and drank from canteens. We walked barefoot everywhere we went. We slept under the stars and danced in the rain. We explored the woods and settled by campfires at night. I didn't plan on seeing a napkin until I came back home, but I wasn't about to tell her.

When it was time, I wrapped my arms around Mama's softness.

"Remember, I gave you a one cent stamp and a nickel to buy a postcard. You be sure to write us when you all go to Annapolis."

I kissed her cheek. "Can't forget to write to the best mama in the world." I gave her my finest smile for her to remember while I was gone.

Daddy walked Reggie and me down to the church. The greatest two weeks of summer were about to begin. Worries about paying the rent and operations on arms would have to wait.

"Did y'all see my new uniform?" Mickey wiggled around in the front seat of the big ol' Ford and sat on his knees to look at us in the back seat.

"You look real fine," Abraham assured. He sat on one side of me, Reggie on the other. I was stuck in the middle.

I raised my voice so everyone could hear over the air rushing past the open car windows. "Nice looking uniform, Mickey."

Reggie nodded in agreement, though he mostly looked out the window.

Mr. Ames, our Boy Scout leader, sat behind the steering wheel. His left arm rested on the door and extended outside the car window, his hand open like he was trying to catch the wind.

"You look good." He smiled down at Mickey.

I'd seen Mr. Ames's two front teeth so many times, I could almost see them now. Both were chipped, so when he smiled, the gap became the opening to a secret cave. Mr. Ames wasn't tall like Daddy. He was what they call stocky, with a barrel chest and arms that bulged under the sleeves of his shirt. And he was about as dark as a colored man could be. Daddy said Mr. Ames was an excellent role model for Reggie and me.

"My brand new uniform," Mickey murmured. He fingered the buttons on his shirt. With each compliment, he'd smiled so wide you could count how many teeth he was missing.

Abraham gave me a knowing look. He was the oldest and wisest boy in the car. I nodded in silent understanding, trying to look as wise. Reggie did the same. We knew the truth. Colored Boy Scouts never had new uniforms. We got second hand uniforms passed down from white Boy Scouts. Our uniforms were faded and patched. And if a uniform had all of the buttons, they didn't match.

But the other truth was, we didn't care. All year we wore hand-me-down clothes from older brothers and cousins. Almost nothing we wore was new, and that wasn't going to change when we joined the Boy Scouts. The important thing was we *were* Scouts.

"Are we there yet?" Billy, the other front seat boy, asked Mr. Ames.

"It's a mighty long ways from Sandtown to Camp Linstead, but don't you worry none. It will be worth it." Mr. Ames pulled off his cap, scratched his head, and put the cap on again. "Camp Linstead sits on the banks of the Severn River, a nice big river. You'll have fun swimming in it."

Abraham squirmed with excitement. "I can't wait to go hiking in the woods."

"I want to go swimming!"

"My favorite is the campfire singing."

We all talked at the same time. Mr. Ames laughed, low and rumbling like a papa bear.

Mickey spoke up. "I can't sleep in a tent this year, but I will next year. Then I'll be a *real* Boy Scout"

"You are a real Scout, Billy." I leaned forward and rested my elbows on my knees. "You're wearing a uniform like the rest of us. You just got to rise up through the ranks. First year you sleep in an old farm wagon, second year you sleep in a tent. And your third year, you sleep in a log cabin." I looked forward to sleeping in a cabin next summer.

I glanced over at Reggie, who was gazing out the window again. Being fourteen sure had him quiet. I thumped his shoulder. "Wake up, cousin."

"I'm awake."

His attitude would never do. I thumped him again. And then, like only a cousin and best friend could, I tickled his neck. I knew this would change things. He curled into a ball of laughter and tried to slap my hands away.

"Settle down boys." Mr. Ames warned, but he was smiling.

Reggie and I panted with laughter. We slumped and squirmed, twisted and turned in the back seat.

Each turn of the tires took us further from the heat and noise of summer in the city, closer to the cool breeze and waters of the shore. Mama always said it wasn't the heat that was so bad in summer, it was the humidity. That never made sense to me. The two always came together.

Camp Linstead was a world away from Sandtown. Even in August, the camp's riverside location felt better than home. Going to camp was better than Christmas, but I never said that out loud, because I didn't want to hurt Jesus' feelings.

"Is that supposed to happen?" Billy pointed out the front window to steam rising from under the hood of the car.

Mr. Ames sighed and muttered. He slowed down the car and skillfully pulled off the country road lined by farmland and sections of thick woods.

"Get out, stretch your legs boys. We'll wait for one of the other cars to catch up with us." A long caravan of automobiles carried our fellow troop members. The cars didn't belong to Sandtown folk. They were on loan driven by our Scout Leaders and leaders from the other side of Baltimore where even the coloreds weren't as poor as those of us who lived in Sandtown.

We piled out of the car, stretched, and ran circles in the grass.

"Here comes someone!" Billy pointed down the road. It wasn't a car but an old green pick-up truck rolling down the highway. We watched as the distance between it and us lessened. It slowed to a crawl as it approached. In the cab were two white men.

"Stay close to the car, boys." Mr. Ames' voice was low and measured. "Get behind me." The truck came to a complete stop opposite Mr. Ames. He took off his cap.

The men in the truck didn't say anything.

Mr. Ames fiddled with his cap. "Good afternoon, gentlemen. Mighty lovely day today."

The man in the passenger's seat pushed back the wide brim of his straw hat, giving us full view of an old, sunken face with a stubbly beard. His lips curled in where teeth should have been. The man behind the steering wheel was a lot younger. He leaned toward the rolled down window. His jaw moved side to side as he studied Mr. Ames and then stared at each one of us.

Even though it was August, my hands felt cold and clammy. We boys had been laughing and squirming before, but now, we were quiet and still.

Finally, the man behind the steering wheel looked back at Mr. Ames. "You making trouble, boy?"

Mr. Ames smiled, but it wasn't his real smile. There was no secret cave. "No sir, no trouble at all. Just taking a break, giving the boys a chance to stretch their legs."

"Where you headed?"

"Camp Linstead, sir. All these fine boys are Boy Scouts of America, as you can see by their uniforms." Beads of perspiration dribbled down Mr. Ames's thick, muscular neck. "We're on our way to summer camp." He swallowed and fiddled with his cap.

The two white men looked at each other and exchanged words we couldn't hear.

A mockingbird sang out from a nearby field.

"Boy, something wrong with your car?"

"Yes, sir." Mr. Ames' head bobbed up and down. "Just an overheated radiator, sir."

Gravel spit out from under the spinning truck tires as they suddenly sped away.

Mr. Ames exhaled. He pulled a kerchief out of his back pocket and mopped his brow and neck. "Okay boys, excitement's over. Go on into the woods and do your business. One of our cars will be along soon."

When I stepped out from the woods back to the roadside, a vehicle from our caravan was pulled up behind our own. The doors swung open. Boys tumbled out, ran into the woods, then milled around the edge of the forest.

Mr. Brown, the owner of the big blue Ford had jugs full of water in his trunk for radiator emergencies. He and Mr. Ames fiddled under the hood of our car.

Mickey ran up beside our leader. "Mr. Ames! Here they come again!"

Instinctively, the rest of us gathered close to our leader. All talking ceased.

The green truck crept by. The old man leered at us and passed his shotgun by the window before he placed it on the dashboard. Once the dented truck passed, it accelerated and left behind a cloud of dust.

Mr. Ames slammed the hood. "Let's go boys! Pile in!" He and Mr. Brown quickly exchanged some words and got back into their cars.

As we rolled down the road, Mr. Brown stayed close behind us, always within sight. We were quiet for a long time.

Finally, Mickey's squeaky voice got everyone's attention, "Are there going to be any white boys at camp?"

Mr. Ames cleared his throat.

"No need to worry 'bout sharing the place, Mickey. The

whites have Camp Linstead all summer in June, July, and the first part of August. The last two weeks of August is special for us, coloreds only. Colored Boy Scouts and their colored Scoutmasters." He grinned at Mickey and tousled his hair with one hand. "Just our people."

"Good."

Nobody else spoke. The only sounds were the hum of the engine and the air rushing past our windows.

Reggie broke the silence. "What do you like most about camp, Mr. Ames?"

"I love the fresh air."

"What else?" Abraham asked.

"Sounds of the bullfrogs at night."

It felt good to think about camp. I egged him on, "Yeah, and what else?"

Mr. Ames rubbed his chin with one hand, his other guiding the steering wheel. "I love the feel of cool, wet sand between my toes."

We burst into laughter. I imagined Mr. Ames' big toes wiggling in the sand like baby turtles digging out from their nest.

He kept talking. "And I like starry night skies, swimming, and watching you boys be like Tom Sawyer and Huck Finn. Truth is, I like most everything at camp."

The wind rushed past the rolled down windows. There was a rthymic thump of the tires rolling beneath us.

"Quit poking me with that bent arm." Abraham protested in my direction.

"I'm not poking you."

"Are so."

"Am not," I insisted.

"Well, move over."

"You move over."

"Boys, that's enough." Mr. Ames barked. He stretched and adjusted his position behind the steering wheel. "Let's practice some of those campfire songs. No use waiting 'til the last minute."

So we sang campfire songs at the top of our lungs. Reggie couldn't sing at all. I already knew that. Abraham sounded good because his voice had changed. But me, I was the best of the backseat boys. As we sang and the car rolled along, worries about white men faded away. And I hoped they'd stay away for a very long time.

———◆———

"It's the only way, Ola. We got to do this ourselves." Daddy stood beside me, a hatchet in his hands raised high in the air. "Hold him still, and I'll chop off his arm."

Mama's face was distorted, her laugh creepy and cold. "That's right, you go on now."

"No, Daddy, no!" I tried to scream, tried to run away from the parents I used to trust.

But my movements were slow. I couldn't get away. It was like moving through molasses.

Like I was wound up in a blanket.

Like I was in a nightmare.

I awoke panting, twisted in my blankets, lying on top of my bad arm. It pulsated beneath me, pounded, begged to be released. I rolled over and freed it. It was half asleep, the pain of prickly pin needles spreading as blood flow returned. The cauliflower masses throbbed even more than usual. I rubbed my head, massaging the headache away, and tried to focus on the events of the past few days instead of the pain.

It had been a great week at Camp Linstead. Every meal

was dished up on my very own galvanized steel mess kit. Each Scout was responsible for washing his own kit to be ready for the next meal. I did the job, but it wouldn't have gotten Mama's approval. And I hadn't used a napkin once since I arrived.

We hiked in the pine woods, identified different types of trees, practiced archery, went canoeing, reviewed our handbooks, practiced first aid techniques, and learned about birds, the weather, and Indian lore. During the worst heat of the day, we swam in the river. A swim net protected us from jellyfish, so with the danger of being stung eliminated, we played endless games of chicken, had water fights, and practiced our swimming strokes. We arrived at dinner worn out and waterlogged, only to be revived by pork and beans or hot dogs cooked over an open fire.

Evenings, we sang around a campfire on the narrow sandy beach. One of our leaders taught us to identify constellations in the stars. And so long as Abraham or Reggie was nearby, I loved to be scared senseless whenever one of the Scout leaders told a ghost story.

One day we drove in to Annapolis, the capitol of Maryland and the nearest real town. We walked along the old, cobblestone streets to the harbor and watched watermen work on their fishing lines, crab nets, and boats. Mr. Ames told us Governor Ritchie, the most powerful man in Maryland, worked in the big, fancy building on the hill at the end of the street.

I stood next to Mr. Ames. I didn't mean to, but I could hear when he lowered his voice and leaned in close to Mr. Brown.

"Word is Ritchie's days are numbered, ever since the Armwood lynching last fall."

My stomach tightened. A lynching?

"The one happened down near Salisbury?" Mr. Brown whispered.

"Yup, the twenty-two-year old boy."

"How far is Salisbury from here?"

Mr. Ames tilted his head. "Guess about eighty miles."

"That's eighty miles too close."

Both men shook their heads solemnly and looked off into the distance. For several moments they were quiet as the other boys chattered. Then Mr. Ames seemed to notice me.

Mr. Ames smiled broadly and showed his secret cave. "Smitty, think it's time to move on?"

I nodded. I didn't want to hear any more about lynchings, no matter how far away they happened.

Twelve boys could make a lot of noise, so Mr. Brown clapped his hands and whistled to get everyone's attention. "Okay boys, let's buy postcards and write to your parents. We have three pencils for you to take turns writing. And as a surprise, your church family took up a collection. Gave us enough money to buy ice cream milkshakes to share."

We cheered, clapped, and hollered.

Mr. Brown nodded toward the five-and-dime store nearby that advertised it had a soda fountain. "Will they serve us?"

"Not sure." Mr. Ames shook his head. "But I know they will over on Calvert Street. Start walking boys."

Lying on my pallet and remembering the rich, chocolate milkshake I shared with Abraham made my arm feel better. Without sitting up, I tried to use my feet to smooth out my blanket. We didn't have the money for a sleeping bag, so I slept on two folded blankets like a lot of the boys did. Reggie, Abraham, and three other boys slept inside our tent. The smell of canvas and mildew mixed with the night air of summer's end. Outside, the quiet stillness was broken only by the song of some bullfrogs in the distance.

"Get off. Get off." Reggie whimpered in his sleep. His legs started running, though he stayed on the tent floor beside me. "Don't! Off!"

"Reggie, man, wake up." I leaned over and shook his shoulder.

Abraham sat up and rubbed his eyes. "What's wrong?"

"Reggie's having a nightmare." My cousin's cries got louder and more distressed, tears streaming down his cheeks.

"Wake him up." Abraham crawled around another boy, who was sound asleep. Once beside Reggie, Abe gave him a hard shake. "Wake up, Reg, you're okay. *Wake up.*"

Reggie woke up panting. In the shadowed moonlight, I watched his eyes darting wildly around, searching the tent. I'd never seen my cousin like this. Even though it was because of a bad dream, it alarmed me. I was glad Abraham took charge.

"You're okay, Reggie. You're safe." Abraham crooned in a voice wise and gentle beyond his years. "Just Smitty and me. We got you."

Reggie sharply inhaled, then seemed to relax. "Oh." He wiped away some of the tears on his face. Abraham helped Reggie sit up, said it would help him get out of the bad dream faster.

Reggie barely whispered. "Wish it were a dream."

My two friends knew I was there, but it seemed more like I wasn't. They had a private conversation of their own. Private only because even though I knew the words, they didn't make sense.

Abraham's hand rested lightly on Reggie's arm. "I saw the marks."

Reggie held his breath a moment. He exhaled, nodded, then chewed on his bottom lip.

"Who?"

My cousin glanced at me. "My mom's boyfriend. He's lived with us a long time."

"What's he use?" Abraham asked.

"These days, a belt." Reggie took another swipe at the tears on his face.

They were quiet.

"Anything else?"

"He always..."

Abraham tilted his head, looked at Reg. "He always what?"

"Always does stuff." Reggie barely murmured. He looked down at his blanket then pounded his fist onto the tent floor, just once, with all his might.

Abraham winced. "I'm sorry."

They were quiet for a long time.

"You?" Reggie asked.

"No." Abraham shook his head. "My brother, though. Sam. He had nightmares, too. Then he grew bigger and beat Dad to a pulp one night. Dad almost died. Before Sam ran away, he warned our father if ever he touched me or my little sister, Sam was gonna come back and finish him off." Abraham sniffed. "Ain't seen my brother since, but he made it safe for me and Alice. Dad never touched us."

They were silent a long time until Abraham broke the stillness.

"Let's try and go back to sleep."

"Abe?"

"Yeah?"

"Would you...?" Reggie stopped then started. "You think...?"

Abraham interrupted. "I'm gonna sleep next to you."

"Thanks."

"No problem." Abe yawned.

Without a saying a word, I lay down on my blankets and wondered about all I didn't understand in life.

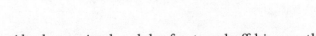

Abraham wiped a glob of oatmeal off his mouth with the back of his hand. "Hurry up and finish eating, Smitty. We gotta go."

"Why you think I'm taking so long?" I grumbled.

They'd been thirteen of the best days of my life, each day a new adventure and fun times with my friends. Reggie, Abraham, and I were inseparable. Plus, I earned two new badges. And I made it through two weeks of camp without losing any pieces to my mess kit. Mama was sure to cluck over that accomplishment. It had been my best time at camp ever.

But that all changed the night before when I learned my job for camp cleanup was to help with the swim net. I must've done something to make God or the Scout leaders mad at me. Last night, I lay awake in the tent and plotted an escape. I'd have a real bad stomachache in the morning. If I pretended to be so sick I couldn't eat my breakfast and moaned as I held my belly, I was sure to get out of cleaning the swim net.

It was a great plan. I'd drifted off to sleep with a smile on my face.

Problem was, I woke up so hungry I ate most of my oatmeal and toast before I remembered I was supposed to be sick. My own stomach ruined my plan of escape. I was doomed. I was mad at myself and mad at Reggie. He had kitchen clean up. Lucky.

"Time to get to your jobs, boys!" Mr. Ames announced from up front. "If you don't finish eating and clean up in two minutes, you'll get extra work assignments."

I ate faster. Maybe cleaning the swim net wasn't so bad. At least I didn't have to help clean the outhouses. That was the worst job in the whole universe.

Abraham waited for me.

I wiped my mouth with the back of my hand. "Ready."

From the back of the room, one of the older Scouts complained about the end of summer cleanup. "Why don't the white Scouts ever close down camp?" he called out. "I been here three years, and every year it's the same."

Soon all seventy-five boys were murmuring. Everyone was complaining except for the Scoutmasters. They all sat together around one table and exchanged looks. A few studied the coffee in their cups. Others rubbed the beard stubble on their chins and said nothing. It felt like everyone was in a bad mood on account of having to leave camp. Or because we had to clean up. It was hard to tell which.

The room got unusually quiet when Mr. Ames stood up, scratched his head, and muttered something about attitude. "The Maryland Boy Scout rulebook says whoever is at camp the last two weeks of summer does the cleanup." He paused and glanced at the other Scoutmasters. "The rules say nothing about coloreds having to cleanup. It just so happens we get scheduled for the last two weeks. Let's be grateful we get to come at all."

Tension hung in the silent air.

"It's only a little work boys, a small price to pay for two weeks of fun."

Strained silence followed.

Finally, an older boy spoke up. "Bet those white boys couldn't handle the work. They'd go home crying to their mommies." He laughed so hard he snorted. Everybody else laughed at that, and the pressure eased.

"You all are proud, hardworking Scouts. You go do the best job ever was done cleaning up this camp." Mr. Ames wiggled his eyebrows. "Now, let's get a move on."

Abraham tagged my shoulder and started running. "Race you to the beach!"

I was right behind him the whole way, zigzagging along the sandy trail through the woods. My lungs heaved to help my feet keep up with my long-legged friend. On the beach by the river's edge, we leaned over, hands on our thighs, and fought to catch our breath.

"You get faster every year, Smitty."

"Thanks." I gasped. "You too."

The blue-green river water looked inviting. I was tempted to go for one last swim as we waited for the others, but lately, more sea nettles had been slipping into the swim area. If one bumped into you, the tentacles stung wherever they brushed against your skin, leaving welts and an intense burning sensation. It didn't sound fun to me. Neither did cleaning the net.

By the time Abraham and I were breathing easily again, Mr. Ames and Mr. Brown plus six other boys joined us at the beach.

"Boys," Mr. Ames said, "this swim net has done a good job all summer, gave Scouts a safe place to swim." He looked at us lined up before him, like soldiers preparing for battle. "Lots of jellyfish have bumped into this net before drifting on down the river. But others got tangled up and are still stuck. Our job is to haul in the net, scrape off all the sea nettles tangled in the lines, and store it for next year."

"Yes, sir!" Mr. Brown must have thought he was in church. "That's right!"

"Some of those nettles in the net been dead a long time, and they can't hurt you. Ones that've been dead a short time can still sting. And the live ones can burn you something fierce." Mr. Ames paused. "And boys, you can't tell by looking which is which." He looked us over as if sizing up our character. When he looked directly at me, I held his gaze and swallowed. My Adam's apple felt one hundred times bigger than normal.

"We need to clean up this net. You might get stung, you might not. Are you man enough to handle this job?"

I forced myself to nod.

I would not let down my fellow Scouts.

I feared those jellyfish.

But my Scout's honor and duty kept me standing where I was.

Mr. Ames's chin went up. He smiled. "I'm proud of you boys. Now let's get to work."

The men waded far into the blue-green liquid and cut free one section of the net. Mr. Ames held onto one end, Mr. Brown the other. They walked slowly back toward the beach, pulling it between them.

Mr. Brown spoke up when they got closer to where we waited on the shore. "Boys, this net moves easily through the water, but as we pull it out, it's going to feel heavier than you'd expect. Check to find a clean spot before you grab on. Let's haul this in and lay it out on the beach."

Just like he promised, the netting was heavy and awkward. Jellyfish were wedged into the net covering a large portion of it. Some of the jellyfish had clear flat swimming discs. In the middle were designs that looked like pink four leaf clovers. Others looked like white bells with maroon markings. The ugliest of the jellyfish had a brown bell section with extra long tentacles dangling from the edges. There were big ones the size of dinner plates, little ones like tea cup saucers, and every size in between.

The mix of jellyfish dangled and danced in the air as the dripping net emerged from the river. We dropped it onto the beach with a thud. The rounded blobs of the nettles' ballooned tops rippled and shook like the bellies of hundreds of fat men. Tentacles overlapped as if they were searching for the liquid they left behind. Sand stuck to the sea nettles made contact adding grainy texture to the odd display. It was an ugly sight.

I looked around. Every one of us stared, wide eyed. A few looked a little nauseated.

"They were there when we were swimming?"

"That's disgusting."

"Sure is."

The mess of jellyfish reminded me of the time Mary had the flu at Christmas, and she got sick after eating Mama's cracker pudding.

"Yup, sure is ugly." Mr. Ames chuckled. "But better in the net than in our swimming water."

I murmured agreement.

Mr. Brown laughed. "Some of you boys look like you have weak stomachs. Go on to that pile over there and grab a tool. We'll show you how to scrape the net clean." He directed us to a nearby pile of sticks, shells, and broken boards.

After a while, I got the hang of holding a section of the net in place with the end of a stick as I used a piece of board to scrape off the jellylike blobs and globs. All the while I was careful to keep my skin away from the tangled tentacles. As we worked on the net, a couple of the older boys took turns using a garden shovel to dig large holes in the sand. The one with the shovel scooped up the piles of jelly fish we'd removed from the net and buried them deep in the sand.

"Dagnabit! Shoot!" From his crouched position beside the net, Mr. Ames shot up and swung his arm back and forth. "Yikes! It smarts, boys, be careful."

He and Mr. Brown walked to where they'd set down their canteens. I hadn't noticed the bottles of vinegar. Mr. Brown dribbled the tangy smelling liquid over Mr. Ames's arm. "That'll help for a little while at least."

The morning sun beat down on our backs as we labored over the second net. One boy got stung. All work ceased as we watched him dance around, swing his arm, and holler. He started to cuss, until Mr. Ames reminded him we were Scouts. The boy grimaced and blinked back tears as Mr. Brown poured vinegar over the emerging welts.

"Take a break for a moment, son." Mr. Brown pushed the cork back into the bottle.

Mr. Ames cleared his throat. "The rest of you, we're more than halfway done. We're almost there, boys."

It felt like we were turning our backs on one of our own as we returned our focus to our work. But we had to get the job done with as few casualties as possible.

Finally, we labored over the last section of net. Juneus, a light skinned boy with good hair, stood between Abe and me with the shovel. He began scooping up the pile of sea nettles we'd scraped off the net. "Mr. Brown, did you hear I earned my archery badge this week?"

"Good for you," Mr. Brown said.

Juneus continued shoveling up sea nettles. The mound of the sandy, jelly blobs and twisted tentacles slipped a little on the shovel blade. Juneus got it balanced again.

"Careful, son." Mr. Brown cautioned. "Looks like you've

got enough there already."

"I'm good." Juneus snickered. "I'm trying to earn my jellyfish badge."

Everyone laughed.

Still hunkered down by the net, I laughed and turned to my side to stand. I needed to ease out the kinks in my back.

I swung the wooden board in my right hand as I turned.

Clunk!

The overloaded shovel blade met my board.

Juneus stumbled. The mound of jellyfish slipped and slithered from side to side on the shovel blade. It swayed dangerously close to me despite Juneus's efforts to keep a hold of the handle and regain his balance.

Voices hollered.

Juneus yelled.

Sea nettles slid.

The slimy damp weight of jellyfish fell on my wrist and forearm then bounced off and landed on my foot and ankle. Wherever the mushroom-shaped heads of the sea nettles landed, the tentacles soon followed. Long strands of tentacles wrapped around my wrist.

I jumped all the way up and yelled, "Juneus, you dummy!" I shook my arm with such force, I thought it might break off from my shoulder, yet the tentacles stubbornly stayed draped around my wrist. It felt like a thousand invisible bees stung me all at once.

Like an Indian doing a passionate rain dance, I hopped from one foot to the other. My right foot escaped the pile of jellyfish that landed on top of it, but not soon enough. The stinging, burning sensation made my foot want to escape from the rest of my body. But since my feet couldn't get away, I jumped wildly from one foot to the other.

"Smitty! Careful!" Abraham leapt away from me.

His warning came too late.

My left foot landed on top of a slick, slimy jellyfish. Both my feet swung up from underneath me and I landed with a thud on the sand, flat on my back. The gelatinous ooze of jellyfish seeped through my shirt and onto my skin.

I wanted to yell, but instead whispered. "Thank you, Jesus."

Mr. Ames bent over me, his broad shoulders blocking the sun. He squinted with concern. "What'd you say?"

I whimpered, fighting back tears of pain and embarrassment. "Thank you, Jesus."

"Why?"

"The jellyfish under my back's been dead a while. It didn't sting."

Mr. Ames and Mr. Brown shook their heads and laughed. Soon all the boys joined in.

Everyone laughed except me. My Scout leaders put their strong hands under my arms and lifted me up. My feet never touched the sand. They carried me straight over to the vinegar bottle.

Mr. Brown dripped vinegar over my wrist, forearm, ankle, and foot. It felt good as it landed on my welting skin, but the relief was short-lived.

Away from the other boys, my bravery slipped, and tears slid down my face. "Why do sea nettles sting, Mr. Ames?"

He looked at me with kind, deep black-brown eyes. Sweat glistened on his cheekbones. "Don't know why, Smitty. I guess there's a reason." He got quiet for a moment, put his hand on my shoulder. "There's a lot in life that stings, son. A lot in this world that hurts. And for most of it, we'll never understand why."

Chapter Six

1935

Smitty, 11-years old

Nazis deprive German Jews of their citizenship

*Maryland Court of Appeals orders the
University of Maryland to admit Donald Murray,
the university's first black student*

One pound of hamburger meat costs 11 cents

"Mama, are you sure my uniform looks good?"

"Smitty, I told you twice already, you're handsome as any man I ever seen."

Mama smiled so wide, I couldn't help but believe her, but I had to be sure. "Clifton, look me over real careful. Do I look good?"

Clifton looked up from the breakfast table. His eyes twinkled, and a smile slid across his face. He liked it when I asked him important questions. It made him feel smart as everybody else.

"Mama's right, little brother. You're the best looking Boy Scout ever."

"Thank you." I was satisfied. It simply wasn't in Clifton

to lie. He told me how he lied once when he was a young boy and got such a bad bellyache that he thought he'd die by morning.

"Let me check your bandage, son." Mama fussed and inspected the white gauze bandage she had wrapped around my arm earlier in the morning. I'd had the operation the month after I'd helped clean the swim net at camp and hardly needed a bandage any more, but Mama insisted. The operation got rid of the hemangiomas and eliminated the pain, but my arm still didn't straighten out.

"What's so special about this morning, Smitty?" Ruby asked, scraping the last of her oatmeal from the side of her bowl.

"Today I go to my first Boy Scout Jamboree," I announced, my mouth full of toast. "Boy Scouts from all over gather for a big meeting once a year in late spring. This is my first Jamboree *ever*."

The past few weeks at meetings our Scoutmasters had talked up this big event. In years past, there were reasons we couldn't go to the Jamboree. I'm not sure what the reasons were, but this year, we could go. From our church in Sandtown, we'd walk aways then take the streetcar to Morgan College. At the college we'd meet up with the other colored troops and hike across Morgan's campus, past Lake Montebello to the big church in Clifton Park where the Jamboree was going to be held.

I glanced at the clock. "Reggie should've been here fifteen minutes ago. We're going to be late."

"Reggie?" Mary who had been half asleep at the table, looked up. "You say Reggie was going to meet you?"

"Yes."

Mary crinkled up her nose and yawned. "Guess I forgot to tell you. He stopped by yesterday, said he wasn't going this morning. He has to work."

"Mary!" I bellowed. This was just like her. Now I was going to be late. "Mama, I gotta go now."

Mama reached into her change purse and pressed two coins in my palm. "Put that money deep in your pocket 'til you get on the streetcar. Run fast as you can to the church."

I kissed her goodbye. "Yes, ma'am!"

I was half way down the street when Mama called after me. "You be sure you mind Mr. Ames, young man!"

◆

Morgan was a school where coloreds could get a college education and go on to have all sorts of fancy jobs, like being a lawyer. As we hiked across the campus, I pretended I was a student there, learning everything there was to learn in the world. Since I wanted to be as smart as Frederick Douglas, I figured college would probably help me.

First though, I had to survive grade school, and I wasn't so sure I could. Problem was, I liked to talk.

One time at dinner Daddy shook his head in exasperation. "Smitty, you talk more than Ruby and Mary put together."

I answered with a smile. "Maybe I'm just more interesting than them."

Mama said I was sassing. Daddy wasn't sure. They couldn't agree if they should punish me. I just thought I was telling the truth.

I liked to talk, ask questions, and make people laugh. Mama said there was nothing wrong with talking except in school, because the teachers expected you to be quiet and stay in your seat. For me, the one thing harder than not talking was staying in my seat.

But I knew I could sit in my seat for the Boy Scout Jamboree meeting, because I'd do anything to be there. I couldn't wait to be surrounded by hundreds of other Boy Scouts as we recited our pledge and the Scout Law. We would stand together for all the good and honest things we believed in.

Daddy first signed me up for Scouts to keep me busy, so I couldn't get into too much trouble. I didn't like it the first week, because he'd made me go. But by the third week, I loved Scouts. Now I was in my third year, and I loved everything about it.

We hiked several miles in the warm morning sunshine until we finally arrived at the church in Clifton Park. Single file, Mr. Ames led us as we climbed the elegant stack of white marble stairs to the set of wide doors with shiny brass door handles. Mr. Ames stood on the top level by the door, his hat in his hands, as he was greeted by a white Scoutmaster. I wiped sweat off my face with my hands, then wiped them on my pants. I checked all my buttons and my shoelaces. I was ready to join my fellow Scouts of Maryland.

From inside the church we could hear the opening ceremonies begin exactly as Mr. Ames had described. We could hear the boys inside begin to recite the Scout Law. Tired of waiting, I wanted to run inside and join in, but forced myself to stand obediently. I imagined the hundreds of Scouts inside standing, reciting the Scout Law. Good Scouts always stood when they said the Scout Law.

Together in one powerful voice made up of hundreds of boys inside the sanctuary I heard, "A Scout is trustworthy, loyal, helpful..."

My lips began to move. I had to join in. "...friendly, courteous, kind, obedient...."

From the step behind me, I heard Abraham's deep voice.

"...cheerful, thrifty, brave..."

I turned and smiled as we recited the last two words together, "...clean and reverent."

It felt good to say the words with hundreds of our Boy Scout brothers, even though they were inside, and we were still outside.

Someone behind me called out. "Come on Mr. Ames, we want to go in."

Mr. Ames looked like he was waiting for something to happen.

The white Scoutmaster stood next to him. Two more men in Scoutmaster uniforms came out from inside the church. The door closed behind them. One man crossed his arms over his chest. The other put both hands on his hips and blocked the door. They all talked with Mr. Ames.

I leaned forward and tried to make out what they were saying, but I couldn't hear. Maybe there weren't enough seats left for our group to sit together. Maybe we had to wait a few minutes, since we were late and might disturb the meeting. Whatever the problem, I knew Mr. Ames would solve it.

But from where I stood, it didn't look like Mr. Ames was saying much. He simply nodded his head and looked down at his shoes.

He studied his shoes for a long time and moved his jaw from side to side.

Both white men stood unmoving.

Mr. Ames cleared his throat. He turned and looked down at us. "Don't make a fuss now, boys. Let's turn around." He put his cap back on his head. "We're hiking back."

Nobody moved.

It didn't make any sense. We'd hiked all morning. We'd barely arrived, hadn't even been in to the meeting, and that was the whole reason we came. I wasn't the only one who was confused. Up and down the steps all of our group looked perplexed.

Abe dared to question, "What do you mean by 'turn around'?"

Our leader closed his eyes for a moment and smiled. But it wasn't his real smile, because you couldn't see his mouth-cave. He breathed deep and steady.

"Abe, no questions. Turn around, walk down the steps, and hike back to Morgan."

My lungs went empty. I began to breathe fast and shallow. This couldn't happen! I looked around to see if any boys around me looked like they understood. All up and down the flight of steps my friends and the boys from the other colored troops looked as confused as I felt. We'd waited months and months to come here.

Abraham swore.

I muttered under my breath.

Mickey started to cry.

"We hiked all this way."

"What's wrong, Mr. Ames?"

"My daddy gave up his newspaper all week so I could ride the streetcar."

"We can't leave."

Our complaints and protests buzzed in the air like a swarm of disappointed bees.

"That's enough, boys, turn around! *Now!*" Our leader slapped us quiet with his voice.

He had never, ever yelled at us.

Beads of perspiration trickled down his face, and the veins in his neck were pulsing. His breathing became fast and shallow as he looked past us, down to the street.

His reaction scared me, though I wasn't sure why. It

almost seemed like Mr. Ames was afraid, but nothing could frighten my Scout leader.

Then, in almost a whisper he pleaded, "Now boys. *Turn. Now.*"

He spread out his arms and blocked the two boys closest to him so they couldn't step towards the church. Gently he waved his arms to shoo us back down the steps.

The two white men stepped forward, closing the gap between us and them.

One of them growled. "You heard him, boys. Turn around." He lifted his chin and curled his lip. "We don't want your kind here."

Our kind?

What did he mean?

We were Boy Scouts, exactly like all the Boy Scouts meeting inside the church.

But we weren't.

We were colored.

While the meeting continued inside the church, we silently walked down the steps. The white marble steps. *White.* Cold and hard.

My feet were heavy boulders inside my shoes. I felt sadder and sadder with each step. We were supposed to walk into the church, not away from it.

A crowd of white people had gathered on the sidewalk below and watched us descend the stairway. Four white policemen stood between us and the crowd.

My heart pounded.

My mouth went dry.

That's when I saw a white boy in a Boy Scout uniform staring at me. He stood between a well-dressed man and woman. The man had pasty skin and wore a pin stripe suit and a gray fedora. His sneering lips curled back, baring teeth like a vicious dog.

The woman's lips pressed together and twisted. She wore a silky dress that billowed in the breeze. The hat on her head tilted to the side like Mama always tried to do but said she could never pull off.

The pale boy's eyes met my own. We were locked in a gaze. We both wore the same uniform, both of us were Scouts. Maybe we even had some of the same badges. I imagined the conversation we could've shared if we'd been friends. He glanced down at the ground. When he looked up at me again, his lips curled, and he showed his teeth like a snarling dog. He looked exactly like his father.

The boy already had the ugliness inside him, so strong it sent chills down my spine. Shame forced me to lower my head and shuffle my rock-heavy feet.

Next to that white boy, I was nobody.

I wasn't a Boy Scout.

I was only colored.

I bit my bottom lip and pressed my fingers to my eyes. I would not cry in front of them.

Sometimes when the ugliness happened, there was a white person who looked at you, and you knew that man or lady didn't think you were a nobody. Now and then, a white person looked at you with kind, tender eyes. Their gazes told you they felt real bad about the way things were. They looked at you like you were somebody. An expression that whispered hope into your soul saying, *It's not your fault. It won't always be like this.*

But I couldn't hold my head up long enough to see if any of the white people around that church looked at us that way. Like every other Boy Scout I'd arrived with, I kept my head down. We walked along the street, the cold stares of the whites chilling our backs.

The policemen followed us. They hooted with laughter and said they'd make sure we got out of the neighborhood safely. They walked behind us and slapped their billy clubs into the palms of their hands. They sneered and snickered. "Bunch a no good, colored boys. Can't scrub clean enough to ever be real Scouts."

Every once in a while, one of them poked one of us with his club hard enough to bruise ribs.

I heard a few boys sniffling, but I swore I wouldn't give in to these men.

When we finally got to the end of the long street, we turned the corner out of the Clifton Park neighborhood. Away from the audience and the taunting policemen, I allowed one lone tear to trickle down my cheek.

My tongue peeked out of my mouth and caught my tear.

It was salty.

Bitter.

Why'd I have to be born colored?

Chapter Seven

March 2008

Smitty, 84-years old

*Alaska's last native speaker of the Eyak language dies,
making the language extinct*

"It's shameful how they turned you away from that Boy Scout Jamboree!" My wife and I have been married 62 years, and she still gets upset by that story. "Didn't *any* white person speak up?"

I've long since gotten over the injustice. "Nah. I'm sure there were folks watching who knew it wasn't right, but what were they going to do? They couldn't change the system. It was too big, too entrenched in society."

"Still, it was very wrong."

I pat her hands resting on the kitchen table. "It's in the past. No sense holding on to all the discriminations I suffered in my lifetime. Holding on leaves you bitter." I steal a glance at Leslie. "When you hold on to bitter, you can't be open to the sweet things that come your way."

Leslie smiles. She understands what I'm not saying.

So does my wife, a good woman. She pours me some

more coffee.

I've been telling my stories to Leslie when she comes and visits. She hasn't made any promises to write, but that's okay. The telling feels good. I watch as she fiddles with her digital recorder and makes some notes with good old-fashioned pen and paper. She looks so much like her father, I call her "Little Irv." She don't mind. I think she likes it.

I sigh. "Little Irv, did you know when your daddy was a boy, he lived near that church?"

She nods her head. "I recognized the name Clifton Park."

My wife's eyebrows arch up. "Do you think Irv was at that Jamboree?"

I laugh. "No, he was never a Boy Scout."

I miss Irv so much, I ache inside. Before him, I never would've believed I could love someone so much, someone who wasn't own my flesh and blood. Who wasn't even my own race. Irv changed all that.

My wife turns another page in my orange notebook. "Here Smitty, look at this award."

I know she's trying to distract me from my grief of missing Irv, my best friend.

We're at the kitchen table looking through my big orange notebook, showing bits and pieces of my life to my young writer friend. The book is stuffed full to the breaking point with a lifetime collection: military papers, certificates, awards, diplomas, church bulletins, and newspaper articles. Each item has been carefully stored in a plastic page protector.

Once I'd entered my adult years, I started to put this book together. Each page is about me. I added to it as often as I could. Guess I kept this book to remind me I'm a somebody.

It's a terrible thing for a boy to grow up feeling ashamed of the color of his skin, of who God created him to be, but it happened too many times. And years later, even though the boy's grown into a man, some of those feelings can remain deep down inside.

I clear my throat to get the ladies' attention. After all, I'm sure they don't want to miss a word. "Because of my skin color, my family circumstances, and my lack of education, I struggled with being a nobody for a long, long time."

They understand, one woman because she lived through it, the other because she listens with her heart.

"But bit by bit, each time I earned something in this book, I realized I mattered. I was a child of God. That fact alone makes me a somebody."

"That's right."

"Yes, sir."

My spirit's warmed. We're having church, the fellowship of believers. "I was child of the Heavenly King, the Lord Jesus Christ. And that encouraged me to work hard for each item in these pages."

My wife pats her hand on a new page and smiles. "I especially like this one, *The Roots of Scouting Award.*"

One of my favorites. In the spring of 2008, the Scouts of Baltimore honored me by establishing The Reverend James H. Smith Scholarship Fund. I've spent my whole adult life giving back to the Boy Scouts. They seemed to have appreciated it.

I'm still proud to be a Boy Scout. And being a Boy Scout is probably what gave me my patriotic spirit.

And I'm proud to be an American, grateful to have lived my life in this country. There've been so many names for us with dark skin: colored, Negro, black.

African-American is what they say now, but not me, I'm black. I wasn't born in Africa, neither were my parents or my grandparents. I was born right here in Baltimore City.

I love my country and served it well.

"So when your Daddy signed you up for Scouts, you didn't want to go?" Leslie asks.

"*Did not* want to join." I shake my head. "I was in school all week, thought that was enough time to have to follow the rules." I laugh. "But soon as a chapter for coloreds opened up, Daddy marched me down to the church and signed me up. I didn't have a say in the matter.

"He was smart. He knew children have too much energy, too much curiosity. If he didn't keep me busy, he knew I'd get into trouble. That's why he had all of us kids work hard around the house and at odd jobs." I sip my coffee, and it feels good . "Daddy had a strong work ethic and made sure he instilled it in each of his children.

"He knew the importance of being an honest, hard worker. I'm grateful. When I ran away, I could've ended up in a whole lot more trouble than I did. But in the end, I couldn't run from all my father had invested in me."

There's a stack of papers on the table next to my orange book, things Leslie's printed off the Internet, notes I've made for her, a few photographs, and an old road map. I unfold the map of Anne Arundel County, smoothing out the creases made over the years.

This morning as I got out of bed, it felt like I had creases in my old, tired body. Too bad I can't smooth out my aches and pains like I'm doing to this map. "Leslie, you spell that road name with an A, not an E. It's Arleigh."

"Thanks, Mr. Smith."

I slide my hand over the map as if I'm stroking a cat. "The other day it was beautiful outside, and I felt good, so I went for a drive in my truck. Drove down to Anne Arundel County to see where Camp Linstead used to be."

Leslie's eyes widen.

"Sure are a lot of traffic lights between here and there, got lots of praying done. Whenever I'm in my truck and stopped at a traffic light, I pray for the person in the vehicle beside me or in front of me. I might be the only person praying for them that day, and I don't want to miss the chance to make a difference in their life. I may not know their name, but God knows their needs."

It's cool today, so I pull my sweater a little tighter around me. Seems lately I'm either tired or cold. Or both.

"Right there." I point to the map on the table and tap with my index finger. "Camp Linstead's long gone, but that's where it was."

The women peer with squinted eyes at the paper map as if they might see some little Boy Scouts run across it.

"Now there's a community called Linstead-on-the-Severn. Big, expensive, waterfront homes, just lovely. I'm sure folks living there are good people. Yet I doubt any kids there ever cleaned a swim net loaded with jellyfish. Probably never slept in an old farm wagon either." The thought makes me chuckle.

"And where's Arleigh Road?" Leslie's slim, pale fingers search the map.

"Right here." I tap with my brown index finger. "Less than three miles away."

My wife leans in and looks closer. "What was at Arleigh Road?"

Leslie grins. "My grandfather bought a piece of land for thirty dollars there, and then he and my dad chopped down trees and built a log cabin. During the summer they went to get away from the heat of Baltimore City, same as Smitty."

Mrs. Smith looks at me with surprise. "Irving was near Camp Linstead as a boy? Same time as you?"

"Yes ma'am. Less than three miles away."

When I was a boy and went to the Boy Scout Jamboree, I was in Irv's neighborhood. And as boys, we both swam in the Severn River. Irving and I grew up in the same city, in separate worlds, but our paths crossed many times decades before we ever met.

I find that pretty amazing now. When we did finally meet, I wasn't amazed, I was irritated. I had no need for a white man in my life. Never had a white friend, and I certainly didn't want one. Life sure is full of surprises.

CHAPTER EIGHT

1937

Smitty, 13-years old

Margaret Mitchell wins Pulitzer Prize for Gone With the Wind

President Roosevelt appoints the first African-American Federal Judge, William H. Hastie, Jr.

A loaf of bread costs 9¢

Even though I already knew the answer, I asked anyway. I was thirteen years old and thought I could change Daddy's mind if I persisted.

He stood by the kitchen counter drinking a glass of water. He'd already said no. Reasoning with Daddy hadn't worked, neither had persuasion

I looked up at my father and tried one more time, desperate. "One pair of new pants, Daddy, that's all. Can't I get just *one* new pair?"

His eyes narrowed. "No."

Desperation welled up. "They're giving them away free, Pop. *Free.*" I had to have some new clothes. Everyone else I knew had gotten some.

He put his empty glass on the counter with more force

than usual.

"When I say no, I mean *no.*"

A government welfare agency had come into town and was giving away free clothing for people in need. The way I figured it, we were a family in need as much as anyone else was. But no matter how much Mary, Ruby, or I pleaded, Daddy would not allow us to get any of the free goods.

"Cousin Reggie got two new pairs of pants, Pop. It didn't cost them one penny." As a family we still struggled to get enough money in the "Rent" coffee can each month. Richard and Clifton didn't live at home any more, but they gave Daddy money anyway when they could. I thought Daddy would be happy I could get new clothes. For free.

Dad exhaled like the steam escaping from the pressure cooker on Mama's stove. He took a few deep breaths. Just stood there. He didn't look at me, but coolly stared past me out through the kitchen door.

I thought I was wearing him down, so I kept at it. I even smiled my most charming smile. "You've said yourself these are awful hard times. Seems we should be grateful for what the Lord is providing."

Daddy went from simmering steam to full-blown boiling over. His eyes narrowed into little slits. His face flushed. He bent down to my level, looked me in the eye, and pointed with his index finger. He wagged his finger so close, he tapped me on the nose. Another time that would've been funny, but I'd never seen my father like this. I leaned back against the kitchen counter. He towered over me and got in my face all at the same time.

"Now you listen to me, son. And you listen real good." His volume increased with each syllable. "Do you know what those welfare people give you when you accept a pair of their *free* pants?"

"A shirt?" My voice cracked. Stupid puberty.

"Not a shirt. A harness! Underneath their *free* clothing is a harness, binding you in obligation to the government. A *harness,* Smitty, like you're a damn mule!"

Daddy took a breath.

I didn't dare move.

His voice was lower in volume, but strong as steel. "The government's not going to give you something for free. That's not the way it works. When the government gives you something you didn't earn, in exchange they take things away from you. They take away your pride. They take away your dignity. And they take your independence. You getting' this, son?" He leaned in even closer. "For a simple pair of pants, you become indebted to folks whose faces you've never even seen."

He leaned away from me, breathed heavily, and ran his hand over his head.

I moved an inch and swallowed.

He came forward by a foot and exhaled like a bull.

"You start taking things for free, and it makes you one of two things, a thief or a slave. They're giving away the pants, so you wouldn't be stealing. But you'd become a slave, obliged to do whatever the government wants you to do tomorrow because they gave you a pair of pants today."

He shook his head. "My great-granddaddy worked in the fields as a slave when he was a young man. He was beaten till he bled. He showed me the scars on his body when I was a little boy." His eyes seemed to plead, wanting me to understand. "You and me, son, we're *free.* Everything we own we have because *we worked* for it. It's ours without obligation to anyone. I don't care how many patches your Mama has to sew on your pants. We *are not* harnessing ourselves to the government so *you* can have some new clothes."

He stood to his full height, but his eyes stayed locked on mine.

I hadn't blinked. I'd barely breathed.

"The only one we will *ever* be indebted to is God Almighty. Do I make myself clear?"

"Yes, sir."

I hung my head.

It was hopeless. Daddy would never understand.

"Now go scrub our front steps while you think about what's more important. New pants or your dignity and freedom."

My head snapped up. "But Mary scrubbed the steps this morning!"

"No buts. You do as I say."

Daddy didn't understand. Things were different now. I only wanted new pants. I wasn't signing up to be a slave. If welfare, or the government, or whoever it was—I didn't care—was giving away free clothing, why shouldn't I get some? I wanted my fair share.

I knew my father loved me—that wasn't the problem. He didn't understand what it was like to be a teenager.

Lately all the girls were smiling at me trying to get my attention. I liked it but it also confused me and, too often, I said the wrong thing. Girls giggled around me and I wasn't sure why. New pants would be a boost to my confidence and my social life.

Clifton and Richard were well into their twenties. They'd both gotten married. When they visited home, I talked to them about girls and stuff. They'd smile and laugh, but I wasn't trying to be funny. I was trying to get advice. Occasionally, they helped me out. More often, Richard would shake his head and say, "You're going to be a teenager for plenty more years, little brother. Better get used to it."

Daddy tried to give me advice. He was always full of advice, but he'd been a teenager so long ago, the rules must've changed since then.

I gathered the supplies and got to scrubbing those stupid ol' marble steps like a man sentenced to the chain gang. Must have already scrubbed them two million times in my thirteen years, and here I was scrubbing them again. The sun warmed the back of my neck and arms. The sand and pumice were gritty in my hands. I scrubbed as I wore my old patched up pants. Obviously, Daddy didn't know what real suffering was. This was real suffering, to be out in public in my old patched up pants. I should have been out shining shoes, making money to help pay the rent.

"Hey, Smitty."

Clarence from the next block over was all smiles. Next to him stood his sister.

"Hey." I barely looked up until I saw Alice. She sure was cute.

She showed off her dimples. "Hi there."

I mumbled something back, embarrassed to be scrubbing the steps while they walked all over town. I threw more sand on the middle step.

Clarence stood in the sunlight, looked down, and brushed imaginary dirt off the knees of his trousers. "Careful with that sand, Smitty, I gotta keep these pants looking good."

If he'd been a hot air balloon, he would have lifted off the ground. "Did you get yourself some new pants, Smitty?

They're giving them away for free down the street."

I grunted. I didn't know what to say. I was sure Alice was staring at all the patches on my pants. She was prettier every time I saw her.

They walked on, Clarence strutting like a rooster down at the market.

I sighed.

There was no way any good woman was ever going to marry me if I had patches on my pants. My social life was doomed before it even began.

CHAPTER NINE

1938

Smitty, 14-years old

Action Comics issues first Superman *comic*

U.S. Supreme Court grants Lloyd Gaines, a black man, the right to attend the University of Missouri Law School. Three months later, he disappears

Cost of a blanket $5

As I tiptoed past Mama and Daddy's room, the floorboards creaked so loud I was sure they could hear it in the house next door. I froze, mid-step, and balanced on my toes opposite the bedroom door. It was open just enough to get me in trouble.

I listened.

Silence.

If I woke Daddy and Mama on the one day of the week they slept past sunrise, Daddy would have my hide. The deep roll of Daddy's snore thundered out from the room, followed by the squeak of bedsprings. Mama probably rolled over in her sleep. I was safe.

Reggie, who had repeatedly tossed pebbles up to my

bedroom window, was waiting out on the front steps. "You dummy, you overslept."

"Good morning to you too." I rolled my eyes. "Thanks for waking me." I stuffed a hunk of cheese and bread wrapped in newspaper into my coat pocket. Without time for breakfast, I was already hungry.

"Let's get a move on." Reggie slapped me on the back and smiled, showing off the gap between his two front teeth. "Don't want someone else to get our job."

The day before, Reggie had stopped by to say he'd lined up work down at the stockyards. It was slaughtering season. The herdsman we'd worked for late last year was back and said he'd hire us again. Most weekends, shoe shining kept me busy, but working as an under-shepherd paid better. Besides, it was an excuse for Reggie and me to be together.

The sun wouldn't come up for two hours, so by the light of the morning moon we half walked, half jogged the three miles to Baltimore's Union Stockyards. My heart pounded with excitement as we approached the entrance to the bustling business center. Fences and pens as far as you could see held pigs, sheep, cows, bulls, and horses. Last time we worked for Mr. Foster, he told us the stockyard spread out across fifty acres of land. The only other stockyard in the United States bigger than Union was out in Chicago.

The unmistakable smell of manure hit so strong, it stopped me in my tracks. The first whiffs of the tangy, ammonia-like odor burned my eyes. I rubbed my nose and turned to get a good look at Reggie, pretty sure of what I'd see. Sure enough, he stood there with his eyes squinted into tiny little slits. His lips were pushed up like he was trying to plug up his nose with his big, full lips.

I laughed and thumped him on the shoulder. "Your face is all smooshed up, fool."

His eyes watered as he shook his head. "How can you take it, man? That stench about chokes me to death."

"You might be bigger than me, but my nose is stronger than yours." I teased, trying not to cough.

"There's enough dung here to suffocate a brother." Reggie's eyes were narrowed and red-rimmed, but his smile was broad and bright.

"The smell of money." I was already pondering a new business venture. I could bring my old wagon down here, load it up with manure, and take it to houses with yards and gardens. Folks would probably pay for good, fresh fertilizer.

Reggie coughed and hacked up something from his throat. "The smell of money, that's right." He wiped his eyes with the back of his shirtsleeve then pointed ahead. "Mr. Foster's over this way."

We zigged and zagged our way through the maze of corralled animals, some of them brought to Baltimore from as far away as Texas. Wooden signs proclaiming, "Every hoof under every roof" hung from above, bragging how the animals were protected from the weather. Mr. Foster brought his sheep from Oklahoma. He told us most stockyards were out in the open without any overhead protection. Animals at Union Stockyards were considered higher quality because they were protected from rain, wind, and snow.

There were as many sounds as there were animals, and they blended into a unique sort of melody. Above the symphony of animals, men hollered commands and made business deals.

I felt an unusual lump of something underfoot and slid the slightest bit. I looked down at my feet and shook my head. Mama would never let me bring these shoes into the house again.

Reggie laughed and slapped the back of his hand on my

arm. "Over there."

Mr. Foster stood next to one of the sheep pens and waved. "Hello Reggie, glad to see you made it."

"Hello, sir. Brought along my cousin Smitty."

Mr. Foster smiled, pulled off one of his rubber gloves, and reached out his hand. "I remember you. You worked hard last time." His powerful hand about swallowed up my own.

"Thank you, sir."

Mr. Foster had big brown eyes peering out from behind a pair of glasses that were perched on his slender nose. An angular, chiseled face was framed by a well-worn, broad brimmed straw hat.

He idly slapped the rubber gloves against his pant leg. "Now gentlemen, let's review your responsibilities."

I quickly bit a mouthful of cheese and pushed the remainder back in my pocket.

"We will herd the sheep from these stockyards to the Union Slaughter House, about four miles from here." He pulled the neck loop of a rubber apron over his head. The apron reached almost to his knees and had big pockets on the front. He slipped the long straps between his fingers and tied it behind his back. "Sheep have a strong instinct to follow each other. Some people believe sheep are dumb because they follow so easily. But the truth is, their instinct to flock together protects them from predators in the natural world, yes? You boys understand?"

Reggie and I nodded.

"Together, they are protected." The wise shepherd climbed over the wooden fence into the pen with his sheep. One of the fleecy animals looked up at him, leaned against his leg, and bleated for attention. He smiled as he reached down to pet her head and stroke her side.

"Alone, a sheep is vulnerable to attack. If this girl ends

up by herself, she will become quite agitated. She knows she's safer in the company of others." He looked back at us. "That's where you and my two herding dogs come in. You all are to keep the sheep together.

"You boys walk alongside them, keeping them safely in the flock. My two dogs do the same." His smile faded. He looked down at us over the rim of his spectacles. "At no time whatsoever will you touch any of my sheep." The subtle change in his voice told me how serious he was about this.

He looked me in the eye. "Do you understand me, Smitty?"

I stood taller, feeling his trust. "Yes, sir."

"Reggie, do you understand?"

"Yes, sir."

"Very good, boys. I want my sheep in perfect condition for shearing and slaughter." Mr. Foster talked on. "If a sheep falls down, is injured, or becomes separated from the flock, you come find me at once."

Mr. Foster looked over his flock. He had a gentle expression, like Daddy's when he said he was proud of me.

This man really cared about his sheep. I bet if they had names, he'd know each one.

"Listen to the sound of my sheep, boys." The baaing and mewing that came from the flock was gentle and constant. "I understand their voices. If you work with me often enough, you will hear if they're content, alone, or scared. These sheep are going to the slaughter house, and I want them to arrive calm, assured they are protected along the way."

He looked me in the eye again, as if I were somebody. "As my under shepherds, you play an important role in the very last hours of my sheeps' lives. Do you understand?"

I nodded and wiped my sweaty palms on my pants. I'd forgotten what a big responsibility it was to be an under shepherd, to help guide and protect these sheep. Did they know they would die today?

My teacher's voice broke through my thoughts. "We'll follow Frederick Avenue to Gilmore Street. Left onto Lanvale, right onto Mount Street. Follow that all the way up across North Avenue. The slaughterhouse is at North Avenue and Retreat Street."

"Same route we took last time?" I asked.

"It is, so you know the way, don't you?"

I nodded.

"Good, but remember, this is all new territory for the sheep." He climbed out of the pen and stood by the gate. "My sheep have never been this way before. Houses and buildings along the roads will help act as borders for the sheep's path, but there are places where it's wide open. Any questions, my young shepherds?"

Neither of us spoke.

"Then let's begin."

Reggie and I climbed into the pen as instructed. Because the sheep wouldn't leave the pen when the gate opened, our first duty was to give them a reason to move. We pushed our way through the milling sheep to the back of the pen. Once there we waved our arms and hollered, unsettling them. Mama was always shooing Reggie and me outside because we were too loud. Hollering at a few sheep came real easy to us.

Mr. Foster stood outside the pen, his two border collies sitting beside him. He laughed at our antics and, when the sheep were riled up, he opened the gates, and those sheep practically tumbled over each other out into the open. They bleated loudly, scrambling about as they tried to find their place in the flock. Mr. Foster whistled commands to the dogs as he walked ahead, his shepherd's hook in hand. The dogs circled and ran alongside the flock, pouncing and barking. Initially, it seemed like total confusion. But by the time we exited the stockyards and were headed down Frederick Avenue, the commotion had ceased.

Reggie and I walked on either side of the flock. The sheep stayed together, since the dogs gave them little chance to stray. The time or two a sheep started to wander from the flock, all Reggie or I had to do was step in its path, and it quickly moved back in with the rest.

The creamy colored coats of the wooly sheep almost glistened in the morning light. Following Mr. Foster, their backs and buttocks gently rose and fell, enhanced by the rise and fall of the road. It reminded me of cold winter nights when Mama would come into my room and shake open an extra wool blanket to lay across my bed. The flock of sheep ambling their way through Sandtown looked like a blanket unfolding over the neighborhood.

"They're pretty, aren't they?" I hollered to Reggie over the constant bleating.

He looked at me like I was crazy. "They're dumb sheep."

I shrugged. He could think what he wanted.

As we turned up Gilmore Street, the front door to one of the row homes opened. A woman dressed in a flannel bathrobe with hair curlers under her head kerchief stood rubbed her eyes. She laughed and hollered to someone inside the house. A moment later, she and another woman giggled with delight as they watched the herd of sheep strolling up their street. The women chattered to each other and waved at me. I stood a little taller as I returned their greeting.

The city was waking up. On the next block the streetcar clanged its arrival. Sounds of folks starting to get busy with the day drifted from open windows, along with the scent of bacon and eggs. My stomach rumbled. A train whistle blew in the distance, probably arriving at Union Stockyards with another delivery of animals.

I heard another sound, a new sound.

Behind me, way down the street a sheep lay all alone on her side. Her strained and panicked cries were different from the contented baaing of the flock.

"Stay calm," I told myself as I ran back to get a closer look. That poor ewe was upset enough for the both of us. Three of her legs frantically kicked in the air, yet her position didn't change.

"Hey little lady, what's the problem?" I dropped to my knees beside her and resisted the urge to pet her as I remembered Mr. Foster's warning.

"What happened to you, girl?" I crooned as smoothly as I could, hoping my voice would calm her down. She baaed even louder than before, like she was yelling at me. Her large, glassy eyes seemed to be insisting I do something.

One of her front hooves was stuck in the gap beside the streetcar track. "Hang on little lady, I'll get your shepherd!"

I sprinted back down the road and past all the other sheep. I didn't know exactly how bad that one sheep was hurt, but I knew she needed the shepherd as much as all the others in the flock. Maybe even more.

By the time Mr. Foster and I got back to the isolated sheep, she had somehow gotten her hoof free from the track. In the process of freeing herself, she'd rolled onto her back. Her legs kicked the air in a frenzy. Her bleating still sounded anxious but was softer than before.

Mr. Foster knelt beside her and placed his hand on her upturned belly. He spoke softly to her, immediately quieting her distressed cries. He rolled her onto her side and held her down with both of his strong hands.

"Tell me your name again, son?" He looked up at me.

"Smitty, sir." I swallowed a lump. Had I done something wrong? "Smitty Smith."

"Well, Smitty Smith, I'm very proud of you. You saved this sheep from a painful, lonely death. You saved her life."

Me?

Saved her life?

His muscular hands stayed on the sheep's side, keeping her from standing. "A sheep rolled onto its back like this is called a 'cast sheep.' It's a very dangerous situation for the animal. You see how short and stocky she is?"

I nodded. She had a large, wooly body with small, skinny legs.

"With this heavy fleece of wool, she can't right herself to stand up. The more she tried to get off her back, the more panicked and exhausted she became. She's worn out now. Not much longer, and she would have died, distressed and alone." Mr. Foster examined her tenderly, using his hands to feel her body and legs. She mewed and baaed at him softly.

He checked her face closely, then looked at me and smiled with those twinkling eyes. "She's a bit scraped up, but she's okay." He looked back down and petted her head. "Just a little weary, aren't you, girl?"

He cooed reassurance as he stood, reached down, and scooped his arms around her wooly body. With one, strong, smooth motion, he lifted her onto all four legs, then held her still. At last she was completely quiet, breathing fast, catching her breath. She tilted her head, as if she was listening to the rest of the flock milling about on the next block.

Dropping to his knees beside her, Mr. Foster examined her face again. She remained quiet and breathed easily as she relaxed in the shepherd's nearness.

"Smitty, did you know sheep can recognize a human

face?" He scratched her under her dark muzzle. "This animal knows the difference between you and me. She's comforted by my presence."

"She sure didn't get quiet when she looked at me."

Mr. Foster laughed warmly. He reached into the pocket of his apron and pulled out a bottle of ointment. Carefully, almost reverently, he unscrewed the cap and applied some oil to the scrape on the sheep's head.

It seemed odd that sheep actually trusted him.

I was in awe. "You look like the Twenty-third Psalm."

"That's right, son. '*Thou annointest my head with oil.*'" He examined her once more. Satisfied, he put the bottle back into his deep apron pocket.

He stood, smiled at the sheep, then at me, and began to walk back to the flock.

The rescued sheep trotted close behind him.

And so did I.

The next day was Sunday. After I completed my duties as altar boy, I sat in front of the church and congregation. As an altar boy, I lit the candles at the start of the service and snuffed them out at the end. I helped the pastor with communion services and easily memorized all the prayers he said, along with the congregation's response. Week after week, I whispered every word right along with the pastor.

But the best part of being an altar boy was all the smiles from the girls in the congregation. Out in the world I was merely another colored kid.

During the sermon, I looked out on the congregation and smiled at my family. Mama and Daddy sat side by side.

On the other side of Mama sat her mother, my Grandma Julia Jones. She had on a hat with a big feather sprouting out of it. The feather fluttered a little each time Grandma Julia's head bobbed up and down as she said, "Amen" and other encouragements to the pastor. Ruby and Mary sat on the other side of Daddy. My gaze drifted to the back of the sanctuary where a painting of Christ as the Good Shepherd hung. I kept picturing Mr. Foster as he'd cared for that cast sheep. He'd really cared for that one animal, even though he had so many others to watch out for. And that sheep trusted him. The memory stirred up my soul.

Ever since I was a little boy, Mama and Daddy had taught me that the Lord is my Shepherd, and he would take care of me. Daddy often read the Twenty-third Psalm to the family, and Pastor recited it in church. As many times as I'd heard those words, it was hard to imagine what they really meant. The day before, I'd begun to understand.

Yet with so many people in the world, why would Christ care about me, one teenage colored boy?

I'd asked Daddy that question once.

He told me that God loved Smitty Smith.

God loved *me*.

I thought about Mr. Foster, the way he so lovingly cared for his hurt sheep.

And I wondered, if I ever got hurt, would Jesus take care of me?

CHAPTER TEN

1938

Smitty, 14-years old

Crystal Byrd Fauset of Pennsylvania is the first black woman elected to a state legislature

While at a conference in Birmingham, Alabama, First Lady Eleanor Roosevelt challenged segregation rules by sitting next to her black friend Mary McLeod Bethune

Lipton's Noodle Soup costs 10¢

Henry and I stepped from the alley outside, through the back door, and into his mother's warm and inviting kitchen.

"About time you got home, Henry. Church was over quite a while ago." Disapproval dripped from the sweet voice.

Henry gave his mother a kiss on her cheek. "Sorry, Mama. Smitty and I ran into each other."

Mrs. Blount glanced up at her son, her face without expression, earrings shining from her ears. She was a petite woman and had nine children. Wearing an apron stained with gravy didn't spoil her beauty. She looked every bit like the dignified grocer's wife she was. She lifted the lid to the pot on the stove. Steam rose from under the lid as she peeked inside at whatever was cooking. When she opened the oven door, the smell of pork roast filled the kitchen.

"Smitty's here, mama." Henry seemed a little worried. "We ran into each other after church."

Mrs. Blount looked at me coolly.

I stood there with a big smile on my face and wondered if she heard my stomach growling.

"Good to see you." She smiled. "Haven't seen you in a while."

"Good to see you too." Hunger prevented my mind from more fascinating conversation.

The door between the kitchen and the dining room was propped open. Henry's older sister Esther walked by laughing with someone we couldn't see. From the buzz of conversation and laughter, it sounded like there were several people in the other room.

"Who else is here, Mama?" Henry peeked around the door.

"Your Aunt Mary and Uncle John. I reminded you this morning they were coming over after church." She opened a drawer and pulled out some serving spoons. "Esther, Minnie, and Bernice got the table set and moved in all the chairs *after* helping me get the meal ready. You'll have to help with clean up, since you weren't here earlier."

"Yes, ma'am."

I probably wasn't supposed to see when Mrs. Blount looked over at Henry and raised one perfectly arched eyebrow. It was time for their Sunday dinner, and I wasn't family.

Biting my bottom lip, I shifted my weight from one foot to the other.

I should've said goodbye and left.

But I didn't.

My polite head was no match for my hungry stomach.

I stood there and smiled like a fool.

A hungry fool.

"Well, Smitty." Henry's voice trailed off. He stared down at the floor.

"Well, well." I echoed. My face was going to crack if I didn't tone down the smile. "Your cooking sure does smell delicious, Mrs. Blount."

'Mm-mm." She spooned white mashed potatoes out of the pot into a flowered serving dish, then added a yellow square of butter on top. The butter began to melt, trickling down the potato mountain. My mouth watered.

Putting the empty pot aside, she wiped her hands on her apron. "Smitty Smith?"

"Yes, ma'am?"

Her back was toward me as she yanked open the oven door.

The fragrance about made me drop to my knees.

Mrs. Blount paused and looked back at me over her shoulder. "Would you like to join us for dinner?"

"Don't mind if I do." I answered quick as I could.

She smiled at me like she meant it. "Good, I'm glad to hear it. Go telephone your parents and let them know. Phone's in the hallway."

With pot holders in her hands, she reached into the oven and pulled out a hefty roast of meat that looked like it weighed more than she did. Once the roast was on a platter, she breezed out of the room and carried it into the dining room. "Girls, set another place for Smitty. He's joining us for dinner. Bernice, bring in the potatoes and the collards please. Minnie, bring in the rolls."

Henry slapped me on the back. "Great! Our phone is that way." He pointed down the hall.

Minnie and Bernice came into the kitchen, both talking at the same time, laughing and giggling. They were pretty girls with graceful figures and bright eyes.

"Hi Smitty." One greeted me, then the other. They'd gotten prettier since the last time I'd seen them. I didn't know if I was weak from hunger or their attention.

"Smitty?" Henry nudged me. "The phone?"

"I don't need to call my parents. They won't mind."

The truth was, we didn't have a telephone. As far as I knew, the Blounts were the only family in Sandtown with a phone. They weren't uppity about it, but they forgot most folks didn't have one. They used it to communicate between their home and Mr. Blount's grocery store, a mile away.

Mr. Blount even had an automobile. They were Sandtown's high society.

Mr. and Mrs. Blount, five of their nine children, Aunt Mary, and Uncle John gathered around the table. The four older brothers had already moved out of the house and up to Harlem, which left two brothers, all three sisters, and plenty of room for me at the table. After the blessing, conversation and laughter filled the room along with the clatter of dishes and silverware.

It was hard to ignore how this family was different from my own. Here, everyone was family by blood. They shared similar facial features and mannerisms. Some of their voices even sounded alike.

My family members were different in every possible way. None of us looked alike. We didn't sound similar either. Our skin color ranged from Mama's deep, dark coffee to Richard's skin so light and hair so fine, he could pass for white. We had different body builds and various face shapes.

Some noses were broader than others. This pair of lips was fuller than that pair. I loved my family, and the differences didn't bother me. But I was almost startled by the similarities within the Blount family.

"Here Smitty, help yourself to some mashed potatoes."

"Put another piece of meat on your plate, you're a growing boy."

"Anyone care for dessert? Smitty?"

Everyone took turns sharing updates on their lives and listened to each other's stories and opinions. Laughter came easily. By the time brownies were served, I had joined in with a story of my own. I decided to tell about how my Grandma Julia recently raised quite a ruckus in church.

I took a deep breath. "I've got a story. You know how sometimes kids say things that embarrass their parents..."

"You got that right, Smitty. One time my youngest daughter here, Bernice—"

"*Daddy. Stop.*" Bernice interrupted. She leaned forward, eyebrows raised, a look of panic in her eyes.

All the sisters giggled.

Mrs. Blount glared at her husband and shook her head, "Don't you tell that story to our company."

Bernice sat back in her chair. She let out a long sigh, then looked at me with the biggest, brightest brown eyes I'd ever seen. "You were going to say?"

For a moment I forgot. "Yes, right. Sometimes kids say things that embarrass their parents, but recently my grandma said something in front of the whole church that made me want to crawl under my chair." I slowly shook my head.

"Which church do you go to?" Minnie asked.

"The A.M.E. church around the corner." They nodded. The Blount family went to the Baptist church. "Never been so embarrassed in all my life.It happened last month during the Sunday evening service. Pastor Brooks was away for a death in his family, so Elder Bailey led the evening service."

Mr. Blount tilted his head. "Fred Bailey?"

"Yes, sir."

"I know Bailey, comes in the store quite regularly."

"For his message, Elder Bailey talked about husbands and wives and how they should treat each other. He went on and on. The whole time he was talking my grandma squirmed in her seat." I squirmed in my chair to show them. "She huffed and muttered to herself as he gave examples of how some men don't treat their wives too well, and that's not very Christian-like.

"She crossed her arms across her chest." I crossed mine. "And made a fuss as she turned away from Elder Bailey. By now, folks were paying more attention to Grandma Julia than they were to Elder Bailey." It was heady business entertaining a family with so many pretty sisters. I enjoyed this.

"Bailey coughed, cleared his throat," I demonstrated. "And he began talking louder, trying to get everyone's attention. The louder he talked, the more my grandma huffed and puffed. It was like they were having a contest."

The Blount sisters giggled.

"Elder Bailey got downright dramatic." I used my hands and gestured like the man. "He looked so disappointed as he complained some men in the church aren't being true Christian gentlemen to their wives. With that Grandma threw back her head and cackled like a hen, *'HA!'*"

Esther leaned forward. "What did Elder Bailey do?"

I paused to make sure I had everyone's attention. It was time for some real dramatics.

"My Grandma Julia sat up straight. She cleared her

throat so loud the rafters shook, then she stood up and looked around to make sure everyone was looking at her." I turned my head from one side to the next, pursing my lips like Grandma did. "Then Grandma faced Elder Bailey and shook her boney, ol' finger at him."

I did my best imitation of her body language, raised my voice several octaves, and wagged my finger. " 'I happen to recall there are some men in this church who have real good wives. Pretty wives. *Christian* wives. Faithful, hard-working women.' Then she put her hand on her hip, stared straight at the Elder, and leaned forward. 'But some of these men ain't satisfied with solely *one* woman. They have *outside* women!' "

"Oh...." One of the Blount brothers leaned forward, laughing. "She said *that*? To the *Elder*?"

"She sure did." I nodded. "I was sitting right beside her."

"What did the Elder say?"

"Come on, tell us." Minnie giggled.

Now it was time for me to act the role of an overweight, pompous man with a booming bass voice. "He puffed up all self-righteous, straightened his tie, and in a thundering voice challenged, 'Sister Julia, would you by chance be talking about me?'

"And my grandma answered." My voice got higher. " 'Elder Bailey, I'm looking right at you, and I'm talking right at you. If the adulterer's shoe fits, you wear it. You wear it for all the church to see.' "

I bobbed my head with a sharp nod and continued. "Grandma Julia sat back down with her head high, crossed her arms over her chest, and stared straight at him."

"What happened next?"

I paused for dramatic effect.

"The Elders silenced Grandma in the church. She isn't

even allowed to say 'Amen.'"

Everyone around the table applauded and howled with laughter.

I shook my head for theatrical effect. "Never been so embarrassed in my whole life."

When the laughter subsided and the last crumb of brownies was gone, I felt stuffed with home cooking and attention.

"Henry, time for you to clean up. You too, Smitty."

"I'm going to stretch my legs." Uncle John stood and excused himself. He gave his wife a look.

"I'll join you." She followed.

Soon all the adults were out of the room, leaving us younger ones to scrape and stack the dishes at the table. When Henry and I carried the load of the plates and bowls into the kitchen, we found the adults squared off in whispered conversation.

When they saw Henry and me, they stopped talking. Henry's parents, his Aunt Mary, and his Uncle John looked past Henry and stared at me.

Silence.

The corner of my lip turned up in a half-hearted smile. I swallowed, not sure why I felt like I was in some sort of trouble.

Mr. Blount cleared his throat.

The uncle murmured something under his breath.

I wasn't sure what I'd done wrong. "Sure was a delicious meal. Thank you again for your hospitality." I tried my best to be charming, already hoping for a future invitation.

Mrs. Blount tilted her head of soft curls to one side. "You're very welcome." Her face was gentle, yet she didn't smile.

No one else spoke.

The quiet in the kitchen was so different from all the laughter we'd shared a few minutes before. The adults looked back and forth at each other, eyes shifting from side to side.

Uncle John nodded his head slightly, a frown on his face.

I glanced at Henry. Something felt mighty serious, but I didn't know what.

Mr. Blount took a small step forward, "Smitty, tell me again your grandmother's name?"

"My grandma?" I smiled, glad he liked my story. "My grandma's Julia Jones."

Mr. Blount nodded slowly, distracted by some faraway thoughts. He looked at his wife then back at us. "All right boys, you're dismissed. The others will finish cleaning up. You all go enjoy some evening air."

I met Henry's gaze. He shrugged. "Thanks, Daddy. Come on, Smitty, let's go."

Mrs. Blount shooed us out through the kitchen door, and we stepped into the cool evening air.

The screen door slammed softly behind us and bounced closed.

There were murmurs from inside the kitchen. One voice strained above the rest. "That's the boy, I tell you. That's the boy."

Henry and I paused on the steps. I looked at him for an explanation. He looked as puzzled as I felt.

Henry shrugged. "Come on, let's see if anyone's singing down at the corner."

"Okay."

That's the boy.

CHAPTER ELEVEN

April 2008

Smitty, 84-years old

Danica Patrick becomes the first female in history to win an Indy car race when she wins the Indy Japan 300

I look at Leslie's digital recorder and make sure the little light is still on. "You know that family never once turned me away from a meal. All those times I just happened to show up at mealtime. Sometimes I stopped by two, three times a week." I shake my head at the boldness of my youth. "They always had room for me at their table." The Blounts had been real good to me. I knew that when I was a boy, but I appreciate it even more now that I'm an old man.

My wife nods. "My parents loved you."

"I even carried around a set of silverware in my coat pocket. I was afraid they might run out of utensils, so I carried my own."

The love of my life laughs, chin up, eyes twinkling. "Oh Smitty, you did not!"

"If I'm lying, I'm flying."

The three of us laugh till we can barely catch air.

My wife's petite frame shakes as she holds her side.

Leslie laughs until tears stream down her face.

I try and catch my breath, yet each time I calm down, I start chuckling again.

It feels good. Laughter's important exercise when you're old.

"Hmm." She shakes her head. "I wonder why Mama and Daddy didn't say anything?"

"Don't know. I've wondered that too."

We get real quiet.

That's the boy.

More than twenty years passed before I learned what that phrase meant, and it changed my life forever.

CHAPTER TWELVE

1939

Smitty, 15-years old

Albert Einstein informs Franklin D. Roosevelt about the atomic bomb's potential

First air-conditioned automobile, a Packard, goes on exhibit in Chicago

Talcum powder costs 13¢

Worn out from a day of selling *Afro* newspapers in sizzling temperatures, I sat outside on the front steps after the sun had set. Baltimore's heat and humidity were miserable. Everyone moved slowly, worn down by the heavy layer of sweat that constantly coated their skin and made their clothes stick to their bodies.

Mama and Daddy's voices drifted through the living room's open windows. In the background I could hear my sisters chattering about something. Their voices seemed too light and breezy for the hot summer night.

Similar sounds came from neighboring houses. Summertime in a Baltimore neighborhood of row houses—with windows and doors wide-open—meant neighbors knew your business more than usual.

Despite my aching feet and exhaustion, I felt restless. Mama said restlessness was part of being a teenager.

Far down at the end of the street, the tight, soulful harmonies of street corner singers lightened the air.

When I was younger, Daddy would take me out after supper to listen to the singers practicing nearby. Small groups of young men sang without instruments or background music, only the magic of their voices. Sandtown had some real talented folks. Bill Kenney sang with the famous group, *The Ink Spots*. Ever since Kenney found fame, Sandtown's street singers tried to follow in his footsteps, find a way out of these hard times.

The screen door squeaked as I stepped into the living room. "I'm going down to the corner. Too hot to sit here."

Mama looked up from her mending. "I don't like you down there. Nothing but trouble with all those young folks together on a hot night."

"Mama, half the songs they sing are gospel."

"Let the boy go." Daddy nodded in my direction. "He's fifteen now, almost a grown man."

"Thanks. I won't be late."

Hands in my pants' pockets, I strolled down the street and nodded to neighbors on their steps. When I passed three pretty girls sitting together, I tried to be cool. They giggled as I passed by. Never knew what to make of girls and all their giggling.

Down at the corner stood the singers, six men in their twenties. They looked casual enough, but I knew they'd positioned themselves carefully for the best blend of their voices. The street corner was their stage, and they made the most of it. Their a cappella harmonies were sung with soulful understanding. A small audience milled about as the singers took a break, talking about what to sing next.

"Hey Smitty!" Reggie stepped up beside me and slapped me on the back.

"Good to see you, Reg." My cousin and I hadn't seen much of each other lately. I didn't recognize the two fellas who were with him. "Where you been?"

He smiled, showing off the familiar gap between his teeth. "Just busy. These are my buddies, Ralph and Herman."

I nodded.

They nodded back. There was no way to know which was Ralph and which was Herman. One was tall with biceps that bulged under his rolled up shirtsleeves, the other short, his belt hiked up inches below his bull like chest.

Reggie and I talked until the bull-man stepped forward. "We're going. Got things to do."

"Yeah. Bye," said the other, and they were gone.

Reggie's brow furrowed. "What?" He held his hands out, palms up, like he didn't know what had just happened.

I thumped him on the arm. "It's all right, man." I was glad the two left. Those fellas looked like trouble to me.

"Hush up, y'all." An attractive girl nearby scolded us. "They're starting."

Everyone got quiet.

The group leader raised his hands to cue the start of their next song. In smooth-as-silk harmony, they sang "Precious Lord, Take My Hand."

A few lines into the song I looked at Reggie, and by the expression on his face, I could see he was as impressed as I was. These fellas were more than good. They were stunning. Their sorrowful music convinced you their world had fallen apart.

They couldn't go on another day.

The Lord was their only hope.

The harmony made me ache inside.

Under my breath, I hummed along to the very end of the song.

The men sang out their last note and let the magic of it suspend somewhere between the humid air and my restless heart.

Their leader lifted one hand, spread out his fingers, then whipped his fingers closed into a fist.

The music ended.

But my restlessness continued.

———◆———

Reggie and I wandered the neighborhood and watched whatever there was to watch. Folks sat out on their steps, talked, and fanned themselves with sheets of newspaper. A young couple sat dangerously close. Somewhere, someone in her family was watching. Or a Neighbor- Mama observed carefully. That's the way it worked in Sandtown.

Bacon perfumed the air as someone prepared a late supper.

"Hear you been hanging out with the Blount family," Reggie said.

"Henry and I been friends a long time. Mrs. Blount sure does know how to cook."

"You be careful." Reggie's typically smug attitude grew serious. "They think they're better than us."

I looked at him. "They do not. Where'd you get a fool-headed idea like that?"

"Mr. Blount drives that big fancy car around Sandtown like he owns a bank or something. He's just a grocer."

"He works hard."

"They've got a telephone in their house, least that's what I heard. What do they need one for? They acting all fancy."

"What's it to you if they've got a telephone?" Reggie wasn't making sense. The Blounts were good people, everybody knew it. "What's got you so cross about them?"

Reggie stopped walking and shoved his hands in his pants pockets. He was quiet a long time.

"It's Minnie." He said. "She's got me cross."

"What are you talking about?"

"I asked Minnie out, and she turned me down. Turned me down like I wasn't good enough for her." Reggie started walking again. His chin was up, proud and defiant.

I tried to catch up with him, but could barely walk for laughing so hard. "*Minnie!* Boy, you *aren't* good enough for her! What were you thinking?" I had a hard time catching my breath.

He glared at me as I howled with laughter.

Minnie was petite, refined, and the color of sweet caramel.

Reggie was clumsy, unsophisticated, and dark as coloreds came.

I stopped and bent down with my hands on my thighs to catch my breath. My side hurt from laughing.

Reggie hadn't laughed at all. He marched back to where I stood and shoved me.

I almost toppled over but caught my balance like a clever cat.

He looked mad, and that made me laugh even more.

"Min-nie!" I teased, dragging out her name. "You are something else, Reggie, thinking a girl like Minnie Blount would go out with the likes of you."

Reggie was angry. Real angry. "I'll get you, cousin."

After we walked the neighborhood we landed on my family's front steps.

"Thought I heard someone out here." Daddy pushed open the screen door and leaned out.

I looked up at my father, the back of my neck straining like when I was a little boy and tried to take in his full height. "Hey Daddy. Just Reggie and me."

"Hi, Uncle Charlie."

"Hello, Reginald. Good to see you." Daddy nodded. "How's everyone at home?"

"Fine."

"And Edna?" Daddy always asked about Reggie's older sister. I hardly knew her. She lived in New York.

"She's good. She likes being a nurse."

Daddy looked off into the night. "Okay boys, don't stay out too much longer." He slipped back into the house, and we heard the stairs creak as he went up for bed.

Reggie and I sat side by side, shoulder-to-shoulder.

Several houses away, some neighbors sitting on their steps buzzed in conversation.

Reggie cleared his throat. "I've got something to tell you." He leaned back, rested his elbows on the top step, and looked me over.

A train whistled in the distance.

"So, go ahead and tell me." I figured he couldn't say much that I didn't already know.

"It's about your family. Your daddy."

I yawned. "What about him?"

He sat forward and scratched his head. "You know all your brothers and sisters aren't really your brothers and sisters?" He looked at me from the corner of his eye. "They weren't born to your parents."

"'Course I know that. Most of them are mama's cousins' kids or something." Why'd it even matter? "We've been raised as brothers and sisters for so long, that's just what we say."

Reggie reached down to the sidewalk and picked up a few pebbles. He shook them around in his hand and took a deep breath. "Smitty, you weren't born to your parents, either. They're not really your mama and daddy."

"Has the heat gone to your head? They sure are my parents. I was born June 24, 1924, at Franklin Square Hospital." The hospital that had *two* maternity wards for coloreds. I always felt a little proud about that.

"The hospital part's true, but your mama ain't your mama. She's your great-aunt. Your daddy is your great-uncle." He cocked his head to the side, a look of superiority on his face. "Why do you think they're so old?"

I wasn't going to take part in his foolishness.

"Think about it. Everyone else your age, their parents are a lot younger. Your parents are old, too old to have had you fifteen years ago."

This wasn't the first time I'd tried to figure out how old Mama and Daddy had been when I was born.

Every time I did the arithmetic, it came out wrong.

For Mama to be fifty years old when I was born seemed a little old, but not impossible.

I was their son, Daddy always said so.

I was special, different from my brothers and sisters.

I was their blood.

Daddy and Mama wouldn't lie about that.

So something was wrong with my arithmetic.

I crossed my arms. "What are you saying, fool?"

Reggie sighed. "Do you get what I'm trying to tell you?"

My head started to buzz.

I closed my eyes.

Go away, Reggie.

He was still next to me when I opened my eyes.

Reggie casually tossed a pebble into the street. "My sister Edna, the one you think is your cousin, is really your mother. I was four years old when you were born. I remember it well."

He tossed the last pebble into the street. "So that makes me your uncle." He brushed the pebble dirt off his hands and leaned back on his elbows.

Then he smirked.

I felt dizzy.

My mouth went dry.

My head pounded.

"Edna had you when she was fifteen years old." Reggie wouldn't shut up.

My stomach tightened in a knot while a sour taste burned the back of my throat.

"You gettin' this?"

I worked hard to control my voice. "I hear what you're saying Reggie, but I don't think too highly of you lying to me."

"It's the absolute truth, I swear. Just sorry I don't know anything about your real father. Nobody ever talks about him."

My real father? Charlie Smith was my real father.

Ola Smith was my real mother, that was a fact.

"Bring me a Bible, and I'll swear on it."

I swallowed. Swearing on top of a Bible was serious business in our family. No one ever threatened that if there was a chance they were lying.

It was the other kids in the family who weren't born to Mama and Daddy. I'm their son, I'm their blood. They said so.

My hands clenched into tight, angry fists. "You're talking like a damn fool." My eyes narrowed, daring him to speak.

"You're the fool, Smitty. Been fooled your whole life. Unlike your parents, I've never lied to you, and I'm not lying now."

The very foundation of my world was crumbling, and everything was closing in on me.

I forced open my fists, uncurled my fingers, and stroked the edge of the cool, white marble steps underneath me. That's when I felt a crack in the marble. I'd never noticed it before.

Had the neighbors heard what Reggie said?

He glanced over at me with a smug expression. "Well?"

I stood and shoved my hands into my pockets.

The bitter taste in the back of my throat grew stronger. I needed to get away or I'd be sick.

I rallied all my strength, turned my back on my cousin, and walked away.

A rusty brown tin can lay on the sidewalk. I stared at that useless can, kicked it, walked a few steps, and kicked it again.

Each time I kicked that can, it bounced down the street and made a hollow sound that echoed in the night air.

The street corner group started singing the same songs over again. "Precious Lord, Take My Hand" floated through the heavy, humid air.

I walked with my hands shoved so deep in my pockets, the stitching started to tear. I didn't care.

Everything around me was gray.

All the houses looked alike.

Nothing was the same.

My life had changed.

Tired and worn I didn't know what street I was on or where I was going.

I didn't care.

The corner singers' song couldn't drown out Reggie's voice.

It hammered in my head.

Edna's your mother. Edna's your mother. Edna's your mother.

I roamed all night.

More alone than I'd ever felt before.

Numb and broken, I pleaded with God, "Please let Reggie be lying."

Mama and Daddy were old.

It hadn't bothered me before.

Were they too old to be the parents of a fifteen-year-old?

I didn't look like either one of them.

But I'd always had Daddy's temperament. Happy. I got that from him.

Folks said we were like two peas in a pod.

I was his.

Wasn't I?

The dawn sky was brightening with morning light when I finally returned home to the front steps where Reggie and I had sat during another lifetime, just a few hours ago.

I reached forward to open the door.

The last time I'd walked through that door, I was my parents' son.

This time I opened the door and stepped into the house a nobody.

CHAPTER THIRTEEN

1939

Smitty, 15-years old

Hitler calls for extermination of all Jews

*Peggy Bolin becomes the first black woman to serve as a
U.S. Judge*

A postage stamp costs 3¢

I slept a few restless hours.

Like always, Daddy left for work before I woke up.

When I went downstairs to the kitchen, I saw Mama, but I couldn't look at her. Didn't say anything to her either, even though she asked where I was all night. Her eyes were puffy and red-rimmed.

I left the house after breakfast and wandered around town all day. I didn't sell any newspapers. I didn't care.

Later in the afternoon, I hung out with Henry. I didn't say a word to him about the night before. I was fine. Nothing was wrong. Nothing had changed.

"Would you like to join us for dinner?" Mrs. Blount called out the living room window to where Henry and I stood near their steps.

I gave her my charming smile, the one I sometimes practiced in the bathroom mirror. "Thank you kindly, Mrs. Blount, but I should be getting home."

It was the first time I'd ever turned down one of her invitations.

She stepped out through the front door and held her hand to her forehead, shading her eyes, trying to get a closer look at me.

"You feeling okay?" Her voice oozed motherly concern.

I swallowed the lump in my throat and kept the smile on my face. "Feeling fine, thank you."

She nodded and assured me my place would be waiting next time. I knew it, too—had my silverware in my pocket to prove it.

———◆———

The back door squeaked as I tiptoed into the house through the kitchen. Since I'd left that morning, I'd shaken everything off my burdened soul. I'd decided the previous night did not happen. If I didn't say anything or ask anybody about it, it could not be true. Mama and Daddy were my parents.

Mama, Mary, and Ruby were seated around the dining room table, heads bowed as Daddy said the blessing.

"And dear Lord we ask you would be with those who protect us throughout the day, the policemen, the firemen...."

I lifted my chair cautiously and tried to pull it out from under the table. I winced when one of the feet caught on the edge of the stupid linoleum and made a loud scraping sound.

Mama looked up at me with sad eyes, blinked, and bowed her head again.

Daddy's rich, deep voice kept right on praying. "And may this food be used to nourish our bodies as we present our bodies for your service, O Lord. In your Son's powerful and holy name we pray, Amen."

"Amen." We all echoed.

Wham!

Daddy's fist hit the table so hard all the plates, forks, and knives bounced up and rattled as they landed back on the table. He stood up so fast his chair fell down behind him.

His cold eyes bore into me. "Young man, you will *not* enter my house late for dinner and casually sit down to eat my food! *Not* after what you put your mama through last night!"

"Daddy, I..."

"Not a word out of you! Not one word!" His chest was heaving up and down in shallow breaths. "You get your hind end out of my chair and up to your room! And *don't* you come out until I say so!"

Mary and Ruby stared, their expressions betraying sympathy mixed with fear. Daddy had never behaved like this before. Ever.

Mama kept her head down.

Somehow, I needed to fix this. "I..."

"Now, Smitty!"

I pushed out from the table with both hands and sprung up. One of the chair legs wrapped around my own, and the chair fell behind me as I fought my way away from the dining room.

The stairs turned from solid wood to fluid waves as they tripped and tangled me. I staggered down the hall and into my room, slammed the door, collapsed on my mattress, and pounded it with my fist until my hand throbbed.

When I didn't have any strength left, I wiped the tears

from my cheeks.

Fool.

Weakling.

No wonder nobody wanted me.

I rolled over onto my back and stared up at the ceiling. Don't know how long I lay there, eyes fixed on the single light bulb that hung in the middle of the room. The only other thing to look at was the old chest of dresser drawers and the plain wooden chair. I was too exhausted to walk over and look out the window.

There was no clock in my room, but I could hear the sounds of the evening routine that drifted upstairs. Chairs scraped over the linoleum when the family finished eating. Dishes and silverware clattered as Ruby and Mary scraped and stacked them.

The front screen door opened and banged shut. Daddy was outside. Mary, Ruby, and Mama talked as they did the dishes. Their voices were muffled, but I could hear Ruby's voice, steady and even. Mary's went all up and down in volume and pitch. Mama didn't say much.

I rolled over on my left side. The bedsprings squeaked. I felt a slight pain in my elbow and rolled on my back again.

Lifting my left arm above me, I inspected the crook of my elbow with the fingers of my right hand. When I was ten years old, Mama and Daddy took me back to the Harriet Lane Home. The tumors in my arm had continued to grow, and at times caused dreadful pain. Some days were so bad I had to stay home from school or miss the Druid Hill Park baseball games.

Dr. Kidlowski operated and removed the tumors. After the surgery, it was hard for me to know if the pain from the procedure had been worth getting rid of the tumors.

It was a horrible experience, more pain than a boy

should have to endure. I missed a whole year of school. As much as I didn't care for school, I begged to go back and be done with my arm. It was almost more than I could take.

Every other day, Mama peeled off the bloody bandages that completely covered my arm. The dressing stuck to my skin, pinned there by my own dried up blood. Mama talked to me in a cooing voice, telling stories trying to distract me from the pain.

She used a fresh towel, warm water, and soap to wash the wounds, cleaning out debris and puss. She constantly told me how brave and strong I was as she tenderly packed in new cotton gauze. But my arm was so messed up, even cotton caused pain. After all that, she wrapped my weak and weary arm in fresh, white bandages. I tried to believe her when she promised the next bandage changing would be easier, but that didn't happen for more than six months. Blood would seep through by the next day.

Once a week we rode on the streetcar to visit Dr. Kidlowski so he could check on things himself. Before the surgery I was thrilled to have a chance to ride the streetcar. But after the operation, my arm was heavy with blood-soaked cotton bandages . The stitches pulled and irritated my skin. Travel over the bumpy cobblestone roads made my arm throb in new ways. I dreaded those weekly visits.

Every evening, the first thing Daddy did when he got home was see how I was doing. "How's my little shadow?" he called through the house looking for me.

He'd find me on my bed in my room or on the living room couch. No matter how weary he was from a long day of hod carrying, he acted so excited, ready to tell me a funny story and make me laugh. I never knew if all the stories were true or not, but it didn't matter. Daddy's attention was what I needed. He helped me feel better whenever we laughed together. And he made sure we laughed a lot.

Daddy held me when I cried too. Cried because of the pain that never seemed to end.

After months turned into a year and healing came, he held me when I cried. This time I sobbed in disappointment because I still could not straighten my arm. The tumors were gone, but my arm was and always would be bent.

I rolled over in my bed again. The mattress creaked. I sighed.

I'd spent a lot of time in that room waiting for Daddy to come up the stairs. Now I lay there and hoped he never would. How would he punish me, and when would he do it? I was too big to wallop with a branch—at least I hoped I was.

I kicked off my shoes and let them drop to the floor one at a time.

Once when I was a little boy, Daddy caught me doing something that deserved his discipline. He sent me outside to bring in a branch so he could spank me. He had me lean over, and with the first whip the branch broke in two. I didn't even feel it.

"Smitty!" He bellowed. "You march back out there and find something that will hold up to your bottom."

He about fell out of his chair laughing when I came back in dragging a large, solid two-by-four.

"Son, I could kill you with that thing!" He laughed till he cried. "You get on out of here before I change my mind."

I dropped the board and ran.

Whatever Daddy was planning this time, I knew he wouldn't change his mind. I'd stayed out all night without a word to my parents.

If they were my parents.

Questions rolled around in my mind and tormented me. Things I'd never even thought to consider before Reggie opened his mouth. And every question led to the same answer—I wasn't worth having.

No one wanted me as a baby.

And I wasn't special now.

My stomach growled. It was dark outside.

I sat up on the bed, and leaned against the feather pillow that seemed to melt behind my back.

The floorboards creaked.

I looked up to see Daddy close the bedroom door behind him. He looked tired and old as he stood there. Even so, his presence filled the room.

"Smitty?" He walked softly across the small room. "What in tarnation were you doing out all night?" His words were firm but loving.

I rubbed the back of my neck and searched for words.

I looked up at him and quickly looked away.

"I..." My voice cracked and I stopped. My jaw clenched as I forced back tears.

Daddy and I'd had our differences before, but nothing like this. The tension in the room was thick as the humidity outside.

Daddy sighed. "Please tell me."

I closed my eyes too late. Tears seeped out from under my lids. I squeezed my eyes tighter and took a breath. If I voiced it, then it might be true. If I didn't say it, then it might go away. I felt sick to my stomach, my heart, and my soul. I didn't know what to do.

Daddy eased himself down on the edge of my bed.

I pulled my legs away from him, pulling them close to my chest. I hid my face on my knees and wrapped my arms around my legs.

He tried again. His voice was soft, concerned. "Tell me what's troubling you, son."

I exploded.

"That's just it, Daddy. *Am* I your son?" The accusation tumbled out before I could stop it. I couldn't take it back. I closed my eyes. When I opened them, I saw an expression I'd never seen on my father—panic.

"What are you asking?"

"Am I your son? Reggie says you're not really my daddy, he says you're my uncle and..—"

"Reggie said what?" Veins bulged on his neck.

"He said you and Mama aren't really my parents, that Edna is my mother."

"He told you that? Damn, Smitty, why that boy told you that, I'll never know!" He stood up so fast the bedsprings under me bounced.

He turned away, ran his hands through his hair, and muttered. "Help me, Jesus!"

He stood with his back to me, facing the wall.

I barely breathed.

When he finally turned around, there was still fire in his eyes, but his voice was controlled and even. He rubbed his chin.

"Yes, Edna gave birth to you, but is she your mother? Who is it has done all your cooking, cleaning, and laundry? *Who*, Smitty?" He stepped towards me. "Who is it sat by your bed at night for weeks after you had those tumors removed from your arm? Who is it nursed you day and night when you had pneumonia?"

He got louder and leaned in closer to me. I leaned back, trying to blend into the wall, afraid he would hit me.

"Did Edna stay up all night with you fixing onion poultice for your chest? Did *Edna* take care of you when you were sick? Is she your mama, Smitty? Or is that lady down the hall, the one with a broken heart wondering what kind of trouble you got into last night—is she your mama?"

How much could the others hear? Could they hear my heart breaking?

"You want to go live with Edna, Smitty? You want to go live with your mother? Fine! I'll pack your bags!" He turned, yanked open a dresser drawer, and wildly started pulling out my clothes.

I jumped off the bed and lunged toward my father. "No! Daddy!" No matter how many questions I had, I didn't want to leave Daddy. His love was all I'd ever known.

He slammed both fists on top of the dresser. His back heaved up and down as he caught his breath, still facing the wall.

I pulled his arm away from the dresser and kept tugging until he finally turned towards me. I fell forward, collapsed into his arms, and sobbed.

He gently rocked me.

I sobbed until I reached a new level of exhaustion.

When he loosened his arms, he placed his hands on my shoulders and guided me back to the bed.

My nose was running and my eyes were swollen. All I had were little slits to look out and see the world. My world that had fallen apart. I crawled back on the bed.

Daddy sat on the edge of the mattress.

Neither of us spoke.

It was the longest silence of my life.

Through my swollen, burning eyes, I watched a button on the front of Daddy's shirt. It traveled up and down each time he took a breath. Mama probably sewed that little button on there, and it wasn't going anywhere. It was safe against his broad chest, like I used to be when I was a little boy and snuggled up against him.

"Son." He whispered. "Smitty."

Our eyes met.

Daddy's deep brown eyes glistened with tears. "You are my blood, exactly like I've always said. We raised you as if you were our very own boy."

I groaned an animal sound that came up from the deepest part of my gut.

He grabbed my shoulders and gave me a shake.

I forced open my eyes.

"Reggie's right, Edna gave birth to you." He looked so sad. So old.

I didn't know what to say.

"Edna was fifteen years old when you were born, same age as you are now. She had recently moved in with Grandpa James and Grandma Julia." Daddy sniffed. "She was way too young to be raising a little baby, and they were too old. Your mama and I—Ola and I—we wanted you the minute we laid eyes on you."

"My mother didn't want me?" It was all I could think about. My own mother didn't want me.

"Oh, don't go thinking like that. That wasn't it. Sometimes life gets too complicated, too big, for a little fifteen year old girl."

"She gave me away?" You give away puppies and kittens. Not babies. Not me.

"It wasn't like that. You were cared for. Different women in the neighborhood watched after you. They were thrilled to hold a little baby again." A corner of his lips curled in a half smile. "But mostly it was Mrs. Evans who cared for you."

"Mrs. Evans?" I didn't know that name.

"That's right." He rubbed his eyes and wiped his nose. "Mrs. Evans lived on Gilmore Street. She knew she was too old to care for you once you got to walking around, but she had you while you were a baby. She loved you something fierce, but it tore me up you weren't with family. Ola, too. Your mama wanted you from the first moment she saw you." Daddy's voice was tender.

My head throbbed.

"You were ten months old when we finally brought you home here. It was a rainy day, and oh, how your mama fussed about carrying you those two blocks in the rain."

He rested a moment, then sighed. "Edna is your mother, she birthed you. Grandpa James is her father, your grandfather. And I'm your grandfather's brother." Daddy nodded. "Reggie's right. Technically, that makes me your great-uncle. But me and you, we are blood, Smitty. And I have raised you as if you were my very own. I couldn't love you any more than I already do. You are my son."

I tried to absorb it all.

"No other baby's ever been more loved than you. It was simply Ola and me doing the loving, not the young girl who brought you into the world."

His words were comforting and heart wrenching.

I sighed, exhausted.

Daddy stood up. "I'll bring you up some supper, then you get some rest."

I was asleep before he came back up from the kitchen.

I woke up to find a plate of fried apples and bread and butter on the chair next to my bed. On the floor beside the chair was a glass of water. I ate quickly then slipped out of my bedroom and padded down the hallway until my feet felt the cool tile of the bathroom floor.

On the way back to my room, I noticed Mama and

Daddy's door was ajar. I paused, wondering if I should thank Daddy for leaving the food by my bed.

Mama's voice drifted out from the room. "Oh, sweet Jesus. Tell me Reggie didn't tell him."

"He did. I wish I could take Reggie and beat him within an inch of his life. Don't care how old he is." Daddy's voice cracked with emotion. "Smitty has always *felt* like my son. He's our boy. He's *always* been our boy."

"I know, baby, I know. Come here." Mama's soft, satin voice crooned. "Come here, Charlie."

For the first time in my life, I heard my father cry. He cried in his wife's arms exactly like I had cried in his. Deep gut-wrenching sobs. I swiped away tears from my eyes and bit my lip trying to make them stop.

I slipped back into bed and drifted in and out of restless sleep.

The sun was shining the next morning, but it seemed nothing could warm me on the inside. I was worthless, and the questions and deep hurts could not be erased with one night's sleep.

Fifteen years ago life got too complicated for a little fifteen-year-old named Edna.

Now that I learned about my mother, life felt too complicated for me.

Chapter Fourteen

April 2008

Smitty, 84-years old

American mathematician and meteorologist Edward Lorenz dies at 90. He coined the term "butterfly effect," theorizing how small actions could lead to major changes

The women are very quiet.

I've told some folks the story about my real mom, but not too many. It hurts too much. Not like it did that day—there's been a lot of healing over the years. Yet there's still a part of me that aches deep down. I don't need to mention that to Leslie though. No sense in that.

"What did you do?" Leslie asks the obvious. Guess I'll have to work on her journalism skills.

"Life continued same as before. Mama and Daddy loved me and provided for me. I sold *Afro* newspapers and learned shoe repair at my uncle's shop. Of course, any money I earned was handed over to Daddy." It feels good to laugh. "We still needed every penny to get by. When school started back up, I still got in trouble for talking. And many evenings near dinnertime I just happened to visit the Blount family."

"Did you ever have to use the silverware in your coat pocket?"

"Not once. They always set a place for me."

My wife smiles as if she were sixteen again. "I might have had a little something to do with that."

Leslie leans forward, props her elbows on the table, and rests her head in her hands. "But how could you get over that news so quickly?"

My wife and I both shake our heads. She answers first. "He didn't get over it, not at all. When we were dating and early in our marriage, Smitty went through real dark periods. It wounded him very deeply."

"She's right. Things continued the same on the outside, but inside, I didn't know who I was. When a boy's fifteen, he's supposed to be counting the whiskers on his chin when he looks in the mirror. When I looked in the mirror, I didn't know who looked back.

"I knew more about who I wasn't than who I was. In a manner of speaking, my whole life had been a lie, and I was the last one to know. I was my parents' great-nephew, not their son. I was Edna's son, not her cousin. And I was Reggie's nephew, not his cousin, either. I barely knew my real mother. And how could Mama and Daddy not really be my parents? Their love was all I had ever known. It was very confusing."

My ice tea has been neglected. I take a sip. "And who was my father? Nobody spoke a word about him. Why? What had he done that no one wanted to remember him? Or was his crime that he helped bring me into the world? There was no way for me to find him, either. They didn't have adoption agencies for blacks back then. Folks just passed their children along, no paperwork or legalities required."

I chew my bottom lip a moment. All these years, and it's

still hard to say some of this. It makes me tired. "In my way of thinking, if being my father was such a sin, then I must've been no good, too. A nobody. These thoughts swirled round and round inside of me day and night. I could be smiling on the outside, but inside was a storm of confusion. Reggie'd hit me with truth, and I had to deal with it on my own. No one ever mentioned it again."

There's so much more to tell, but not today. "I think we're done for now."

<hr>

"I'm in the living room!" I feel like I needed to enjoy some elegance, and our living room offers plenty.

The ladies come in from the kitchen. Leslie leans down and says hello with a kiss.

I pat the velvety white sofa cushion. "Have a seat."

Her eyes widen.

I enjoy a hearty laugh. "You're just like your father, always wearing blue jeans. It's all right, set yourself down. The furniture won't turn blue."

Hesitantly, she does as I say.

"I'm ready to keep telling my story." I clap my hands and rub them together with enthusiasm. "You ready to write my book?" I give her my charming smile.

"Maybe."

"That's enough for me!" This is wonderful news, real progress. The joy inside me overflows. "I better start wearing cardigan sweaters and smoking cigars. I'm going to be an author."

Leslie turns on the digital recorder, and I'm ready to talk. "After I learned the truth about my unwanted birth, the main thing that changed was I began calling Mama 'Aunt Ola' and Daddy 'Uncle Charlie.' The expressions on their faces told me it broke their hearts, but I did it anyway, at least when I remembered. I guess it was my way of acknowledging the truth of the relationship. The blood relationship. Even though I fought it, my deepest part loved them as my parents."

"It broke their hearts even more when I decided to quit school and leave Sandtown. Mama and Daddy protested because I was under age, but in the end, I had my way. I was barely seventeen years old when I joined the Army."

Leslie's scribbling down notes. Folks just might hear my story someday. So many people feel down on themselves and need encouragement, and that's why I want my story told, to give hope. There's always hope.

"In 1941 Adolf Hitler was making all kinds of misery in Europe, but that was the farthest thing from my mind when I joined."

"But you were under age, right?"

Can't help but chuckle a little at that. "Yes, I was too young to join the military, but Uncle Sam didn't mind about that or my bent arm. Guess because there was trouble brewing they made exceptions. Plus, I didn't tell them the truth."

We enjoy a laugh over that one.

"For fifteen months I worked in the Army's port battalion, a dockworker loading and unloading ships until I was wounded in battle."

Leslie's eyebrows arch up in surprise. "You were wounded...in battle?"

I must look like a real hero to her. "Yes ma'am. One rainy evening, I ran to catch the bus, fell, and broke my arm. I did battle with the pavement, and the pavement won." I've gotten a lot of good use out of that line over the years. "In the process of treating the broken arm, the doctors somehow discovered I was under age. They couldn't keep me. My Army days were done, but they were kind to me. I got an honorable discharge with a certified disability. They packed me up and sent me home."

Leslie tries to put the pieces together. "And then you two married?"

"No. I joined the Merchant Marines. I knew they wouldn't turn me away, because so many Merchant Marines were black. I wanted to honor and defend our country like the white men in uniform. Wanted to prove I was as much of a somebody as they were."

My wife jumps in. "But the Lord wanted you back in Sandtown."

"Yes, he did." I nod in agreement. "But I didn't go. I ran away from him like I ran away from my parents." It's wonderful to look back and see all the ways the Lord refused to let me get away.

I show Leslie a few photos of my time in the service. "The Merchant Marines took me out to Port Orchard, Washington, which seemed like the other side of the world from Sandtown. I developed my love for cooking as a food preparer in the steward department. Saw parts of the world I never dreamed I'd see—Europe, the Philippines, even Japan."

I was a good cook and felt at home on the ship, but deep down I knew I was trying to run from God and from the truth of who I was. Underneath it all, I figured if the Lord let me be hurt so deeply, why should I concern myself with him? Oh, I prayed and sometimes read my Bible like Daddy taught me, but it was just motions. My prayers seemed to bounce off the ceiling, as if even God didn't care about me.

But when you believe you're a nobody and that even

God doesn't care, you do things that reflect how little you regard yourself. I did some things that reflected how little I thought of myself. I stole things, money mostly, from my fellow marines. My fingers got mighty sticky, and I always seemed to get away with it. No one ever suspected me.

But I knew.

Not only had I become a nobody, I'd become a lying, cheating, stealing nobody. I felt so low without any hope of being anything more. I could talk smooth and look confident on the outside, but on the inside, I was dying.

Now that I'm an old man, even a great-grandfather, I know Mama and Daddy never stopped loving or praying for me. I may not have been born to them, but I was the son of their loving hearts. That's what really mattered.

The Lord heard their prayers. Even as I wandered away from Sandtown and all my parents taught me, he took care of me. He was my Shepherd. As I tried to run from his love, he kept me from straying too far. I was like a wounded little lamb. Long before I knew it was happening, the Lord Jesus began to anoint my wounds with the sweet oil of his love. Exactly as I'd seen Mr. Foster do for that little ewe when I was a boy.

Then one day the good Lord used my sweet mama, my Aunt Ola, to lead me back home to the love I so desperately needed. But in using her, my heart was broken once again.

CHAPTER FIFTEEN

1945

Smitty, 21-years old

West Point graduate Colonel Benjamin O. Davis, Jr.
is first African American to command a military base
(Goodman Airfield in Kentucky)

Nat King Cole is first African American to have
a radio variety show

Minimum Wage: 40¢ per hour

The creased pages of Daddy's letter trembled in my hands as I read the next sentence written in his careful pencil print:

> *She's gone, son, gone home to our Lord.*
> *She died on Mother's Day. She loved you as*
> *if you were born of her own womb. You may*
> *not believe that, but it's true. Don't ever forget*
> *it. She was your mama in every way possible*
> *except for the labor pains and birthing.*

The sheets of paper slipped from my fingers and drifted

to the barracks' floor. Numbness washed over me like an ocean wave in winter, crashing over my gray-rock soul. As the wave receded, a groan came up from way down inside of me. Again and again, I pounded my fist into the mattress of my cot, like I did as a boy and I was angry with Daddy. I was a world-traveling man, twenty-one years old, but at that moment, I felt like the little boy from Sandtown.

"Hey, you okay?" someone called after me. I didn't look to see who.

The barrack's door slammed behind me, and I escaped into the cool summer night. I needed air. Under a sky smeared with stars I wandered, kicking things and crying until I gasped.

Mama was gone.

I didn't get to say goodbye.

I broke her heart when I left Sandtown. Now it was her turn to break mine.

My heart ached in a way it never had before.

I sat on a small hill beside the baseball field, amazed at the tears pouring out from inside of me. Tears that, once I gave in to them, seemed to slowly soften my hard heart.

Exhausted, I wiped my nose on the back of my sleeve.

Smitty, you know better than that. Here, use my hankie.

I could hear her voice as if she were sitting beside me. How many times had she scolded me for wiping my nose on my shirtsleeve?

I smiled, sniffed, and wiped my face with the palms of my hands. It didn't matter the grass was damp. I stretched out, put my hands behind my head and crossed one foot over the other.

Mama.

Gone.

It didn't seem possible.

A lone tear slipped down the side of my face and landed in my ear.

Now you wash behind those ears, young man. Tomorrow morning, we're off to church. Want you clean for the Lord's Day.

I could almost feel the big, scratchy towel Mama would wrap around my skinny, little body once I stepped out of the bathtub. She'd pull me close and rub me dry.

She smelled of fresh baked bread, mother sweat, and baby powder.

She loved the Lord Jesus, there was no doubt about that. Often she spoke to me about heaven and described great reunions that would happen there one day.

Her *one day* had come.

Gazing up at the stars, I wondered what it would be like. Was she happy? Did she get to see her parents and all her brothers and sisters like she had talked about? Was heaven real? Or maybe it was no more than a good story used to reassure little boys?

My thoughts wandered and swirled with memories that made me smile.

When the realization of her death hit once again, my lips quivered. I'd never be able to thank her for loving me. For keeping me covered in the rain when she and Uncle Charlie picked me up from Mrs. Evans' house and took me home.

Never again would I get to thank her for feeding me, raising me, even disciplining me. For the million things she had done to love me.

Things she did, not because she gave birth to me, but because she chose me.

She wanted me.

When it seemed nobody else wanted me, she did.

I had traveled thousands of miles from Sandtown, trying

to leave home and all its hurts far behind me.

But in my grief under a canopy of stars, her death reminded what my heart had known all along.

Ola Smith was my mother.

"Thank you." I whispered as I stared up at the night sky.

A dazzling falling star arced across the heavens in a blaze.

You're welcome.

It was too late to go home and rebuild my relationship with Aunt Ola, but I knew I needed to try with Uncle Charlie. I felt bad about how I'd left home. I felt even worse about who I'd become. I was ready to go home, but was Uncle Charlie ready for me?

CHAPTER SIXTEEN

1946

Smitty, 22-years old

Harold Delaney marries his bride, Geraldine East

Delaney, a black chemist, worked on The Manhattan Project, the scientific project that led to the development of the atomic bomb, which ended World War II

A man's dress tie costs $1.50

Cold beads of sweat broke out on my forehead as my breathing quickened. "Jesus, help me." I half-prayed, half-swore as I squirmed behind the steering wheel of Mr. Blount's car. Tonight I followed the same routine I'd followed most nights since coming home from the Merchant Marines, but I'd never had reason to sweat like this.

Because all my siblings had moved out of the house, it was only Uncle Charlie and me at home. After dinner he was content to sit on the front steps with the neighbors, but I still had energy to burn, so I walked to Mr. Blount's grocery store to pay him a visit. It was a long walk, which gave me time to think. At first I walked to his store and hoped one of his pretty daughters would be there. But after a few times with no daughters at the store, I discovered I liked talking with Mr. Blount. He seemed to enjoy me, too. We'd talk sports and neighborhood news. When closing time came, I drove him home in his car. Why he trusted me, I do not know, but I wasn't about to turn down driving such a fine machine.

Tonight seemed like all the other nights until he locked up the store and forgot to turn off some of the lights.

"Give me a minute while I go in and take care of things."

"Yes sir, I'll be here."

He slammed the door behind him, leaving behind his canvas money sack. That bag whispered my name. Called to me. It mocked me and told me I'd always be a thief.

A moment later, I began to sweat.

My fingers shook as they touched the bag, stroked the canvas, and pushed it around to test things out. Sure enough, that sack felt heavy with coins and bills. I wondered how much money was right under my fingertips. It felt like a lot.

For me, money was scarce. Repairing shoes was steady work, but not much pay.

In the military I'd become skilled at stealing from my fellow marines, enough money to help me out, but not too much. Sometimes, the fellas didn't even notice money was gone. And when they did discover they were short on cash, they never suspected me.

Would Mr. Blount realize money was missing if I helped myself?

And if he did, would he suspect me?

When all was done, I fussed with my hair and my overcoat, made sure everything was precisely right.

Mr. Blount got back in the car. "Lights are out and everything's locked up. Let's go home."

The engine purred like a kitten.

"How's your daddy getting along these days without Ola?" Mr. Blount asked. "She's been gone almost two years now."

"Doing fine, I guess. He misses her terribly, but he's getting by." I was silent for a moment remembering Mama. "Few days ago, I even heard Daddy humming."

"That's good." Mr. Blount fiddled with the moneybag.

"Business good today?" My face and neck warmed with a wave of shame. This man trusted me. If he knew the real me of the past several years, he never would have left that money behind in the car.

"Business is always good on Saturdays, folks preparing for Sunday dinner. Long day." He yawned as I pulled in the alley behind his house. "Want to join me for a bite of something to eat?"

"Don't mind if I do."

Minnie had moved out of Mr. and Mrs. Blount's home and joined her brothers in Harlem, but Esther and Bernice still lived there. All the boys, including Henry, had moved to Harlem. Mr. Blount was the lone man left in his household. I guess that was the reason he welcomed my visits.

Inside the kitchen, he put the canvas moneybag on the counter and went straight for the refrigerator.

I smiled as I slipped off my overcoat, pleased I hadn't stolen one penny of his money.

He put a plate of cold leftover meatloaf and potatoes on the kitchen table in front of me, then poured two glasses of milk. "How's your job going?"

"Fine. I work with some mighty good soles." I enjoyed the overused shoe repairman's pun.

The door between the kitchen and dining room swung open, and in breezed Bernice.

"Welcome home." She planted a kiss on her father's

161

forehead, then poured herself a glass of milk. She sure was pretty. She had the biggest brown eyes I'd ever seen, a smile that could light up a room, and a pleasing petite figure with plenty of curves in all the right places.

I gave her my most charming smile. "Hello, Bernice."

"Nice to see you again." She smiled at me.

I plain forgot to chew the food in my mouth.

She left the kitchen as gracefully as she'd come in. As the door swung back and forth, I stared at the place where she'd disappeared.

Mr. Blount laughed low and quiet. He gave me a sympathetic thump on my shoulder with his fist. "Have some more meatloaf, son. Get your mind back on food."

Mr. Blount could see my interest in his daughter was growing. The problem was, I didn't know if his daughter had a clue.

———◆———

"You're awfully quiet."

"Me? Quiet? Naw..." I lied.

Bernice and I strolled slowly down the street, hand-in-hand, so as not to hurry the autumn evening away.

She glanced at me. "We're getting married in a few weeks."

"Mm-hm." Her hand fit so perfectly in mine. I hoped I'd never get over the thrill she gave me.

"I'm going to be your wife." She was so delicate and feminine.

I stopped walking, pulled her a little closer, and took in a deep breath of her scent. "Don't I know it."

Her big brown eyes gazed up at me. "And a husband

doesn't keep things from his wife."

"No, of course not." I agreed. I'd agree to anything with her in my arms.

"Then start now, Smitty. Tell me what's troubling you."

I didn't know what to say, so I gave her hand a gentle tug and started walking again.

The September air was cool and clear for our evening walk, the only date I could regularly afford. The sound of the neighborhood was our serenade. We passed giggling girls playing hopscotch on the sidewalk. Their parents sat on the front steps and smiled as we walked by. Cigarette smoke drifted past from a group of men across the street.

Bernice knew me so well. She could read my mood as easily as she could read the newspaper. She knew how to talk to me, too. Time and again she talked me through my dark, stormy spells.

I was glad to be home in Sandtown, and I loved Bernice. But all the questions and struggles deep inside of me came back up to the surface the day I came home.

I was finally at peace with Aunt Ola and Uncle Charlie, my mama and daddy. They were the parents who raised me. Yet all the unanswered questions about my biological parents tormented me.

Bernice knew how to prod me on with her gentle talk, and she knew when to be quiet. We walked for a few minutes in silence before she spoke again.

"Is it about your mama?"

"Yup." I swallowed the big lump in my throat. It was hard to admit my struggle.

Everything was hard to admit. The confusing family relationships went round and round in my head, bewildering me to the core. With such a twisted family tree, what did it make me?

Who was I?

What about me even mattered?

Here I was, seven years after learning the truth about my birth, getting married in a few weeks, and I was as confounded and confused as the day I learned I was a nobody. It never went away.

I stopped, shook my head. "It just seems..." The words caught in my throat.

Bernice turned to me with dewy eyes and a gentle expression. "Go on."

I swallowed and tried again. "It seems when a fella gets married, his mama should be at his wedding."

"Do you mean your mama, Aunt Ola? Or your mama, Cousin Edna?"

"That's it, Bern, sometimes I don't know who I mean." I rubbed my hand over my face as I tried to sort through my thoughts. "I know Mama can't come to the wedding, huh?" We both laughed, and that helped.

I took Bernice's hands in mine. "Sweetheart, Aunt Ola would be mighty proud of me marrying a woman like you." I kissed her fingers. "But what do I do about Edna, the mother who birthed me?"

Bernice thought a moment. "How well do you know her?"

"Hardly at all. She moved away when I was a little boy, only four years old." That familiar ache twisted at my stomach. My mama by birth didn't even stay around to watch me grow up. I only saw her when she came home for the holidays. And most of my life I'd thought she was my cousin.

My fiancée nodded. "Well, would you invite someone you barely know to our wedding?"

"No, guess not. Wouldn't make sense."

"Smitty, things don't always stay the same. There might come a day you'll know Edna better. She'll be less of a stranger, and it won't be so painful to think of her as your mother." Bernice paused, letting that thought sink in. "Maybe one day she'll even be someone special to you. Now's not the time, but maybe one day."

She tilted her head and studied me.

"I don't know if I want to know her," I countered. "She didn't want me, so why would I want her?"

"You don't want to know her now, but one day you might feel differently. Time will tell." Bernice stopped, looked up at me, and placed the palm of her soft hand alongside my face. Her hand was velvet. I couldn't stay angry when she looked so beautiful.

"Let the Lord be the judge. Things are not always as they seem. Edna was barely fifteen years old when you were born. That's terribly young to be a mother."

Bernice was right, but I didn't think I'd ever want to know Edna better. She'd tossed me aside like I was yesterday's newspaper.

"Bernice, why are you marrying me?"

She put her hands on her hips and looked me square in the eye. "What kind of a question is that? I love you."

"And I love you. But for me, you're a step up. You're pretty, intelligent, graceful, and the grocer's daughter." I tugged on her arm and guided her to a bench. She sat, and I slumped down beside her. "But for you, I'm a step down. Son of no one, family all mixed up. I work shoe repair, have a lame arm, and can't even afford a place of our own." I shook my head in disbelief and kicked my foot. "What kind of man brings his bride home to live with his Uncle Charlie? I want to do better for you, Bernice, really I do."

She opened her eyes wider than normal, and her jaw

jutted out in defiance. "Now you listen to me, Smitty Smith." She was fired up now. "You are going to be my husband, and I'm going to be your wife. We are equals at the foot of the Cross, and that is all that matters." She took my hand. "Plus, I love and respect you, and so does my family. Even my daddy."

Her eyes softened, and so did her voice. "You are an intelligent, hard working, wonderful man with a great sense of humor. I am proud to walk down this street with you for the entire world to see. You and me, we're going to do just fine." She smiled at me with that smile. "And you, Mr. Smith, are going to be somebody who makes a big difference in this world, I just know it."

I was quiet as I replayed her words in my head. "You forgot handsome."

"What?"

"You forgot to mention I was handsome," I teased with a quiet laugh.

"Oh Smitty, you are so very handsome." She laughed and gave me a quick hug.

We continued on our walk. I felt better with each step, with Bernice beside me, her hand in mine.

"You really think I'll be a somebody some day?"

"I *know* so." She was emphatic. "You're already the best somebody in my world."

We walked a few steps before she continued. "If you think all this talk is going to get you out of marrying me, you had better think again. I'm going to be Mrs. James Henry Smith. We're going to be together until the end of our days, each and every wonderful day from now until then."

I pulled her close and stopped her talking with a kiss. I was the luckiest man alive.

———◆———

After tugging on my shirt collar, I adjusted my tie and threw a worried glance at the preacher.

Rev. Thompson smiled. "Don't worry. Brides always need to fuss a little longer on their wedding day."

It was a Wednesday afternoon in October 1946. Together, Bernice and I and all our wedding guests had walked to the preacher's house. She was in the upstairs bedroom getting ready, taking too long. My mind raced with worry. How was I going to support her on a shoe repairman's income? Should I have paid more attention to the people protesting our marriage? They said it wouldn't last more than two weeks. Maybe they were right.

Before I could work out any answers, Mrs. Thompson came down the stairs. "The bride is all ready." She beamed a reassuring smile at me before she smoothed her skirt and sat down at the piano against the stairway wall. The piano bench creaked under her impressive weight.

Mrs. Blount and Grandma Julia, our only wedding guests, fussed from the couch. I looked to the top of the stairs and didn't blink. After a few measures of "Here Comes the Bride" from the out-of-tune piano, Bernice appeared at the top of the stairs. She stood there a moment like all brides do, pausing to take it all in.

She was stunning. I forced myself to breathe.

"Oh, simply beautiful." Grandma Julia wept softly.

Mrs. Blount murmured her agreement. With a demure smile, Bernice glided down the stairs clothed in her finest Sunday dress, hat, and gloves. When we'd walked to the preacher's house a few minutes ago, she was wearing the dress, but she'd carried her hat and gloves. Now, all adorned, she somehow looked different. She was a bride.

My bride.

She stepped beside me and looked up at me with adoring eyes, and my chest expanded with pride. The only thing between us was the small bouquet of daisies she held, a gift from the preacher's wife.

We turned to face the minister.

"Smitty, Bernice." Rev. Thompson's voice was deep and reverent. "You two have decided to honor the Lord by joining in holy matrimony. Marriage with the papers to prove it." His smile was as broad as his belt. "That's good, that's real good."

"Praise the Lord!" Grandma Julia witnessed with enthusiasm.

Mrs. Blount gently laughed. "Amen."

Pastor Thompson looked directly at Bernice, then me. "Are you ready to proceed?"

"Yes," Bernice answered.

"Yes, sir." I held Bernice's hand a little tighter.

A few words from the preacher, the vows, a kiss, and we were married.

Mr. and Mrs. Smith.

There were no cameras and no receiving lines to greet the guests. We couldn't even afford a cake, but we were as married as any other husband and wife. As legally wed as President Truman and his wife, Bess.

Rev. Thompson shook my hand and slapped me on the back. The women hugged and kissed Bernice first, then me, then each other.

The six of us moved into the kitchen where the ladies had set up a little reception of cheese, knockwurst, and cookies. We talked, laughed, and enjoyed the refreshing taste of Kool-Aid as it slid down our throats. It was a grand celebration, the best wedding reception I'd ever attended.

After the last of the knockwurst was gone, I thanked Rev. and Mrs. Thompson then turned to my bride. "Are you ready to go home, Mrs. Smith?"

She smiled in her warm, inviting way. "Why yes, Mr. Smith, I believe I am."

Everyone laughed, and I was grateful—it covered the sound of my hammering heart.

We marched through Sandtown like a royal parade of four. Mrs. Blount and Grandma Julia led the way in front of Bernice and me. She strolled with her arm linked through mine. The older women proclaimed to all within earshot that we had just gotten married. Folks shook our hands, slapped me on the back, then congratulated and kissed Bernice. Instead of going back to where they came from, they fell in line behind us, joining in the celebrated announcement each time another neighbor was in sight.

By the time we arrived home to Uncle Charlie's house, we had a small crowd behind us.

I held Bernice's elbow as she gracefully walked up our front marble steps. She turned to the crowd. "Thank you all so much for celebrating with us. I'm a very happy woman."

I thought I saw the daisies quiver the slightest bit.

Mr. Sampson from three blocks over spoke up. "Not too long, Smitty's going to be a very happy man."

The crowd laughed.

Bernice blushed.

Mrs. Sampson slapped him on the shoulder. "Hush up, fool."

Mrs. Blount climbed the steps and gave Bernice one last hug and kiss. Grandma Julia did the same.

A moment later, I closed the door, separating my wife and me from the rest of the world and our worries.

Answering the questions of what we would live off of or how long our marriage would last would have to wait until later.

Uncle Charlie was at work.

We were alone.

Scared.

Young.

Eager.

I was now a husband with his bride.

And my wife made me feel real good about that.

Chapter Seventeen

May 2008

Smitty, 84-years old

Average cost of a new house: $238,880

"Did you have a good nap, darling?" Bernice looks up from the kitchen table where she's reading the newspaper.

"Feeling refreshed." I got worn out when we went to the doctor's this morning. He needed to check me over, see what this cancer's doing. I know one thing—it sure does make me tired. I'm beginning to suspect Bernice knows I'm stretching the truth when I say I feel refreshed.

"Where do you want to sit when Leslie comes over?" Bernice eyes me, evaluating.

"Anywhere's fine."

"We'll sit in the sunroom and enjoy the view of the yard. How's that sound?"

"Perfect." Before my nap, I thought we'd have to cancel our interview session, but I think I can do it now. Besides, I enjoy the time, reflecting on my life. That's one blessing from this cancer. I've slowed down enough Bernice and I have talked a lot lately, looking back on the good times and the bad. We have a lot to be thankful for.

We tell Leslie the story of our wedding day, and I think she enjoys it.

My bride of sixty-two years stirs the cream in her coffee. "Remember Uncle Robert refused to come to our wedding?"

I laugh and imitate what I remember of his voice. " 'I will *not* bother to get all dressed up for a marriage that won't last two weeks! A mixed marriage never lasts!' "

"Mixed marriage?" Leslie asks with a puzzled expression and a furrowed brow.

Bernice delicately taps her spoon on her coffee cup. "Yes, we were a mixed marriage because I was a Baptist and Smitty was raised in the AME church, the African Methodist Episcopal. Several people were terribly concerned our marriage wouldn't last because we were from such different backgrounds." She laughs. "At least that's how they saw it."

"I think it's safe to say we just might make it."

Bernice sighs. "I do wonder why my parents never told us what they knew when we were courting. Or even when we were first married. All those years they knew about you, Smitty, and they never breathed a word."

"Guess they figured it wasn't their business."

"Still, it puzzles me." Bernice's voice gets high with emphasis. "We might never have found out."

"Well, we did find out." I smile and think back on that day so many years ago.

Bernice, still bothered, leans forward toward the coffee table and talks directly into Leslie's recorder. "All those hours we spent on the front steps, they might have told us then."

I reach over and hold her hand, calm her down. "We certainly did spend a lot of time on your daddy's front steps, didn't we, Bern?"

Memories of our humble courtship flood my heart.

"We certainly did." She smiles, and the world brightens. "Those were good times when we were courting, sitting and talking on those steps. That's all we did."

I clear my throat to make a correction. "You do remember I saved enough money to take you to the movies a few times?" I did the best I could to treat her well.

"I remember." She nods after a sip of coffee.

"And once, I even took you to the circus. I thought that was a mighty fine date." I turn to explain to our young writer friend. "Because I always tried to be the dapper dresser, I wore a necktie on that date."

Bernice starts laughing.

I ignore her and continue. "She answered the door and grinned from ear to ear. I thought she was so happy to go to the circus with me that she couldn't help grinning. It sure made me feel good."

Now Bernice is laughing so hard she's holding her side. "I was happy to see you, darling, but you were wearing a *necktie.*" Her small body bounces up and down to the rhythm of her laughter. "To the *circus!*"

"We were going on a date. I wanted to impress you." All these years, and she still doesn't get it.

Bernice tries to catch her breath, playfully pushes my shoulder and howls with laughter. "Smitty, *nobody* wears a necktie to the circus. *Nobody!*"

"Well, I did."

"You sure did, darling." She wipes tears from her eyes. "You sure did."

The telephone rings. We dig it out from underneath our loveseat cushions. Blasted wireless phones.

Bernice covers the mouthpiece with her hand and turns

to me. "It's the doctor's office. They need to do another scan." She gets up from the loveseat and heads to the kitchen. "If you'll just give me a minute to get to our calendar."

I sigh, resigned, and then look at Leslie. "Our social calendar sure is full these days."

We sit in comfortable silence, something only real friends can do. She understands about these kinds of doctor appointments.

"I know your marriage lasted longer than two weeks," she says, "but how did you make it financially?"

I glance toward the kitchen, decide Bernice is fine, and settle back in my seat. "I didn't think we would sometimes. I worked as much as I could at whatever job I could, every day but Sunday. And still sometimes, we got down to our last two nickels.

"Of course when we married, I worked shoe repair, but that wasn't going to get me too far. After that, I used the G.I. bill to take a course in histology. Today they call it microanatomy. Provident Hospital was one of the first all black hospitals in Baltimore over there on West Biddle Street. I prepared slides from autopsies for the scientists and doctors to study. Can't really say I was feeling better about myself then, but I'd moved up from shoe repair.

"At the same time, I worked as a host at a nearby funeral home, also drove the hearse. Some days, I worked all day at the hospital and evenings at the funeral home. And then, I worked nights managing a stock room at Glenn L. Martin Airfield. It was the 1950's and the first time I worked at a place where there were white people. I never worked with them, of course. But they were around."

Leslie nods as she listens. I think she understands there's a lot I'm not saying. Not because she's white, that ain't it. There's nothing I could add to all that's been said in history books, movies, and such.

It wasn't easy being a black man in the 1950's. Life was segregated. My world was the black world. Living in Baltimore, we had it better than those living down South, and from what I understand, things were easier for blacks farther up North. Truth is, there was nothing I saw in any white people that made me want to live in their world. Yes, I wanted the same rights and privileges, but associate with whites voluntarily? No, thank you. Except for Dr. Kidlowski, I'd never seen a reason to trust a white person. The longer I lived, the more I saw, the less I trusted any of them.

I wait for the young writer to indicate she's ready for more. "We had three beautiful daughters born close in years—one right after the other, like stair steps. Being a father was wonderful, but it also stirred up all my hurt. How could my biological parents have given me up so easily? Each time one of my girls was born, I fell in love. Those perfect little faces, the soft skin, and the tiny curled fingers. No way could I imagine giving up any one of them. Yet my biological parents had simply handed me over to an old woman in the neighborhood. It hurt every time I thought of it. Bernice always knew how to talk with me when I got to feeling low about my parents. I was blessed to be with such a capable woman."

Bernice comes back in from the kitchen and sits beside me. "We're moving along in our story, I hear."

"Why don't you talk for awhile? Let me rest."

She studies me and nods. "After our first daughter was born, we moved out from Uncle Charlie's to a place of our own in the Gilmore Street housing project."

Leslie interrupts. "You lived in the projects?"

My wife laughs. "Yes, but back then, welfare was so much different than it is today. It was to help you take a step up, get you on your way. Too often today, welfare gets folks trapped in a lifestyle of dependency on government handouts—exactly what Uncle Charlie had warned Smitty against. When we were in welfare housing, there was a strict time limit of how long we could live there. When that time came, you *had* to leave, ready or not. Welfare was in place to help you move up in the world, but *you* had to do the work to get there."

What made me think I could keep quiet? After all, I'm a preacher. "We saved every penny possible. When we left the projects, we moved directly into a house we bought for ourselves. It was quite an accomplishment and a great feeling."

"It sure was." Bernice beams.

"We struggled to pay the mortgage and other bills, but we paid. Occasionally, we had to do without our telephone and newspapers. And let me tell you, I missed my newspapers."

"Oh, but Smitty, they were good times as a young family, weren't they?"

"Oh yes."

Leslie's been writing notes and looks up. "What happened to your daddy, your Uncle Charlie?"

"He did what I'm doing now."

She stares back at me. "What is that?"

"Getting' old."

We laugh aloud, and I enjoy the burst of energy. Never have enough lately.

"Time marched on. Our girls started to grow up and Uncle Charlie was an old man. Plus his eyesight began to fail. He walked around with a white wooden cane letting folks know he didn't see so well."

I can't help but sigh as I think of the man I loved so

dearly.

When I was a child, Uncle Charlie opened his heart and home to me.

He did it again when my bride and I needed a place to live.

In Uncle Charlie's later years, it was my turn to open my home to him.

Chapter Eighteen

1955

Smitty, 31-years old

Rosa Parks is arrested in Montgomery, Alabama after refusing to give up her bus seat for a white man.

*The Montgomery Bus Boycott begins.
It continues for 381 days until the U.S. Supreme Court rules buses to be integrated.*

Average Cost of a new home $10,950.

Good smells from the kitchen distracted me as I tried to concentrate on our budget book. We were getting down to the last of our money for the month too soon before we'd turn the page on the calendar. In addition to the regular expenses Uncle Charlie had bills from the eye doctor we needed to figure out how to pay. I pushed the papers aside, grateful when Bernice called everyone to the dinner table. As hard as I tried to get us ahead, we were always behind. It seemed I'd always come up short the rest of my life.

"Carolyn, Sherry...you too, Yvonne, you all sit down now." Bernice instructed. "And no fussing at the dinner table." The girls were all in school now. Carolyn was in third grade, Sherry was in second, and Yvonne was in kindergarten.

Bernice placed a platter of ham on the table. Delicate drifts of steam rose and perfumed the air. Uncle Charlie balanced his cane against the table and eased his aging body into his chair. Bernice and I were the last to sit.

"Uncle Charlie, would you say the blessing?"

We held hands around the table and bowed our heads for prayer.

Uncle Charlie was near ninety years old and still surprisingly strong. His voice filled the room. "Dear Lord, these are some dangerous days we're living in, so we ask you to bless..."

It seemed like just yesterday Daddy prayed over our meals when I was a boy, surrounded by those I called my family. Now, here I sat with my own wife and children. I was grateful to have Uncle Charlie with us, to give a little back to the man who gave me so much.

I opened my eyes and closed them again, satisfied the girls were behaving.

A split second later Sherry giggled.

"Hush." Carolyn whispered not-so-quietly to her younger sister.

I glanced up in time to see Sherry jam her elbow into Carolyn's ribs.

"Ow!"

Yvonne giggled at her older sisters, then slapped her hand over her mouth.

Bernice gave them *the look*.

Uncle Charlie prayed on.

"Be with our beloved preacher and church family. Give us hearts to reach out to others in need of your love. For it is in Jesus' holy and powerful name we pray, Amen."

"Amen." Everyone echoed.

One by one, we piled our plates with ham, collard greens, and mashed potatoes. My fork met my mouth at the same time Carolyn dropped hers with a clatter. She sighed and rested her chin in her hands.

"Carolyn, baby, what's the matter?" Bernice asked.

Ham bathed my mouth with flavor.

"My food's cold." Carolyn whined, pouting.

Uncle Charlie cleared his throat and dabbed the corners of his mouth with his linen napkin. "Such a shame these modern kitchens can't make food hot enough to stay warm through a quick little blessing." His eyes twinkled despite the dimness of his sight as his broad, bent shoulders begin to shake. Soft chuckles gained momentum until finally his old body bounced up and down, and he laughed aloud.

I finally understood his mirth. "I know how you feel, Carolyn. When I was a little boy, Uncle Charlie prayed over every meal. My food was *always* cold. Some things never change, do they Daddy?"

Daddy laughed and I joined in. "Girls, I don't think I ever ate a hot meal until I met your mother's family." Uncle Charlie's tradition of long prayers and cold meals had been carried on to another generation. I was grateful we were together again. We laughed until we wiped tears from our eyes as three bewildered little girls stared at us.

Bernice smiled warmly. "Eat up girls. Let your daddy and Uncle Charlie have their fun."

I still delighted in Uncle Charlie's company, conversation, and upbeat personality. How would I provide for my wife, my girls, and an old man? Would I ever prove myself, my worth, to Uncle Charlie like I wanted to?

And how much longer would he be with us?

◆

It had been a long night working in the stock rooms, moving and loading supplies. I walked through my front door Saturday morning, tired to the bone. Bernice sat in the living room mending a dress that had been Carolyn's and was now Sherry's. In time it would go to Yvonne.

"Hello, beautiful." I leaned over and kissed my wife.

"Welcome home, dear." She put down her sewing. "How was your night?"

"Good. Busy. No complaints. Where are the girls?"

As if they'd heard me ask, peals of laughter burst from upstairs, followed by the sound of little feet skipping down the hallway above. Next came the tap-tap-tap of Uncle Charlie's cane on the floorboards, followed by his laughter and more squeals of delight.

"Give you one guess who that is playing with the girls." Bernice laughed. "After breakfast, I sent them upstairs to change out of their pajamas. I think they've been having too much fun to have bothered." She picked up her sewing. "Old as he is, I don't think there's another person alive who enjoys children like Uncle Charlie does. Mind you, I'm not complaining, but Smitty..." Her voice trailed off.

"What?" I eased myself down on the sofa.

"I can't put my finger on it, but Uncle Charlie doesn't seem like himself." She stopped sewing for a moment. "Oh, it's probably nothing." She worked the needle and thread again.

After a moment of suspicious quiet, there were more pattering footsteps and taps of the cane, followed by laughter. There were plenty of troubles, but for me all the world felt right when I heard my girls' laughter and the rhythmic tapping of my Uncle Charlie's cane.

"Sound like things are okay now." I yawned.

"Yes, dear, I'm sure you're right."

But that night the world changed.

Bernice had already put Yvonne to bed. It was my turn to get Sherry and Carolyn settled down for the night. They were sprawled on the bare wooden floor of the living room, playing the game *Sorry!* Uncle Charlie rested in his favorite armchair with his eyes closed, humming along to a Glen Miller tune coming from the radio beside him.

"Carolyn, Sherry, time for bed."

"Aw, Dad. *Please....*" The familiar nightly routine had begun.

"No fussing, girls. Give Uncle Charlie a good night kiss."

Hugs and kisses were exchanged between the girls and their great-great uncle. First Carolyn. Then Sherry. Then Carolyn again. Uncle Charlie soaked up all the loving they were willing to give. For a wise old man, he seemed oblivious to the girls' bedtime stalling techniques. Or maybe he was wise enough not to care.

"Okay girls, that's enough. Bed." I shooed them toward the stairs.

Uncle Charlie unfolded his height from his chair and stood. He smiled, his face still moist with kisses.

"Think I'll go get a glass of milk and turn in early myself." He jostled the cane in his hand in his time-to-get-a-move-on way and walked toward the kitchen.

After bedtime prayers, I tucked the blankets around each of the girls the way they liked, Carolyn's blanket snug and tight, Sherry's loose with plenty of wiggle room. I kissed each one and closed their bedroom door behind me.

Down the hallway, Uncle Charlie opened the bathroom door and made his way to his room. His white cane tapped out a rhythm on the floor as he hummed a familiar sounding tune. He was the music in our family.

But all songs end.

That night my daddy propped up his cane in the corner of his room for the very last time.

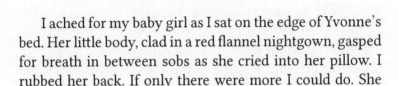

I ached for my baby girl as I sat on the edge of Yvonne's bed. Her little body, clad in a red flannel nightgown, gasped for breath in between sobs as she cried into her pillow. I rubbed her back. If only there were more I could do. She had to cry it out.

Maybe she could cry for me, too.

It had been a long day for all of us. Uncle Charlie's funeral and the reception that followed both comforted and exhausted us.

At last, Yvonne rolled onto her back. Her eyes were red and swollen, her little face wet with tears.

"There, there, Vonnie. Here use my handkerchief to wipe your face." I pulled the fabric square out of my pants' pocket, resisting the urge to let her use the sleeve of her nightgown.

Her lower lip quivered, but her tears had almost run out. "I miss Uncle Charlie."

"I know you do, baby. I miss him too."

She took the hanky. "Why did he have to die and leave us?" She finished drying her face, and gave the handkerchief back to me.

"Eventually, we all have to die."

"But he's in heaven, right? With Jesus?"

"Yes."

She took my hand and played with my fingers, so big

compared to her own.

"And he's with Aunt Ola?"

"Yes, he's with her, too."

"Will you and me go to heaven when we die?"

"Yes."

"How do we know? I want to be sure."

The same as Uncle Charlie had explained to me so long ago, I explained it to my daughter.

"We're all sinners, can't ever be good enough to go live with God. So his son Jesus came to live on earth with us. He died on the cross for our sins, and then—"

"He rose from the dead!" Yvonne finished for me, her hand flying up in the air for emphasis.

"That's right." She'd been listening in church. "And because Jesus conquered death, our bodies die, but we can live in heaven with him forever."

She bit her lower lip. "But I want to be *sure* I go to heaven." She insisted. "How can I be sure I see Uncle Charlie again?"

"You want to pray the prayer Uncle Charlie prayed with me when I was a boy, so you can be sure?"

She nodded, folded her hands, and closed her eyes. "Ready."

Once again, I was struck with the Gospel, so simple a child can understand, yet those who refuse are baffled by it.

"You say the words after me."

Yvonne nodded and kept her eyes closed.

"Dear Jesus, I know I'm a sinner..."

She said the same.

"...and I need you."

She squeezed her eyes tighter.

"Please forgive me of my sins. I accept you as my Lord and Savior."

Her expression relaxed. A little smile crept across her face.

"Please come live in my heart," she said in her little voice. "And help me to live for you. In Jesus' name, Amen."

She smiled at me, her eyes glistening with new tears or leftover ones, I wasn't sure.

"I feel good inside!" She reached up to hug me. "I'm going to heaven!"

I leaned over and wrapped her in my arms. It was one of those rare times I couldn't get any words out.

She kissed me on the cheek. "I love you, Daddy."

"Love you, too." I stood and walked toward the door. "Time now for some sleep, young lady. In the morning, you tell your mama about asking Jesus into your heart."

"I will. Leave the door open a crack."

"Always do."

Outside her bedroom door, I paused, grateful for what I had shared a moment ago with my youngest. Bernice was going to be so happy to learn about Yvonne's prayer.

I walked down the hall to the empty room at the far end.

I pushed the door open, sighed, and leaned against the doorframe.

Was it possible today had been a dream? I'd wanted so much to find Daddy in his room listening to his radio like so many other nights. Maybe the deep weariness of grief was all a mistake and Daddy was simply playing his game of hide-and-go-seek with the girls.

The quiet of the empty room overwhelmed me.

It all felt so wrong.

Daddy's cane stood in the corner like a slim, white, wooden sentry guarding the vacant room.

I stepped through the doorway.

A floorboard creaked.

The bed was perfectly made up. The top blanket smoothed over the mattress showing where it was worn down, curved to the size and shape of Daddy's body.

I stood in front of the cane and gazed down at it. Slowly, I wrapped my fingers around the cool, smooth wood, slender and strong like the man who had depended on its protection and support.

I eased myself down and sat on the edge of the bed.

Almost reverently, I examined the cane more closely than I ever had before. There were nicks in the wood from unexpected encounters, but they were secret stories I'd never know. In some places, the white paint was worn thin, and the deep brown wood underneath peeked through. The cane's curved top felt polished from years of contact with Daddy's fingers and palm. I wrapped my hand around it and tried to imagine the feel of Daddy's hand against mine. Then I slid my hand down to the very tip, the small rounded bottom of the cane.

My daddy's cane.

Closing my eyes, I tried to remember back to when I was a boy. Mama and Daddy had told me all sorts of things about heaven. I tried to imagine them there, free from the burdens of this earth. Restored. No longer needing a cane. Daddy singing loud as he could with the angels, Mama singing right beside him.

I wanted to feel comfort.

All I felt was pain.

Tears rolled down my cheeks as a fresh wave of grief, anger, and exhaustion washed over me.

I was making my way in the world.

I was proving my worth, providing for my family, even if sometimes it felt like we were barely getting by.

I would somehow drown out the confusion and doubts

that still mocked me deep inside.

Hard work was going to change me.

Make me a somebody.

I'd wanted my father to see what I made of myself, to see the man I could become, not the baby he'd taken in, the nobody.

Now that chance was gone.

My daddy was gone.

I tapped the bottom of the cane on the floorboards a few times, my own private tribute to the man who used to walk with this cane and make it tap so rhythmically.

My daddy no longer needed his cane.

But I still needed my daddy.

CHAPTER NINETEEN

1957

Smitty, 33-years old

Jackie Robinson retires from the Dodgers rather than be traded to the New York Giants

Senator Leon Butt's bill barring blacks from playing baseball with whites is unanimously approved by the Georgia Senate

One dozen eggs costs 28¢

The deep, rich aroma of Maxwell House coffee filled the kitchen. I sipped from my coffee mug and sat at the kitchen table in my robe and slippers reading the Saturday morning edition of the *Baltimore Sun*. Uncle Charlie and I used to discuss world events as we shared the paper on mornings like this, but he'd been gone almost a year now. I missed him every day.

The ringing telephone interrupted my thoughts. I lifted the receiver out of the phone cradle mounted on the wall.

"It's Uncle John. How are you this fine morning?" We talked a moment or two before he got to the purpose of his call.

"I wanted to ask a favor of you." He paused and cleared his throat the way old men do. "You know Hawkins Point?"

"Sure do." Hawkins Point was the Baltimore shipyard down by Curtis Bay. Years ago, it was a huge, busy place on account of the war, and it continued to provide work for plenty of folks.

"Could you pick me up in your car and drive me down there? I'd like to show you something."

What could possibly be at the shipyard that John would want to show me?

"It would mean a lot," he added.

"Sure, sure." My flannel robe was awfully comfortable, but I could do this much for him. "Let me sort things out with Bernice. How about I pick you up in half an hour?"

Thirty minutes later, John slid into the passenger seat.

"You sure you know where I'm talking about?" His eyes sparkled behind his glasses. "Hawkins Point?"

"Yes sir. Let's go."

When we arrived at the shipyard, John sat forward and peered out the window, quiet as he concentrated on our surroundings. He seemed to know his way around, so I followed his directions until he directed me to pull over.

"Yes, this is good." He got out of the car and glanced around. His jaw was set.

"Follow me."

The cool, mid-March air held a hint of spring. The wind held a brackish smell, the combination of fresh and salt water so unique to the Chesapeake Bay. If you could smell hope, it would smell like that air.

John walked over the uneven ground with a sense of purpose to the nearest man in the area.

"Excuse me." He explained he was looking for an old friend. He'd lost track of where the friend lived, but knew the man still worked in this area of the shipyard.

"That's Walter over there at the sawhorse." The man pointed out a lone worker.

"Been too many years since Walter and I saw each other," John told me as we walked toward his old friend. When we were closer, John paused a moment to study his friend before being seen. Bent over some boards of lumber, Walter concentrated on his work and hadn't noticed our approach.

Satisfied, John hollered above the noise of the shipyard. "Walter Brown! Hey, Walter!"

The man looked up and watched as we came closer. He was average height, around John's age, and dressed in well-worn work pants. His flannel shirt was missing a few buttons, and a long underwear shirt peeked out from beneath the flannel. Flecks of white sawdust clung to a thin layer of sweat on his coffee-colored face under a broad brimmed straw hat.

"Hey there, John! Good to see you, man." Walter smiled like he meant it. He kept hold of the saw in one hand and reached out to John with the other. I stood to the side, watching as they slapped each other on the back and sized each other up.

John turned his attention back to me briefly, introducing me to Walter. "Smitty here's my niece's husband. He was kind enough to bring me down here so I could find you. You and I were good friend as boys, weren't we, Walter?"

"Sure enough. Grew up together," Walter added with a nod. "Haven't seen each other in a quite a while though."

It seemed more like they were explaining things to themselves than to me. They laughed and carried on as they exchanged news about family and friends, who married whom, and who had passed on. They had plenty to talk about while I stood there, ignored.

Finally, there was a moment of silence. John cleared his throat, and his expression grew serious. He stepped toward me, took hold of my elbow and pulled me into their huddle.

"Walter, do know this young man?"

I was in my thirties with a wife and three kids I struggled to support. I hardly felt young.

Walter studied me a moment. "No, can't say I do."

"You remember Mr. James Jones?"

"Oh yes, I was good friends with his family." Walter gave a tired smile.

"He had a son went by the name of Leroy."

"And another son Curtis, that's right." Walter pushed his hat back slightly to get a better look at me.

John pressed on. "Mr. Jones had some daughters. There was Patience, Gloria, and Edna."

Walter's expression softened. "That's right."

Some seagulls called out in the distance. A truck horn sounded not far away.

"Edna had a son, a baby boy." John didn't take his eyes off Walter.

Walter turned his head, looked off in the distance. He took off his hat and wiped his brow with the back of his sleeve before putting his hat back on. His smile faded as he cocked his head to the side and looked his old friend in the eye.

"What are you getting at, John? I've got work to do."

John looked down at the dirt and shuffled his feet. He coughed and looked up. "Walter, that's the boy."

Nothing else.

There was a long silence between the two of them.

I wasn't sure why, but the phrase, *That's the boy* seemed familiar.

Walter chewed on his lower lip a moment. "What are

you saying?"

Controlled but intense, John continued. "Walter, this here's Edna's son. That's the boy."

As if moving in slow motion, Walter carefully placed his saw across the boards he'd been working on. He lifted his shaking hand to his cheek and rubbed his face. Flecks of sawdust rained down.

No one spoke.

Walter studied the dirt for a long time.

Way back in my memory, I recalled the first time I'd met Bernice's Uncle John. I was fifteen years old and at the Blounts' for Sunday dinner. All the adults huddled in conversation when Henry and I left the kitchen. "That's the boy," someone had said. The words chilled me then as they did now.

Still staring down at the dirt, Walter asked, "That's the boy?"

John turned to me, his eyes gentle and glistening. "Yes. Walter, this here is Edna's son."

When Walter looked up, tears streamed down his face, making clean streaks of brown through the white flecks of sawdust. His hand trembled as he reached toward me. He didn't touch me.

"They told me the baby died at birth." His words were barely a whisper.

It unsettled me to see this strong, hard-working man cry. I couldn't make sense of the secret code these two men used to communicate. They seemed to be discussing me, and I couldn't figure out what they meant.

My breathing became shallow.

My stomach twisted.

"They told me the baby died at birth." Walter uttered again, only louder. "For more than thirty years, I believed he was dead. It never did feel right."

Walter looked at John who looked squarely back at him. Walter's whisper could barely be heard. "Is this my son?"

"That's him."

My tongue smoothed over my lips and went back in my mouth.

I chewed my lower lip.

I stared at John.

Years and years' worth of hurt and confusion were packed in the question I couldn't bring myself to ask.

John seemed to understand as he stared back at me and slowly nodded.

John turned back to the man, who stood crying. "Walter, this here is your son. I'm certain of it."

Walter spoke in whispers. "My son was born on June 24, 1924."

That was my birthday.

I nodded.

"James?" Walter gazed at me through his tears. "James?"

I nodded.

"James Henry?"

I nodded again.

John had introduced me as Smitty. Yet this stranger knew my name. And he knew my birthday.

"James, I'm your father."

A ship blared its horn somewhere out on the water. Seagulls cried as they came close, then faded away. Soon, the blood that pounded in my ears silenced everything. When the pounding cleared from my ears, it moved down to my throat.

I couldn't swallow or speak.

Couldn't move.

Sunshine glared in my eyes, and tears welled up in

self-defense.

Shocked.

Unprepared.

I stared at John.

"Smitty, this here is your father. I'm certain of it."

I look intently at Walter. Stared at him. Studied him. And I could see it. Somewhere around his eyes and cheekbones, I could see a shadow of my future self. When I looked at Walter, part of me looked right back.

I didn't know if I wanted to laugh or cry.

Walter stepped toward me and opened wide his trembling arms. I stepped forward and collapsed into his embrace. The sturdy, hard-working arms of this stranger, my father, wrapped around me as if I were a little boy.

He rocked me as we cried.

We were both in shock.

We sobbed and laughed.

It was everything all at once.

"They told me you died, James Henry. I wanted to hold you, to see you, but they told me you died at birth." He said it again and again, his voice choking out the words between sobs. "I thought you were dead, son. I thought you were dead."

His muscular but weary frame relaxed in my arms. It was his turn to break down, weak and overwhelmed as I supported him. I nuzzled my face in his shirt collar and felt the flannel against my skin. I inhaled the smell of his sweat—my father's sweat.

When we finally pulled away from each other, I had sawdust on my face, too.

We laughed.

For the first time in my whole life, my father and I laughed together.

I could see myself in him.

A mirror of the future me.

After more hugs and slaps on the back, Walter finally turned to John. "How? How did you know?"

"Smitty joined our family a while ago, married my niece Bernice. When we first met him, he was fifteen years old. He told us a story about his grandmother, Julia Jones."

"Julia." Walter repeated, nodding his head.

"When he told us about her, I understood then why he seemed so familiar. He favors you, Walter. He was the spitting image of you when you were a boy. I knew it that first Sunday I met him, and I told the others, 'That's the boy, that's Walter's boy.'"

That's the boy.

I shook my head in overwhelming joy and disbelief. "Why now, John? Why not before?"

He shifted his weight and stared out across the water. "Let's say not everyone agrees with my making this introduction. For a long time, I was told to mind my own business. And I did." He turned to me and grinned. "But your grandma's gone now, and I'm getting on in years. My turn to do what I think's right."

In an instant, my life had changed.

My father had wanted me all along.

CHAPTER TWENTY

1961

Smitty, 37-years old

Pulitzer Prize awarded to Harper Lee for To Kill A Mockingbird

Frank Robinson becomes the first baseball player to win MVP's in both major leagues

First class postage stamp costs 4¢

My suitcase was in the car, and my family gathered around to see me off.

"Don't go, Daddy. Please don't go." Yvonne locked her arms around my waist.

"I've got to get back to school, baby."

"Then take me with you!" Yvonne was tired, and it showed.

I pried her arms off me. "I need you to stay here, help out your mother and your sisters."

Yvonne's expression cooled and her chin went up as she looked away. She probably felt I'd rejected her. It didn't seem right for a father to be so far away from his family. She was too young to understand that it also hurt me to say goodbye.

Bernice stepped forward, put her hands on Vonnie's shoulders, and gently pulled her away from me. Our crying daughter snuggled under her mother's protective arm.

"Darlin', your father will be back in five days, you know that. This is exactly like the other times." Bernice gently rocked Yvonne back and forth as they stood. "You let him go do what he needs to do. Soon he'll be living with us again, all the time."

I leaned forward and kissed Bernice. She smiled with strength and understanding. She would do nothing less.

Carolyn and Sherry looked at me, wide-eyed. "Girls, you all mind your mother. Don't give her any trouble while I'm gone.

"Yes, sir."

"Yes, Daddy."

I got in the car, drove down the street, and left my family far behind.

———◆———

The engine purred like a kitten as I hummed to the rhythm of the wheels rolling down the highway. I liked to drive, but the commute from Baltimore to Greensboro, North Carolina, got tiring week after week.

Still, thinking about where I was going—if Uncle Charlie could see me now!

So much had changed since he'd died six years before. Now, I was close to finishing my first year of preacher training school at Bennett College. When I reached my goal, I'd be a United Methodist Church preacher with the papers to prove it.

The anticipation kept me going. Too often, Negros (that's what we went by now) had a hard time improving their lives with education because segregation set out to make it difficult. However, I was determined to accomplish all I could. My daddy raised me to work hard to better myself. When I was a boy he tried to prepare my siblings and me for what we would face as adults. we needed to better ourselves. We needed to be ready for when more opportunities opened up for our people, and I was grateful.

I was doing my preacher training through an at-home study program through the Methodist Church. One requirement of the course was that I be in seminary classes each summer. In the Baltimore area, if a Negro man felt the call to the ministry with the Methodist Church, he got his classroom training at Bennett College in Greensboro. In 1873, the school was established on land purchased by some emancipated slaves. Even though it had since become an all women's school, it was arranged for those of us Negro men going into the pastorate to be educated there.

The white Methodist men in Baltimore went to seminary in Washington D.C., an easy hour and a quarter drive from my home. Instead, I drove seven hours one way to Greensboro. Monday through Friday I attended classes, lectures, studied, and took tests. Friday afternoons, I'd drive home to Baltimore to be with Bernice and the girls. Sunday afternoons I drove back to Greensboro and my little dorm room.

Bernice was supportive, but it was hard on her, too. Not only did she have to handle the three girls on her own, but money was scarcer than ever, and she pinched pennies like an old pro. Never complained, though. She reminded me the Lord would take care of us. And so far, he had.

I shifted my position behind the steering wheel. Dusk

was settling on North Carolina fields. I reached forward to the dashboard and pulled out the knob for the headlights. Beams of bright light broke through the dimness and showed me my way.

Yes, I was finally finding my way, on the highway and also in life. The nobody struggles I'd battled for so long were weakening since I'd gotten right with the Lord. My relationship with him helped me see my worth as his child. Walter fathered me. Edna birthed me. Uncle Charlie and Aunt Ola raised me. But first and most importantly, I was a child of God.

Seminary was an exciting season in my life. I learned new things and faced new challenges. I still caught myself wanting to discuss with Uncle Charlie the things I'd been learning until I'd remember he was no longer with us.

I didn't need to wonder what he would have thought about me becoming a preacher. He'd approve. After all, my call to the ministry came through Uncle Charlie a few years after he'd died. For the rest of my life, I was sure I'd never forget when I was sick with double pneumonia and Uncle Charlie paid me a visit. It changed my life. The Lord sure does work in mysterious ways.

◆

My girls seemed so much younger then, but it happened only a few years before I began driving down to Greensboro.

The sound of splashing water filled the gray, musty bedroom where I lay in bed. Bernice dipped the washcloth in and out of the bowl and squeezed out the excess liquid. She patted the cool cloth on my forehead. It felt like hope on a wet piece of terry cloth.

My wife, my lover, my nurse.

My Bernice.

She talked to me in a low, soothing voice the way she used to croon to our babies as she rocked them to sleep. "Some of the ladies from church are downstairs."

The fever that raged through my body quickly warmed up the washcloth. She rinsed it in the bowl again.

"In a few minutes I'm going to join them as they pray for you."

"Tell them thank..." Before I could finish my sentence, deep, rattling coughs stole my words and my breath.

Bernice's slim, strong mother-arms helped me sit up higher. She held a bowl under my chin. Rusty brown sputum came up from my lungs and slimed its way to the bottom of the bowl. Pain shot through my right lung.

Exhausted, I sank back into the pillows that propped me up even when I slept. My chest heaved up and down, shallow and quick. New layers of perspiration melted into the already damp sheets. Fresh pajamas and bed sheets didn't stay that way for long.

I opened my mouth to speak.

"Save your strength."

I agreed with a slight nod of my head.

"Baby, you've got to get better. The girls and I need you with us." She cleaned me up, dabbing the washcloth around my mouth.

"When you were a child, you got through double-pneumonia, you remember?" Bernice's voice caught, and she stopped talking. The room was silent except for the crackling of my lungs.

"Do it again, please. For us. For me." Underneath Bernice's soothing rhythm of words, I heard fear in her voice, the same fearful tone I'd heard in the doctor's voice the day before.

"Drink some water now, darling."

I felt a drinking glass against my lips.

"The doctor says it's important you stay hydrated. Fever robs you of your liquid."

It was difficult to make the water go down, but I swallowed.

Refreshing.

Then tiring.

"That's good." Bernice stroked my hair. "That's enough. It's all right."

The back of her fingers felt like velvet as she ran them down my cheek. She leaned forward. A whiff of her favorite lotion graced my nose. Her soft, full lips blessed my forehead with a kiss.

She walked to the windows and made sure the curtains were drawn shut. "I'll check on you again soon as the ladies leave. They promised they wouldn't stay long. Try and get some sleep."

I wanted to nod my head in response, but the pillows' resistance was too much.

I hoped she saw me blink.

Yes.

Sleep.

———————◆———————

My sleep was light and restless, then heavy and deep.

I woke long enough to hear a soft knock on the door.

One of the kids sending a secret message.

Or maybe Bernice.

Why didn't she come in?

Come in, I thought and slipped into sleep's darkness.

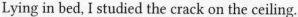

Lying in bed, I studied the crack on the ceiling.

I'd discovered it a few days before. Didn't know how long it had been there.

It seemed bigger now. Longer. Wider.

I closed my eyes.

I needed to tell Bernice about the crack. It was growing.

The house might split in two.

The rain would come in.

And snow.

Snow would feel good.

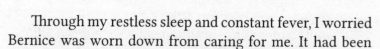

Through my restless sleep and constant fever, I worried Bernice was worn down from caring for me. It had been four weeks since I'd gotten sick, maybe five.

I missed the girls. They were allowed in my room once daily for brief visits. They were quiet when they came in. Even Sherry's spunky personality grew subdued when she saw her daddy lying in bed.

I missed their bright eyes and sunshine giggles. I missed being with them at the dinner table.

I wondered, if I got well, would I still have a job?

If I didn't pull through, how would my girls get along?

But more than anything, I was consumed by a bone-weary exhaustion.

My lungs labored for each breath.

Sometimes breathing brought sharp pain.
My body burned and ached from fever.
I wanted to fight.
For her. For us.
I wanted to give up.
I wanted relief, freedom from fever.
Strength to breathe.
Each breath tired me more than the one before.
Sleep.

———◆———

Someone tapped on the door and woke me.
Why was Bernice knocking? Before she always walked in.
"Come in." My voice was weak.
The coughing came and left me panting.
I was cold. Chilled. I pulled the blankets up to my chin.
My eyelids felt swollen and dry. They scratched like when I got sand in my eyes at Camp Linstead.
Forcing my eyes open, I blinked to clear out the Camp Linstead sand.
The room was filled with bright white light. My eyes quickly closed tight. Yellow spots danced on the inside of my eyelids.
I kept my eyes closed. "Bernice?"
She didn't answer.
The room was silent except for the wheeze of my lungs.
Maybe she didn't hear me. "Bernice?"
Tap, tap, tap.
There was someone in the room with me.
I felt someone there in the same way I had smelled

Bernice's lotion.

I shivered. I was so cold.

Tap, tap, tap.

Why did Bernice knock on the door when she was already in the room? Say something Bernice. Put your warm hand on my forehead. I need you.

Tap, tap, tap.

Please. Warm.

Tap, tap, tap.

No. Not Bernice.

Tap, tap, tap.

Daddy?

Tap, tap, tap.

From across the room, the sound came closer to my bed. It sounded like Daddy's cane. How I missed him. I missed the rhythmic sound of his cane as it tapped on the floorboards.

Tap, tap, tap.

With all the strength I had left, I fought the fatal fatigue and opened my eyes.

Who was in the room?

Who sounded like my daddy, my Uncle Charlie?

At first, I couldn't focus my eyes.

Everything was so bright, but not painfully bright like before.

I blinked.

My eyes focused.

I scanned the room and saw him.

There at the foot of the bed stood the man who raised me, tall, broad, and strong. He looked like the healthy hod carrier I so adored when I was a little boy. He stood with his cane in hand. He didn't need the cane. It was more of an ornament, a badge of honor. A symbol.

He looked directly at me.

Inside me, the chills of fever were replaced with warmth. Not the heat of fever, but the life-giving warmth of pure love.

Tap, tap, tap.

He walked a little closer and peered at his boy.

His son.

Me.

"Daddy..." I couldn't say any more. The bedsprings squeaked under the force of my coughing. My chest heaved and strained. Weary muscles. Tired of breathing.

Tap, tap, tap.

He came closer.

I lingered on every detail of his face. The strong line of his jaw. The breadth of his nose. His high cheekbones and twinkling brown eyes.

He was tall and strong again, not like the old man who'd died down the hall. His clothing was pure white, shimmering like sunshine on diamonds. It draped around him like a royal robe. His golden brown skin was radiant. He looked the same, but he looked even more like Uncle Charlie, more alive than ever before.

He took a few more steps, and the robe swayed and moved with him like beautiful music.

He stood very close, looked directly into my eyes, and held my gaze.

I yearned to explain how I'd become so ill, that the pneumonia was getting worse even though I wanted so much to get well.

I wanted to tell him about my worries. He could help me think through things. He would know what I should do.

Uncle Charlie needed to know about how I met Walter, about my half-brothers and sisters. Walter and I became friends, and then he died so suddenly. Uncle Charlie needed to know that no matter what, he would always be my daddy.

So much had happened since he'd died. I wanted to tell him all of it, but I didn't have the strength for even a sentence.

He smiled at me. His eyes danced with delight.

In that room, we were two men.

One man already dead yet more alive than ever before dressed in heaven's robes.

The other man barely alive, maybe dying, in flannel pajamas soaked with fever-sweat and sickness, buried under a pile of blankets.

We smiled at each other, and I knew he knew and understood all I wanted to tell him. He knew every detail and more. Just like when I was a little boy, Uncle Charlie seemed to know and understand me better than I did myself. It was all communicated with one look between daddy and son. Peaceful in his presence, I rested. Didn't ask why or how he was there. I simply soaked in the reassurance of my daddy's company. It was the best feeling I'd had in a long, long time.

Pain stabbed at my lungs as I coughed and heaved.

I didn't want Uncle Charlie to leave. I was afraid I would cough him away.

Instead, he leaned his white, wooden cane against my bed, then reached deep into his shimmering robe. First, he pulled out a bottle, a brown medicine bottle without any labels. Next, he pulled out a shining, silver spoon. I remembered the tonic he used to dispense from a medicine bottle when I was a boy, but we never had a spoon as shiny as this one.

He carefully poured a dose of liquid from the bottle

into the spoon. As if I were his little boy again, he held the spoon in front of me. He lifted it a bit, his signal to open my mouth. I did. He slid the spoon into my mouth and watched as I swallowed. The warm, pleasant liquid trickled down my throat.

One drop of the fluid dangled from the corner of my mouth. My tongue rescued it, and I felt the healing warmth of that tiny drop join the rest and spread throughout my body.

Still holding the bottle and spoon, Uncle Charlie stood above me. With a look deep and strong he said, "Preacher, the Lord is going to use you. Now preach. Go preach my God."

Preach?

I had dropped out of high school.

I was a stock room keeper, not a preacher.

I was sick.

Maybe dying.

But maybe those weren't good enough excuses for my strict daddy.

"I'm not prepared."

Uncle Charlie's eyes twinkled. "You will be."

As if that settled everything, he straightened up to the full height of his younger years. Slowly, deliberately, he slipped the bottle and spoon back into the deep, unseen place in his robe.

He took the cane from its resting position, looked at me, and smiled again, almost chuckling.

I smiled, too.

It was the most real and natural interaction as any other I'd had in my life. It seemed irrelevant that Uncle Charlie had been dead for years.

A moment later, he jostled the cane in his time-to-get-a-move-on way.

After one last smile, a smile that seemed to know all the answers, he turned and walked away.

And then he disappeared.

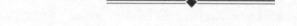

I lay in bed awake, unsure when I awoke or if I'd really been asleep.

My pajamas were drenched with sweat, but I no longer shivered from fever.

I began to cry. For so many years of my life, I'd been angry about my background. My pain and anger were buried deep, yet they were always inside me.

I blamed God.

How could he let me be born a nobody?

Why didn't he do anything to stop my mama from giving me away?

However, this dream encounter with the man I adored and missed so much unlocked my heart. It opened me to the possibility that this world was so much more than I could see or understand. Maybe God was God, even though I didn't understand all he allowed. The Lord was trying to get through to me, and I finally welcomed him.

"Jesus, I know you're my Savior, known that since I was a boy." I half-prayed, half-whispered the words. "But I've been running from you. Trying to do everything on my own, holding on to all my hurt and anger. I give up, Lord. I surrender. I'm yours."

The words choked out of me.

For the first time in my life, I cried for joy.

I cried for the peace I felt inside, peace I'd never known

before.

My life belonged to Jesus now.

For however many hours or years I had left, I was his.

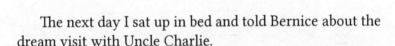

The next day I sat up in bed and told Bernice about the dream visit with Uncle Charlie.

The day after that, I sat at the dining room table and ate dinner with my family.

And the following day, I started planning to become a preacher.

Chapter Twenty-One

June 2008

Smitty, 84-years old

Tiger Woods wins 14th major championship in sudden-death playoff, Torrey Pines Golf Course California

---

Forty years after that dream encounter with Uncle Charlie, I'm sitting at the kitchen table with Bernice and Leslie, but I can still recall that dream so vividly.

"So what did you do?" Leslie asks.

"I prepared to preach."

"Just like that?"

"Just like that."

"They were challenging years." Bernice says with a little chuckle. "The first year he worked and studied at home during his off hours. In order to participate in the classroom portion of the program held during the summer, he quit all his jobs." She smiles and shakes her head. "The little money we had coming in stopped altogether. At the start of his second year, he was given his first church assignment. I had also started college to become a schoolteacher. The two of us and all three children were in school at the same time. I don't know how, but somehow we made it."

Today, we're drinking iced tea. I take a sip before continuing. "Segregation made my seminary schooling a real challenge, having to drive to Greensboro and back. But in another way, desegregation made the last year of my training even harder."

I rattle the ice cubes in my glass, shake it up a little.

"Go on." Bernice encourages.

"Wesley Theological Seminary in D.C. was where the white men attended school while I commuted all those miles to Greensboro. As desegregation started to come into place, I was allowed to finish school at Wesley. It was a much shorter drive to D.C.—that was the good part. But it was the first time I'd ever shared a classroom with white folks."

I study Leslie and see she's trying to process what this means.

Bernice nods sagely. "It was 1965. There were fifteen white men and three black men in Smitty's graduating class."

"I was 41 years old. All my life I'd gone to all black schools, lived in all black neighborhoods, had jobs with all blacks, and gone to all black churches. My world was the black world. And there, at the end of my seminary training, I was in a classroom with *whites*. And supposed to be an equal." I give a gruff laugh and shake my head. "Wasn't nothing equal about it."

I pause and look at Leslie.

She's the daughter of my best friend. Little Irv.

I can trust her, so I go on.

"I'd like to say that since my classmates and I were all studying to serve the Lord, it was a comfortable situation. I'd like to say that, but I can't." I shake my head at the irony. "Too many of us, both black and white, allowed society's distorted views and ill feelings to creep into our hearts.

I'm not saying anyone was intentionally unkind, but it was worlds different than life today. As a black man, I was walking on eggshells in seminary. Had to be on guard, careful what I said, where I sat, who I trusted."

Leslie nods. "So who could you trust?"

I think a moment. "The two other black men."

We laugh, but it's the truth.

I let my young friend ponder the words I'm saying.

And the ones I'm not.

I'm glad I was able to tell her this. Last time we set up an interview, I had to cancel on her, because I wasn't feeling up to it.

It's near impossible for young people today to appreciate how things used to be. Doesn't matter what color skin they have, it's so very different now.

"I'm grateful Uncle Charlie raised me to believe things were going to get better. He was right."

Bernice pats the overstuffed orange notebook that sits on the kitchen table. "This book is part of the way Smitty made sure things got better for us. I'm real proud of you, darling."

She looks at me with those eyes of hers, and my heart beats faster.

I can't help but grin. "Yes, this book holds all the certificates I earned attending classes at various colleges and universities. After I graduated from seminary, I earned my GED. A little backwards, but that's how it happened. Then with all these other classes, little by little, I became a somebody with an education.

"Uncle Charlie knew that for a child to feel proud of himself, the child had to do something he could be proud of. That's why he had us kids working so young. Same goes today. What we do and the education we get affects how we feel about ourselves and the opportunities that become available to us."

I think about some of the young people I know today and slowly shake my head.

"When I was a boy, black people struggled *hard* to get an education. Now the schools are wide open for everyone, but some kids don't even bother to go, and their parents don't seem to care. It's sad."

I force myself to redirect my thoughts and laugh. "Who would've thought that when I was sixty-seven years old, I'd be presented with an honorary doctorate degree? I also earned awards from mayors and congressmen, and my churches gave me beautiful banquets of appreciation. It was all wonderful."

My heart overflows with thanks. I've had a good life.

"But when I first started in the ministry, there was a time when I had some serious doubts about what I was doing. On top of that, something was very wrong with Bernice."

Chapter Twenty-Two

1965

Smitty, 41-years old

The Sound of Music *premieres and becomes an instant hit*

*Martin Luther King, Jr. leads 25,000 people marching
for civil rights to Montgomery, Alabama*

A gallon of gasoline costs 31¢

"I'm real proud of you, darling." Bernice sat next to me as I drove.

I held the steering wheel with one hand and used the other to squeeze her hand. "How does it feel to be a preacher's wife?"

"Wonderful!" Her laughter fills the car. "They sure did put on an impressive dinner to welcome us to the church."

"Now I understand why some preachers get so broad around the belt."

Our three girls slept soundly in the backseat, worn out from a long, full day.

We had almost an hour to drive before we'd arrive home.

From now on, Sundays were going to be a long day with plenty of driving. For my first pastoral assignment, I was given a circuit of five churches in Mt. Airy and Damascus, Maryland. The churches were in the same general area, but each one was a good forty or fifty miles from our home. My starting salary, modest as it was, would help cover the cost of gasoline.

Bernice turned to me. "Explain to me again how you'll be pastor to *five* churches."

It was a little overwhelming.

"On the first and third Sunday of the month, I'll preach at two of the churches, like I did today. On the second and fourth Sundays, I'll preach at the other three. Eventually, we'll try to get all five churches together on the first Sunday of the month for communion." I chuckled, still amazed I really was a Methodist pastor. "The District Superintendent suggested that idea but admitted it wouldn't be easy to get all five churches to agree."

One of the girls sighed, shifted, and went back to sleep.

"Well, if every Sunday is as full and exciting as today was, we won't have any trouble getting the girls to bed." Bernice sighed. "Me neither. I'm exhausted." She closed her eyes to rest.

It had been an exciting day, and I'd enjoyed it immensely.

I felt at home in the pulpit, coaxed on by amens and affirmations from the congregation. I enjoyed studying the Bible and crafting a sermon to share what I'd learned. For me, preaching was fulfilling, exciting. It stirred something deep inside of me. And I loved people, getting to know them and learning to love them for who they really were. Already I was looking forward to next Sunday.

There was a small part of me that wondered if I enjoyed the idea of being a pastor too much? I wanted to honor God, but had my motives taken a wrong turn somewhere? Did I enter the ministry to make myself feel important? Did my desire to leave behind my nobody life and become a somebody put me where I really didn't belong?

It was my first Sunday on the job, and here I was having serious doubts about the whole thing. My thoughts swirled around as I drove. I surrendered my concerns in prayer. *Lord, I think this is your path for me, but if I've got it wrong and you have another path, please show me. Whatever I do, I want to honor you. Amen.*

How would God answer?

I had no idea, but I was confident he would.

What I was not confident about had to do with my wife, propped up against the passenger side door, sound asleep. If this was the wrong path for me, how would I ever tell Bernice?

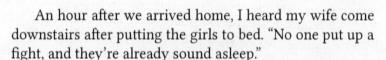

An hour after we arrived home, I heard my wife come downstairs after putting the girls to bed. "No one put up a fight, and they're already sound asleep."

"Mm-hm..." I was half asleep myself, stretched out on the couch with the Sunday newspaper draped across my chest. My right arm held the paper in place, my left arm hung over the side of the sofa.

"Smitty! Oh my Lord!" Her shouts woke me with a start. *"Smitty! Wake up!"*

Bernice's eyebrows were arched high on her forehead, her eyes wide with alarm. She stood motionless at the bottom of the steps. Her outburst had startled me so much, I scrambled to a sitting position.

I glanced around the room, but nothing seemed out of the ordinary. "What's wrong?"

She didn't move or speak. Her expression was frozen.

I stood, and the newspaper fell to the floor.

"Oh Smitty. Oh Smitty." She seemed in a near panic.

I walked toward her. "Bernice, you're scaring me. What's the matter, baby?"

Slowly she lifted her right hand and pointed at me. I glanced down at my shirt. Nothing there. Maybe the day's excitement and activity was too much for her, and she was more tired than we realized. Or she was getting sick, and a fever was affecting her behavior. I reached out to put my arms around her.

Her gaze shifted down. Her right hand kept pointing at me as her left hand came up in front of her, fingers spread signaling me to stop.

I stopped.

I didn't move a muscle, unsure what was going on.

Lord, please let her mind be okay.

The corners of her lips turned up slightly, then slowly blossomed into a beautiful, big smile.

She looked up. Her eyes danced with excitement as they met mine.

I'd never seen her like this.

Breathlessly she whispered. "Don't you see, Smitty?"

"See what?"

"Your lame arm. Look."

I looked.

I blinked, shook my head to clear the cobwebs, and looked again.

My lame arm was no longer lame.

My left arm had been bent and frozen in the same position for forty-one years. Now it was stretched out, as natural and straight as my right one.

Normal as could be.

I gawked.

I laughed.

I stretched both arms to their full length. No pain.

I bent my arms and straightened them out again. Like two dancers, each imitating the other, whatever my right arm did, my left arm copied.

Tears welled up in my eyes. "It was bent this morning, wasn't it, Bern?"

"Sure was. When you were up in the pulpit this morning, it was bent like it's always been." Bernice slapped the palms of her hands up to her cheeks, cradling her face in wonder. "Smitty, the Lord *healed* you!"

I laughed and couldn't stop.

I tested my arm in every position I could think of. All the while, Bernice and I laughed and cried.

It was better than Christmas morning.

"He sure did. Will you look at that." I couldn't stop staring at my arm as I moved it around. I hadn't even told Bernice about my concerns from earlier that evening. By healing my arm the Lord let me know I was on the right path. I was overjoyed.

Yet even in my joy, I was old enough and wise enough to know there would be struggles ahead.

CHAPTER TWENTY-THREE

1968

Smitty, 44-years old

Presidential candidate Senator Robert F. Kennedy of New York is shot at a campaign celebration and dies the next day.

The Supreme Court bans racial discrimination in the sale and rental of housing.

The scent of Bernice's brownies perfumed the car and made my mouth water. "Those smell so good, I'm tempted to pull over. We can picnic, just the two of us."

"The ladies would not like that." She laughed. "Besides, we're late as it is. It's already after seven o'clock. We were supposed to be there at six forty-five."

We were on our way to Lucy Blackwell's house in Damascus for the Methodist Women's Circle Meeting. It was the women's monthly meeting, but as the pastor, I was always included in the fellowship and food, two of my favorite things. We parked the car, got out, and stretched. As I put on my jacket and straightened my clerical collar, Bernice carried the plate of brownies to the house.

"Hello!" We called as we pushed open the front door. "It's Rev. Smith and First Lady Bernice."

From the cars outside, it looked like all the others had arrived before us, but it was eerily quiet for a gathering of women. I followed Bernice into the crowded kitchen.

Never one to shy away from making an entrance, I called out, "Hello, Ladies!"

No one answered.

Their backs were turned. Everyone was huddled by the kitchen counter.

"Hello?" Bernice questioned more than greeted.

One by one, each woman slowly turned to look at us with tears rolling down her cheeks. A few twisted handkerchiefs in their hands. One chewed on her thumbnail. Another hid her face in her hands and quietly sobbed.

Clarence, Lucy's husband, was a big, powerful man who worked construction. He stood with his arm around Lucy, frowning, his brow deeply furrowed.

They stared at us.

And said nothing.

The kitchen clock ticked.

The radio was on. Words buzzed in the background.

Finally, Lucy spoke in a whisper. "He's been shot."

"Who?"

"Martin Luther King..." Lucy couldn't get out any more words. She covered her mouth with her hands and cried harder.

Someone finished for her. "He's dead."

I felt like I'd been kicked in the stomach.

Bernice steadied herself against the counter.

Clarence's chin quivered. "He was..." His deep voice cracked. He looked away, took a breath, and pulled Lucy closer. "He was in Memphis. Someone shot him on his hotel balcony."

Bernice and I turned toward each other. Our eyes locked.

She knew I was thinking the same thing she was.

I rattled my car keys and cleared my throat.

It couldn't be possible.

I took a breath and deliberately spoke slow and even. "Are you saying Martin Luther King, Jr. is dead?"

Clarence nodded, one lone tear glistening against his skin. "He's gone."

The grief in that kitchen could almost be held in your hand.

It was displayed on the drawn faces, twisted in despair and disbelief, in the quivering chins.

"Ladies and gentlemen, in case you just joined us, allow me to update you on the situation."

Instinctively I turned toward the radio. Bernice and I heard it for ourselves.

My wife's trembling hand reached out and held mine.

I turned and stared out the window into the darkness.

Moments ago, it was a peaceful Thursday evening in April, holding all the promise of spring.

But this news brought a heavy bitterness to my heart.

Sorrow and grief were sure to be the burden of every Negro man, woman, and child in America.

Years had passed since Bernice and I met Dr. King. We'd gone to a Ministers' Alliance Meeting held at a Baptist church on Edmondson Avenue. He preached about the dream of equality in America, for the discord between blacks and whites to cease and freedom be available for all. It was a stirring message of hope and purpose that left the sanctuary buzzing with expectation.

After Dr. King preached and the program was over, we waited our turn to meet him. He had a firm handshake and looked me right in the eye with a way that made me feel we'd known each other for years. He'd been so confident that the dream of equality between blacks and whites would one day become a reality.

After such an inspiring meeting, it was strange to return to the fiercely divided reality of Baltimore.

Later that year Bernice and I watched on television as thousands upon thousands of people gathered at the Lincoln Memorial to hear Dr. King preach. His *I Have a Dream* speech was probably one of the greatest history has ever known. Like every other black parent, Bernice and I shared King's dream that our children would "not be judged by the color of their skin but by the content of their character."

Lucy twisted off the radio with a turn of its knob, fiddled with her handkerchief, and blew her nose. "I'm sorry. I simply can't bear to hear it again."

Silently, we filed out of the kitchen into the living room.

Martin Luther King had spoken of a new kind of hope, and that hope had spread throughout the Negro community. Many white Americans supported civil rights, and blacks and whites marched together in peaceful protest of segregation and the inequalities imposed on us with dark skin. The whites who stood up with us were appreciated and needed, but the risks they took were small compared to those of the blacks who marched. If the whites were arrested they were still given a certain level of respect, their physical pain was minimal. For the blacks, too many of them ended up brutally beaten while in jail.

In the North, blacks seemed to be more accepted, regarded more as equals. In the South, they were tormented by the Ku Klux Klan's threats and lynchings. Baltimore fell somewhere in the middle, geographically and in the ways folks suffered. We were denied jobs, housing, and service in restaurants. We had to use separate water fountains and bathrooms. The police could stop us simply because we were black. In more rural areas, there was activity by the KKK, but not near as much as further south. Even so, a black man in Maryland was well aware of the places he wasn't safe to travel alone.

Sadly, not until all of humankind was at the foot of the Cross would everyone truly be equal.

"Reverend Smith?" Clarence cleared his throat. "Seems like this might be an appropriate time for prayer."

My throat felt dry. *Lord, help me to pray and give comfort.*

We stood in a circle and joined hands.

"Lord God Almighty..." I paused, unsure. "We come before you shocked. Saddened. Confused." Deep within me, my own soul felt twisted. Pinned down. Fighting an unseen enemy. "We don't understand why your servant of peace has been taken away from us so violently. He was so young. He inspired us with hope, Lord. Now he's gone."

Someone cried.

"Comfort his wife and children, Father." *Comfort me, I'm angry.* "Help them to lean on you." *Lord where are you in all this? He was a preacher, a minister.* "We pray your servant's death would not be in vain, but somehow let it be used to bring peace between the races." *Will peace ever happen? It feels so hopeless.*

"Soften the hearts of white folks who are prejudiced and bitter against us." *I feel bitter, like I'm still the young Boy Scout turned away from the Jamboree. It's no better now than it was then.*

"And for us who have suffered simply because we're Negro, we also ask your healing mercy." *Healing for what? For being black? That's what you made me. Healing from prejudice? No sir, my own prejudice is what protects me.*

The echoes came. "Yes, Lord."

"All of us, Negro and white, need your mercy, Lord. Protect us from having bitter hearts." *Have mercy on my own hardened heart.*

"Guide us this day in our sorrow. In your Holy Son's name we pray, Amen."

It was a horrible day for the nation.

And it was a terrible day for me.

I had learned to trust God with so much of my life.

But I promised myself I would never trust a white man.

CHAPTER TWENTY-FOUR

July 2008

Smitty 84-years old

*115th Wimbledon Womens' Tennis: Venus Williams beats
Serena Williams (7-5, 6-4)*

"With this cancer tiring out my body like it does, these days it's a challenge to get to church. But so far, I haven't missed a Sunday. I might nap the rest of the day, but I love going to church."

I study my white writer friend. "Your parents raised you in the church."

"Yes, that's right." She nods her head.

"When you were a girl, how long were you at church on Sunday?"

Leslie thinks a minute. "We were home around noon, and then had lunch."

Bernice understands. "You were in the *white* church." She grins. "For us in the black church, it was an all-day affair. We started with Sunday school, a class for every age. Next came the worship service. After worship, the children would play and the women set up our potluck dinner. Everyone brought some kind of dish to share, and on pretty days we ate outside."

I sigh happily. "By the time we'd eaten and things were cleaned up, the kids were worn out, the sun was setting, and it was time for the evening service. We arrived at church early in the morning and didn't leave till night time."

Leslie shakes her head. "That's a long day."

"But they were good days." I smile at the memories. "I loved being a pastor. My greatest joy was finding the good in each person, trying to love them as the Lord loved them. Some folks were more challenging than others, but I always tried."

Bernice reaches across the table for my hand. "Remember how generous everyone was?" She turns to explain. "Our first churches were country people with farms and big gardens. They'd give us all sorts of fresh food."

"Oh, but there was nothing as grand as hog killing season." My mouth starts to water. "We made all day parties out of it."

Bernice's eyes twinkle.

Leslie jerks her head back. "Hog killing?"

I can't help but tease her. "You ever made chitlins or hog maws?"

"Me?" She sputters. "I'm white."

"You sure are, darling." Bernice's petite frame keeps rhythm with her laughter.

I take my time and explain how chitlins are made out of the small intestine of a freshly slaughtered pig. "You have to thoroughly clean out the intestine, that's very important so you don't get sick. It takes a lot of cold water to clean them." I'm leaning forward, using my hands to demonstrate. "After they're all cleaned, you bring them to a boil in a pot of water with some spices, onion, and maybe some white wine vinegar. Cover the pot and let it simmer for three or four hours. I'm getting hungry just thinking about them— nothing like some delicious chitlins." I sit back, satisfied that I've shared such important, cultural knowledge. "Now hog maws are fixed in a similar fashion as chitlins, but hog maws are made from the stomach of the pig."

Leslie has a frozen smile on her face.

I can't seem to stop talking. It's either the preacher in me or the love of good food. "And hog's head cheese isn't really a cheese, it's more like a meat jelly. Like the name says, it's fixed by using the head of the hog."

"Oh Mr. Smith, stop!" She looks a little green.

It feels good to laugh at my white friend. "Today, some folks make it with the shoulder of a pig, but then that would be pig shoulder cheese, wouldn't it? Certainly can't taste as good as hog's head cheese."

Bernice and Leslie are laughing with me.

"It was hard for me to believe there were black folks in our churches who didn't know how to make chitlins, so I taught them. Then we'd enjoy a scrumptious meal together. Leslie, you don't know what you're missing!"

I'm feeling better than I did when we started this interview. The laughter and love in this conversation must be good for me.

"I always loved getting to know people by sharing a meal together. Hog killing season was good for that. Jesus did that a lot, ate with folks I mean. Being a Jew, I don't think he had chitlins or hog maws." I pause to give them a moment to laugh at my joke.

"But you can really get to know someone by breaking bread together, especially if you eat in their home. I always loved being invited over to folks' homes for a meal, didn't you, Bernice?"

"Sure did."

Leslie shifts in her chair. "I still can't get over it, you were at church all day? Every Sunday?"

I turn to my wife. "Maybe the teacher can explain."

"Don't you forget, I was also a principal." Bernice teases. "Yes, they were long days, but you see, church was a safe place for us. During the days of the Civil Rights movement and the start of desegregation, church provided a secure haven for the black community. We understood each other. We could loosen up, not worry if something we did or said was going to get us in trouble. There was plenty of stress and tension for us out in the world, but together on Sundays, we could relax."

The sunlight coming through the windows in the living room draws my attention to a display of family photos. Among the blood relatives is photo of a man who changed the world.

My mood changes and my smile fades. "There was one time, though, we were together with church friends on a historic day when the world changed. I changed too. I made a promise that hardened my heart for decades."

I point out to Leslie the framed photo on the wall of Martin Luther King, Jr. I shouldn't say it was a photo. I think I'd cut it out of a magazine, but that didn't matter. Something deep inside me still stirs when I look at his young face, think of all he represented and the challenging times following his death.

"Where we you when you learned about his death?" Leslie asks.

Bernice and I tell her the story. "That was a very dark day for our country."

Leslie bites the end of her pen. "Weren't there riots after

Dr. King was killed?"

"Sure were, in more than a hundred cities across the country." I shift in my chair. "Baltimore had an especially hard time with riots for almost a week. Sometimes it's called "The Holy Week Uprising," because it all happened just before Easter. Don't think I'll ever forget it.

"Initially things were quiet in Baltimore. I think everyone was in shock. Let's see...he was killed on Thursday, April fourth. On April fifth we heard over the radio that some rioting had begun in Washington D.C. Well, us pastors got to phoning each other, telling each other to brace for trouble. Sure enough, things started in Baltimore the next day, Saturday April sixth."

"What kind of things?"

"Oh, thugs out on the street, breaking store windows, looting, starting fires. It was a sad, sad time for the law abiding people of Baltimore. A part of me understood. Everyone was fed up. Housing was bad for blacks and unemployment was sky high. Folks were frustrated. The man who symbolized hope for the future was shot down in cold blood." I take a sip of water to moisten my throat. "Not saying anything that was done during the riots was excusable. But most of those people involved in the riots were probably out of work, bored, and on edge anyway. They just needed an excuse to cause trouble. They wanted their frustrations to be heard."

Bernice shuffles through papers, finds what she's looking for, and turns it so Leslie can see. I glance at the map and let Bernice explain.

"Most of the trouble was in the poor, black sections of Baltimore on the west side and east side. Here, you see. Not too far from Sandtown at all. I felt so sorry for all the shop owners whose stores were vandalized. Some were completely destroyed. They were just trying to make a living."

I can't help but laugh. "Like everything, there are two sides to the story. One or two of those shop owners weren't exactly going to win the award for "Most Upstanding Citizen.""

"How do you mean?" My wife is still innocent at times.

"One store that went down, the owner had an illegal drug business on the side. Rumor was his store went down due to a bad deal. The riots were a convenient time to make him pay." I pause while Leslie scribbles notes. "And there was another store that went down because they cashed checks."

Our young writer looks puzzled. "What would cashing checks have to do with anything?"

I'm glad there are young people still interested in history like this. "Plenty of people didn't have savings accounts in the bank. They didn't have enough money for that, or they didn't trust the banks with the little they did have. So when they got a paycheck from an employer, they didn't have a bank where they could cash it."

"Okay." She tilts her head and waits.

Bernice continues. "The liquor store would cash checks, but that wouldn't do for some people. Imagine a good little Baptist woman—a strict teetotaler—going into a liquor store. So there were a few general stores that would cash the checks, but they'd charge a hefty service fee."

I took over from there. "And that didn't go over so well with some of the poorer locals, seeing their mama get taken for a large percentage of her paycheck. That's why one of the other stores went down to the ground in flames."

"How long did the riots go on?"

"The worst of it was the first few days. The police

couldn't handle it all, so then the National Guard was called in. A curfew was put in place. And a restriction that no alcohol, firearms, or other such items be sold, but that didn't quite do it. Governor Agnew appealed to the President. Thousands and thousands of uniformed federal troops with guns slung over their shoulders were sent in, and marched down the streets of Baltimore. Heavily armored military vehicles followed behind the troops. That scene did a good job of getting things settled fast. You know I love my country, and I was a military man myself." I start to smile at the memory. "But I do remember the expressions on some of those white soldiers. They were mighty wide-eyed at seeing so many black people on the street. Lots of folks out just to look because they'd never seen a soldier. It worked both ways." It still makes me chuckle.

"The troops set up camp in the parks. Row upon row of Army pup tents in Druid Hill Park and Patterson Park. Imagine, soldiers camping out in my old baseball fields. Something I never dreamed I'd see.

"When all was said and done, three people had died and hundreds were arrested. But if I remember correctly, the ones who died were not killed by the troops. One store owner shot a looter, and another looter shot a store owner. And the last fellow was a drunk whose body wore out when he couldn't buy any more liquor. Mighty sad, but at least it wasn't the government shooting its own people."

"Wow." Leslie's slack jaw says it all.

"As a member of the clergy, I spent some time on the street trying to calm folks down, at least before things got too bad. People around town knew me and the other clergy because we made it a point to know them all year. I'm not sure I made a difference, but I did try to talk reason into a few young men.

"The problem is, part of me was with them. I wasn't going to do anything illegal, but I was heartbroken about King's assassination, and I was angry. I had to direct my anger at someone." I've been serious up till now. "Lord knows, if I directed it to my wife, I wouldn't have had long to live."

Bernice lightens the mood with a laugh. "You got that right."

I'm serious again. "So the logical one to be angry at was whites."

Leslie looks at me, nods. I wonder how this makes her feel.

"It was very wrong." Her daddy and I talked about this sort of thing. I know I can trust her. "My bitterness helped no one, least of all me, but my heart hardened. I'd not interacted with many white people, because we lived in different worlds, so I had no experience. I didn't have any white friends. White people were some kind of vague, powerful presence out in the world. It's easier to hate a vague people group you've never met than to hate someone when you're shaking his hand and he's smiling right at you."

No, I didn't want any white man to enter my world.

But one did anyway.

CHAPTER TWENTY-FIVE

1981

Smitty, 57-years old

*American Charles Chapman is the first black person
to swim the English Channel*

*Paul McCartney and Stevie Wonder record
"Ebony and Ivory"*

A gallon of gasoline costs $1.35

Ready to get off the telephone, I paced the kitchen as far as the phone cord would allow.

"Let me check with my wife." I answered flatly. "I'll get back to you."

I hung up the phone, stared at it, and shook my head. Best for me to simply forget that interruption. Wouldn't be hard. I needed to get back to what I was doing before the phone rang.

"Who was that?" Bernice asked, breezing in from the living room.

I didn't answer. Why did a wife need to know every detail of her husband's life?

"Smitty?"

"Huh?" I grunted, pretending I hadn't heard her.

"Who was that?"

"Nobody." I fiddled with the papers and files I had strewn all over the kitchen table.

Bernice twisted the handle on the can opener. "Well, it couldn't have been nobody, darling. You said you'd check with me and get back to them." Bernice hadn't caught on that I was not feeling like my usual charming self.

I focused on my papers.

They were very important.

Silence.

At least for a moment.

"Smitty, what is wrong with you?" She put down the can opener, and posed with both hands on her hips. "Who was that on the phone?"

Might as well spit it out. "That was Irv Basil, one of the pastors in our church cluster."

She turned back to the can of tuna fish. "That name rings a bell. Why do I know that name?"

"He pastors a church in Pimlico, needed my help a while back."

She laughed. "Oh yes, now I remember. That was something, wasn't it?" She used a fork to scoop the tuna into a bowl. "What do you have to check with me about?"

I heaved a frustrated sigh. "He and his wife invited us for dinner." There. The big secret was out.

She placed the bowl of tuna, bread, plates and a bag of potato chips on the table and started making sandwiches. "Nice. When do we go?"

"We don't."

"What?"

"I think we're already busy that evening."

As she reached for the calendar on the kitchen counter,

she asked for the date.

I sighed and told her.

No conflict. She could not have been happier. You would have thought the President invited us to the White House to have dinner with the Pope.

I pushed my papers aside.

Oblivious, Bernice chattered on. "I always enjoy getting together with other pastors' wives. We'll call them back and tell them it's a date."

"No we won't."

"Why not?" Her eyebrows lifted. "You've always enjoyed dinner with other pastors and their wives. Said the best way to get to know someone is have a meal in their home."

"Yup."

"Why is this different?" She pushed a plate with a tuna sandwich and chips in front of me.

"You don't want to know."

"Yes I do. Why you don't want to go, Smitty?"

Bernice eyed me with an expression that reminded me of Aunt Ola. When I was a boy, all Aunt Ola had to do was give me *the look,* and I'd behave.

Feeling like I was ten years old instead of nearing sixty, I sighed. "Because they're white."

Silence.

I knew I owed her more of an explanation, but I was having a hard time explaining it to myself. Here I was, a minister of the Gospel, and I didn't want to enter a white man's home for dinner.

It wasn't that I'd been suffering any great injustices lately because I was black. Quite the contrary. This was the 1980's. Things were worlds different than when I grew up in Sandtown. Now, Bernice and I lived in Randallstown, a respectable suburb of Baltimore that was home to a variety of people groups. We had a lovely single family home with a big yard where Bernice enjoyed planting flowers. Yes, we'd come a long way since living in my bedroom in Uncle Charlie's house.

I'd experienced my share of wrongs because I was black. Even though I preached to others about letting go of bitterness, sometimes I couldn't do it. We had a few neighbors who were white. I waved and smiled at them as I passed by. In the city I regularly reached out to drunks and drug addicts living on the streets. I demonstrated more of Jesus' love to them than I did the white neighbors who were holding down full time jobs. Shameful, I knew I was supposed to love them all the same.

Yet for all this reasoning, I did not want to go to the Basils' for dinner. "I don't want to get involved, Bern. Being in the same denomination, same church cluster, same meetings with whites, I've gotten used to that. It's the way things are now. But going into their home for dinner?" I shook my head. "I don't know."

"You know it's not necessarily easy for them," she said slowly. "There are a few young teachers at school, white teachers, who come to me as principal for advice and encouragement. They've agreed to teach in the city, trying to do their part, but it's hard on them. They get called names sometimes, get threatened. They're misunderstood." She munched on a potato chip. "On the auditorium wall we have painted the quote from Martin Luther King, the one about his dream to have his children judged on content of their character, not the color of their skin. Whenever a white teacher comes to our school, I have to remind myself that quote applies both ways. I need to study their character, not their skin color."

I fingered a potato chip and dropped it back on the lunch

plate. "Working together is one thing, but I don't think I want to become involved beyond that. Irv said he wants to become 'better acquainted, friends.' I don't exactly feel the same."

"Well, it's too late now." She said sternly, shaking her head.

"How do you mean?"

"You should have thought about that before you rescued Irv from complete ruin. You saved that man's life!" She shot me another Aunt Ola look. "I'd say you're already involved."

She was right, it was too late.

A white man wanted to be my friend.

———◆———

My years in the ministry flew by. Somehow, I was in my late fifties, assigned to my last full-time church appointment before retirement. I'd never fully retire. Instead, I planned to substitute in the pulpit for pastors on vacation, continue as a hospital chaplain, and serve wherever God called me. As a grandfather, though, the thought of taking a nap once in a while sounded like a nice idea.

My life had gone full circle. I was pastor of a United Methodist Church in Sandtown, the very neighborhood where I'd grown up. It felt good to be back. The faces had changed, but much was the same. Proud, poor people tried to do their best even as life presented endless challenges and heartbreaks.

Every month I went to *cluster meetings*, where the pastors of neighboring Methodist churches got together. We discussed what happened in our individual churches and got the latest news from the denomination. There were a variety of churches in the cluster, from large well-off white congregations to small poor black churches struggling to keep their buildings from falling over.

The August cluster meeting was held in one of the more prosperous white congregations, Reverend Waters' church. When I arrived, folks were chatting before the meeting began. I headed down the right side of the sanctuary and slipped into a pew polished so fine, it was easy to slide to the middle.

I ended up beside the newest pastor of the group, who'd been introduced to us last month. Irving Basil was tall and white with dark brown hair and glasses. A graduate of Johns Hopkins University, he'd had a career as an electrical engineer with Westinghouse. He entered the ministry in his late-50s—his second career.

Irv sat next to Rev. Waters, and they were talking intently.

Irv leaned in a little toward the experienced minister. "But brother, are you born again?"

Rev. Waters' extra flesh under his chin waggled when he pulled his head back in surprise. "Irving, I have been a Methodist preacher for more than fifteen years." He sounded like he was scolding a child.

Irv smiled. "That's nice. But do you know Jesus?"

Rev. Waters cleared his throat, stood up, and marched away.

I sat back and tried to keep my laughter quiet as I could. I didn't do very well.

Our kitchen phone rang one cool November day. It was

Irv. We chatted now and then at cluster meetings, but no more than I did with the other white pastors. It was the necessary interaction related to my job, nothing more. I didn't want more.

Usually Irving was quick to laugh, but today, he sounded anxious.

"Smitty, I'm in a predicament."

"Okay."

"My wife's not too pleased with me about a church issue. I don't know what to do, and I want to do what's right."

I didn't know what to say, so I waited. Finally, he continued.

"I'd appreciate your advice. I'm confident you have the wisdom I need. Would you be willing to counsel me?"

I pulled the phone receiver away from my ear and gave it a glance. Did I hear right? In all my life, no white man had *ever* come to me asking for advice. In my generation this sort of thing did not happen. On top of that, Irv was a career professional, a well-educated white man. I barely knew more about him than his name.

I scratched my head, hesitated, and wondered what Uncle Charlie would've done.

I said a quick prayer then I took a deep breath. "I'll do what I can."

It turned out we lived only a few miles from each other. We set a time to meet over coffee the next day. I hung up and wondered what I'd gotten myself into.

———————◆———————

After pulling open the first glass door that led into the Pikesville Diner, I stepped in, and let the rain drip off my coat.

Irv waved from his spot near the dessert display. With one big step, he was in front of me, smiling, holding open the interior door with one hand and reaching out for a handshake with the other.

"Hello, Brother Smitty!"

We shook hands and stood for an awkward moment, surrounded by the buzz and activity.

"Two? Follow me please." The blonde waitress with an outdated beehive hairdo sauntered down an aisle with tables and booths on either side.

Irv was dressed in a pair of slightly worn denim blue jeans held in place with a brown leather belt. He peeled off his yellow windbreaker and hung it on the hook beside our booth. Underneath his blue plaid flannel shirt a bit of white T-shirt peeked out at the collar.

I slipped off my formal black raincoat, hung it on another hook, and topped it with my black wool fedora. I hoped the rain hadn't stained my new black dress shoes, but I decided not to comment when I noticed Irv's work boots. Unbuttoning my suit jacket, I eased down in to the booth opposite Irv.

We ordered coffee and a couple slices of pie— pecan for me, apple for him. As he got into his story, I began to understand his dilemma.

Irv's enthusiasm to turn Baltimore City upside down for the Lord was to be admired, but you might say he was a bit wet behind the ears. Even more, he was a white collar professional who lived in the suburbs, ministering in a rough, mostly black area of the city.

Irv's brown eyes sparkled as he described a man who was new to his small congregation. "His name is Robert Blue. He came into church one Sunday morning as the service was going on, said he was drawn in by the power of my preaching." Irv beamed.

"You all have a sound system?"

"A modest one, but often it doesn't work."

Now a black preacher, who's all fired up and preaching in a church with a good sound system, *might* be heard out on the street. But Irv, he was white. An electrical engineer. He didn't seem the kind of preacher who'd be heard outside the walls of the church.

"Every Sunday I give an altar call. It may not be done in all Methodist churches, but I feel a responsibility to do that." He sipped his coffee and spilled a bit of it when he placed the cup back in the saucer. "That day Robert walked down the aisle with tears rolling down his face. I felt like Billy Graham. I was so happy I thought I'd burst." Irv's laughter was warm and open.

"Robert comes to church faithfully week after week and always has an encouraging word for me. Usually he lingers after the service, says he hates leaving the good Christian fellowship of the church for another long week."

"Excuse me Irv, but is Robert white or black?"

"He's black, and that's another thing I find so encouraging." Irv was all enthusiasm. "Our little church is a white congregation, all older people, in the middle of a black neighborhood."

I knew the church and the neighborhood.

"The church continued to be white even after the demographics of the neighborhood changed. I've reached out to the neighbors. A few have visited, but Robert's the first black person to keep coming back. That's very special to me, Smitty. I want to reach out to the community, keep the church open for the generations to come."

Wholeheartedly devoted to the ministry, Irv was

running into it like a puppy trying to run from the living room to the kitchen and missing the turn, sliding across the floor, all smiles and tail wagging, with his big feet scrambling to get some traction.

"One Sunday," he said, "Peggy and I invited Robert to join us for lunch at a nearby restaurant." Encouraged by this faithful, new congregant, Irv picked up the bill.

"It didn't take long for Robert to feel like part of the family. He joins us every Sunday after church, coming home with us for Sunday dinners. We talk for hours after the meal. I enjoy hearing about his career as a medical doctor and all his world travels. He spends the day with us, usually ends up staying for supper, too. He's wonderful company."

I drummed my fingers on the tabletop. "You and I live pretty far from your church. Does this fella have a car?"

"He rides home with us after church, then I drive him back to his apartment at night."

"A doctor who doesn't own a car?"

"Hmm." Irv tilted his head and seemed to ponder that a moment.

"Just exactly where does Robert live?" I knew the area well. Some parts of that neighborhood were getting mighty rough for a white man to be driving through at night.

"Well, that's embarrassing." Irv became quiet. I couldn't help but feel a little sorry for him. "I don't know his exact address. He has me drop him off a few blocks away from the Mission House where he volunteers for the night shift. He ministers to the homeless men who come in late at night. He likes to get a walk in after such a filling meal. Otherwise he'll fall asleep during his night duty."

I sometimes preached at that shelter and knew it well. They locked the doors at eight o'clock.

I finished chewing a bite of pecan pie as I tried not to

squirm. "While your wife is fixing Robert nice home cooked meals, and you're driving him all around town, what's he doing for you?"

Irv brightened. "He's been delightful, very kind and encouraging, often thanks us for our hospitality with gifts. He gave me some dress shirts and Peggy a few nice sweaters." The white- collar-professional-turned-inner-city-preacher swiped his napkin across his mouth to catch a few crumbs. "Quite a few times he's given us huge beautiful blocks of cheese, like you might find in a restaurant. Delicious smoked cheddar."

Cheese? I was beginning to smell a rat.

"So why are you telling me all this?"

Irv stirred his coffee. "Well, you've been a pastor for a good while. You know the city and its people."

I nodded. "That's right."

"Peggy's become uncomfortable around Robert ever since..." He looked away.

"Since what?" I pressed.

"Robert fell on some hard times, got a little behind on things. He needs a place to live." Irv tapped his spoon on the rim of his coffee mug. "We have a spacious wood paneled basement. I figure it could be made into a nice apartment for Robert. When I mentioned the idea to him, he was delighted."

"I bet he was." Apparently the seminary Irv attended needed to add a class on street smarts.

"One evening, she was extremely upset after I returned home from driving Robert back to the city. She couldn't put her feelings in to words, which struck me odd, but she cried and cried. I thought that maybe it was hormones. The only way I could calm her down was by promising to get counsel from a more experienced pastor."

He pushed his empty pie plate aside. "To be honest Smitty, Peg, insisted I speak with a black pastor. Even though I grew up in the city, she thinks I might be missing something culturally because we're white and live in the suburbs."

"Well, there's all kinds," I said. "He might be fine." I doubted it, but... "Could be nothing wrong. Plenty of good, honest people in the city."

"I know that's true." Irv agreed.

"On the other hand, it sounds like Robert's worked out an awfully nice arrangement. Goes home to the pastor's house after church, has a nice meal, and then you drive him around town like you're his chauffer." I savored my last bite of pie. "Could be you have a real character on your hands."

I slid aside my empty pie plate. I studied Irving a moment and looked him in the eye, a small act that required great determination on my part. "If you want, I could meet this Robert Blue. Get a look at him. Size him up for you."

Irv exhaled a long sigh. "I would so appreciate that, Brother Smitty."

I held my laughter inside, but a smile crept across my face. I'd kept my distance from the other white pastors in our church cluster and the general conference. It was easy to do. But with this fella, something was different.

Irving pulled out a worn leather wallet and left money on the table to cover the bill. We stood to leave.

"Thank you." Irv said, laughing at his own relief. "Thank you so much."

And before I knew what was happening, he wrapped his arms around me in a big bear hug right there in the middle of the diner for all to see. Another first for me.

Chapter Twenty-Six

August 2008

Smitty, 84-years old

*Barack Obama becomes the first African-American
to be nominated by a major political party
for President of the United States*

As I tell this story to Leslie, her brown eyes twinkle like her Daddy's used to do. "I remember hearing about that guy, Robert Blue. What happened?"

My sides start to shake with laughter. "Poor ol' Irv, he'd been had. That Robert Blue set bait on a hook for your father and was waiting for just the right moment to reel him in."

Bernice is giggling, too. "We laugh now, but it was quite serious." Still, she keeps on laughing.

It feels good to laugh. I wipe the tears from my eyes. "Your father and I figured out a way I could meet up with him and his new friend. Soon as I laid eyes on Robert Blue, I could tell he was slick as they come. He was all charm and smiles as he sat in the passenger seat of the pastor's fine automobile with his legs stretched out and his hands behind his head."

I imitate the pose for the ladies. "But when Irv introduced me, it was clear he knew I was suspicious." I have to settle my laughter before I go on. "I don't fault Irv, because that Robert Blue could've fooled the Pope."

Bernice continues. "Smitty remembered Robert said he volunteered at the Mission House in downtown Baltimore. Over the years, Smitty preached there quite regularly, so he knew the director very well. A few phone calls and Robert Blue was found out."

"Found out?" Leslie asks.

My laughter is under control now, so I can explain. "Robert didn't volunteer at the Mission House. He *lived* there. He *was* homeless."

Leslie's eyes grow wide.

"But that's not all." I continue. "He'd never had a career in medicine or traveled the world. He'd battled very serious psychiatric problems his whole life. The State had a file on him thick as an encyclopedia. In fact, the mission director said the guy was likely *dangerous*." I stop chuckling as I think about what might have been. "Robert seemed to have some sort of plan in the works. Lord only knows what would've happened if he'd moved in with your parents."

Leslie, who looks like she doesn't know whether to laugh or cry, simply shakes her head.

"Ol' Mr. Blue heard I was questioning the mission director and disappeared. Neither Irv nor the mission ever heard from him again."

Bernice starts chuckling again, her eyes welling with tears. "Yes, it was serious, but those gifts!" She's laughs so hard she's got her arm wrapped around her stomach. "Those gifts were stolen goods, stolen from the mission! Irv and Peggy were wearing hot clothing!"

Leslie's eyes might pop if they get any wider.

I'm laughing, too, but I go on. "That's right. The mission director said he'd wondered where things were disappearing to. He could figure how Robert stole the clothing, but he never could figure how he snuck out those blocks of cheese from the kitchen." I have to wipe my eyes again. "They were twenty pound blocks of cheddar cheese! Twenty pounds apiece!"

Leslie puts her hand over her mouth and joins in the laughter.

"Your parents returned the clothing to the mission, but they couldn't return the cheese. They were wearing it around their waists." Bernice says. "They'd both put on quite a few pounds!"

We laugh until our sides ache.

When you laugh, you're really living.

I think because I helped him with the Robert Blue predicament, Irv felt devoted to me, and after that, he was ready to be my faithful friend, whether I was interested in friendship or not.

I'd always been accustomed to white men looking down on me for my color, insulting me, or trying to rip me off in a business deal. I'd never trusted a white man before I got to know Irv. I'm sure there have been others like him, but I didn't know them. Now I wish I had. Irving treated everyone with respect. In his eyes there weren't any nobodies—everybody was a somebody. Even me.

Irv knew quickly he could trust me, but I wasn't so easily won over. I look back now and try to think of one particular situation where I finally trusted him. It didn't work that way. It was bit by bit. Irv proved to be honest and true every time. He was highly educated but unpretentious and had an earthy sense of humor. He provided for his family and had enough money to be quite comfortable, but he was happiest digging in his garden wearing old blue jeans and muddy boots. I hardly ever saw the man dressed up.

Leslie interrupts my thoughts. "So did you all go to my parents' house for dinner that first time they invited you?"

"We did." Bernice nods. "And we had a lovely time."

"I was reluctant to accept the invitation, and I think your father sensed that, because he invited another pastor and his wife to join in the dinner party, another *black* pastor. That made a real impression on me." I glance at Bernice. She's smiling with me. "Soon after that, Bernice and I invited your parents to a dinner party we had at Christmas. The house was full of family and friends and the two of them. Their two pale faces stood out from the crowd, but they didn't seem to care."

Leslie smiles. "No, they wouldn't."

Irving's friendship was a new experience for me. I'd never before met a white man who didn't seem to be subconsciously reminding me that he was white and I wasn't.

Since we lived only a few miles from each other, Irv and I took turns driving together to cluster meetings. He'd pick me up in his big, old van he used to go camping. I'd pick him up in my Cadillac. Little by little, we shared about our church experiences, concern for our kids and families, our pasts, and our hopes for the future. After several months of this, I'd almost forgotten he was white. He was just Irv.

"Another cookie, Leslie?" Bernice passes a plate from the coffee table to our friend.

"I remember when I'd stop by to visit my parents. Often, Dad would be talking with you on the telephone."

"Yes, yes. The days before email." I understand the need for email, but nothing can replace the sound of someone's voice. "We got to calling each other on the telephone every few days. I still remember the first time the phone rang and I perked up, thinking, 'I hope that's Irv.' It was someone else. So after that conversation, I telephoned Irv just to say hello.

"That's when I knew I'd finally surrendered to our friendship. Never in all my days did I expect to have a genuine friendship with a white man. But there I was." My eyes brim with tears. "Through friendship with your dad, I finally experienced what it meant to truly be equals with a white man."

I'm smiling on the outside through the tears, but that familiar grief and twisting of my stomach stops me from being able to say more. I glance over to Bernice for help.

She understands. "Of course you know what a dear friend your mother is to me, but I'll say it for the voice recorder." She leans forward toward the recorder. "Peggy is one of my dearest friends. We got to be friends through our husbands.

"Peggy didn't go to college, so she was quite impressed by my college education and career as a school teacher and principal. It doesn't matter that we had different backgrounds, we can talk for hours. Sometimes when Smitty and I were together with Irv and Peggy, I felt like we were all teenagers again. We went on double dates to the movies and to concerts. And we took some wonderful sightseeing trips together. One to Louisiana, one in Texas, and one in the Carolinas."

My tears have passed, and I'm ready to laugh again. I finish the cookie I've been nibbling, even though I don't have much of an appetite. "There was one particular time that still makes me laugh today. We were coming home from downtown Baltimore after a concert at the Meyerhoff Symphony Hall. Going to the symphony was one way to make sure your father got dressed up."

Leslie laughs. She knows. Her daddy had no concern about clothing style.

"I drove us to the concert. When it was all over, we piled in the car to head home. I sat behind the steering wheel, Bernice was up front with me. Your parents sat in the backseat of my Cadillac. We're all settled ready to pull out of the parking garage when Irv cleared his throat and in a very sophisticated voice said, 'Home, James.' Then he howled with laughter and said, 'I've always wanted to say that.'

Bernice nods her head, laughing. "We all erupted with laughter. Oh, it was a good time. Smitty played along and gave Irv the chance to know what it was like to be high white society with a black chauffeur. Of course it was silly. After all, the Cadillac was ours, and Irv and Peggy drove beat up old cars."

I'm starting to feel real tired. But this has been a good interview session. "True friends can laugh at their differences without hurting each other. Irving and I often found humor in our different backgrounds. We also shared our perspectives on racial issues. I think we helped each other understand things better."

It's amazing to think Irv and I both grew up in Baltimore City in the 1930's, yet we lived in very different worlds. As boys, we wouldn't have been friends. Yet sixty years later, we became the best of friends.

Yes sir, Irving was my very best friend.

CHAPTER TWENTY-SEVEN

1990

Smitty, 66-years old

Ground breaking begins for the construction of Baltimore Orioles' new Camden Yards Stadium

Nelson Mandella is released after 27 years imprisonment in South Africa

Lost in the melody of one of my favorite hymns, my brown fingers danced over the ivory white keys of our baby grand piano. I loved to sit in my living room, play the piano and sing. Blues, jazz, classical, I loved it all, but hymns were my favorite. They were timeless, just like the God they were written about.

The kitchen doorbell rang adding a dissonant note to my music. Hoping Bernice was in the kitchen, I ignored it and kept on playing.

My fingers stretched over the last chord.

A thunderous two-people applause broke out behind me.

"That was beautiful!" I knew Irv's voice without even turning around.

"Look who was in the neighborhood and stopped by."

Bernice patted Irv on the shoulder, then left us alone to visit.

I slid off the piano bench and stood to my full but modest height. "Good to see you, Brother Irv." He wrapped me in a bear hug, a ritual I'd come to love. I felt the smile on my face that always came when I was with my best friend. "Have a seat."

We padded across the plush white living room rug and eased our bodies down on Bernice's white sofa. I used to tease her about letting me sit on it from time to time. I did a quick survey to make sure Irv had on his formal blue jeans, not his dirty gardening ones.

Irv explained how he had been out shopping at the Home Depot not far from our house. He animatedly described the latest seeds and gardening tools he'd picked out for the coming season. One topic led to another until finally it got down to our girls. Each of our youngest daughters was in their thirties and still single. As fathers, we shared the desire for our daughters to be happily married to good men.

Irv asked the same question he asked last week. "Any men in Yvonne's life?"

"If there are, they're invisible." I laughed. "How about Leslie?"

"None. I know I'm old, but I don't understand today's young men."

"Me, either. My Yvonne would be an excellent catch." I leaned back and sighed. We sat in relaxed silence for a moment like only good friends can do.

On the coffee table was a framed photograph, new to our living room display. Irv leaned forward and squinted. "Who's that?"

My somewhat sunken chest filled with gratefulness. "That's my daddy, my Uncle Charlie."

Irv picked up the frame and studied the old black and

white photo.

I moved over closer to get a better look at the face of the man I missed so much. "Greatest man I ever met. Hard worker, always happy, loved the Lord with all his heart."

Irv turned and smiled at me. "Sounds like you."

"He made me who I am. I'm grateful." I leaned back, looked at my friend, and asked him a question I'd wondered for years. "What about you, Irv? What makes you so different?"

He smiled broadly and posed, his hand on the side of his shirt as if he wore a formal tuxedo in a magazine advertisement. "My handsome good looks."

After a shared laugh—would that we were as handsome as we'd once been—I pressed him. "I've always wondered, what made you different in your attitude toward blacks?"

He grinned. "My daddy."

"Yeah?"

"My father only had a third grade education, but he was an intelligent man. He worked as a printer in a print shop. I was a boy when he repented of his superior attitude toward blacks."

"How do you mean?" Irv was full of stories, but I'd never heard this one.

"It must have been around 1934, because I was nine or ten years old. One evening at the dinner table, Daddy told what happened that day at work. He started off laughing—and ended up crying." Irv looked away and rubbed the side his jaw with his hand.

"Go on."

"It was getting near Christmas Day," Irv said. "Everyone who worked at the print shop was white, except for Leroy. He swept the floors, emptied the trash, that sort of thing. Daddy joined in together with some other men at the print shop to give Leroy a ham for his family's Christmas dinner. The men made a big production of giving Leroy that ham. It was tightly wrapped up in newspaper to keep it fresh, like they did back then.

"Leroy was so excited, so grateful to the men for their kindness. He talked about what good Christians they were. When Leroy walked away with that heavy ham cradled in his arms, the men howled with laughter and slapped each other on the back. It wasn't a ham, it was a big rock shaped like a ham."

My friend chewed his lip a moment before continuing. "When Daddy told the family about the practical joke he'd been a part of, he was overcome with shame. He started crying right in front of me, my sister, and my mother. I'd never before seen my father cry, but when he realized the cruelty of what he and the others had done, he got down on his knees and prayed for God's forgiveness right there in the dining room. The next week when my father was paid, he bought the biggest, best ham he could find and gave it to Leroy. We didn't have much for Christmas that year, but Leroy had his ham."

Irv's eyes looked dewy.

"After that, my father bought Leroy a ham for Christmas every year. I was fourteen years old when Daddy was put in the hospital. Brain tumor. My family hardly had any money to spare, but that Christmas, Daddy told me to buy a ham and carry it over to Leroy's place. I did it again the next year, too, even though by then, Daddy couldn't speak any more."

Irv rubbed his hand over the soft sofa cushion like he was stroking a favorite pet. "When my father died Leroy came and paid his respects. Everyone else came to the front door, but society's rules said because Leroy was black, he had to walk through the back alley to the back kitchen door." Irv sniffed. "But he was there to pay respects for my father. Leroy was there."

Irv stared down at our white carpeting.

"Smitty, I was sixteen years old when my father died. I felt so lost."

"I was lost at fifteen when I found out Uncle Charlie wasn't really my daddy."

Irv nodded. He knew the story well.

I sighed. "Thankfully I found my way back to Uncle Charlie."

"Our daddies were good men."

I nodded. "Your daddy would be proud of you, Irv."

He smiled. "Thank you." He seemed to savor my words before he spoke again. I wondered if Irv spent his life trying to prove himself to the father he'd lost as a boy. "My daddy taught me that every person is due respect simply because they're God's child. That was part of my father's legacy."

"You've carried it on well, my friend."

"I don't know, but I hope so."

I knew.

I'd never had a white friend before, never met a white man I could trust before Irv. But was it that Irv was so different, or had I changed? Were there other white folks along the way who could have been my friend? It was sad to think, I'd never know the answer.

Chapter Twenty-Eight

1999

Smitty, 75-years old

Rosa Parks is awarded the Congressional Gold Medal for her life efforts in fighting racism

South Carolina removed its provision against interracial marriage

Average cost of a new home: $131,750

"Smitty, welcome. So good to see you!" Peggy smiled and unlocked the front screen door to the Basils' home. Her rosy face gently pressed against my ebony cheek as she greeted me with a hug and a kiss. "Irv's out back in the garden. Let me call him for you."

"I'll go out myself and see what the farmer's up to. Got to see how my collards are coming along." Every summer Irv planted plenty of greens, so I could eat my fill.

I had spent the morning at my desk paying bills and reviewing sermon notes. I was scheduled to preach the next few Sundays for various pastors on vacation. It was a beautiful summer day with unusually low humidity and clear blue skies—much too pretty to stay inside. I was itching to go for a drive. My Cadillac stayed at home in the driveway—this was a pickup truck kind of day. I liked to ride in my little white truck, roll down the windows, and feel the wind rush past.

First, I drove out to the more rural areas of the county and took in the sights. More than a few fields seemed to melt away as new townhouses sprang up overnight. Things were always changing. As I headed back nearer my neighborhood, I prayed my traffic light prayers for the folks around me. That was my habit.

Eventually I pulled into the Basils' driveway for a friendly visit. Folks have gotten so busy these days, they seldom stop by and visit each other anymore, but Irv and I liked to do just that. Their house sat on a large parcel of land. Great big old oak trees towered above, shading part of the fenced-in green lawn with a playground-sized swing set in the very back of the yard.

As I turned the corner past the house, Irv came into view. His was an impressive garden, and Irv worked hard at it. He stood tall in the middle of the large square plot, dressed in his trademark blue jeans, white V-neck T-shirt, and broad-brimmed straw hat. Using a garden hoe, he worked at the dirt in between rows of tomato bushes. Round green fruit dangled from the vines, waiting to ripen into red, juicy tomatoes.

"Hello, Irv!" I hollered as I made my way across the grass, glad I had on my tennis shoes for added stability.

"Hello brother!" He smiled and laughed as he pushed back the brim of his hat and wiped his brow with a kerchief. "What a pleasant surprise." Stepping over the chicken wire fence surrounding the garden, he reached out to shake my hand. He'd been working hard and had an impressive sweaty glow. I decided I'd pass on our usual bear hug.

"How are my greens coming along?"

"These are your rows here." He motioned with his hand, gloved in well worn canvas gardening gloves, and proudly pointed out rows of full, leafy greens. Each type displayed their own unique leaf and shades of green. "Collards and kale are here. And I planted some turnips, too. You like turnip greens?"

"Oh yes." My mouth was already watering. Irv grew the best greens I'd ever tasted. "Your garden looks real fine, Farmer Basil."

He pulled his shoulders back and stood a little taller.

"Bernice and I wanted to invite you and Peggy to join us. We're going to hear our nephew Tony preach. He'll be coming to town next week, and he's preaching at the Assembly of God church in Timonium. Think you'd like to go with us?"

Irv looked genuinely pleased. "We'd be honored. We'd love to go."

"Maybe Leslie would like to join us, too." Irv had mentioned their daughter often listened to Tony's preaching on the radio.

"Oh, I'm certain she'd want to come. We'll let her know."

Peggy emerged from the kitchen door carrying two tall glasses of fresh iced tea. "Time for you to sit in the shade awhile," she said.

We sipped cold tea under a warm summer sky, breathed in the smell of freshly dug dirt, and talked the talk of two best friends.

It was a good day to be an old man.

<hr>

The Assembly of God church held a large congregation with so many programs going on throughout the week, it could make your head spin. Any one of the churches I'd been pastor of throughout my career would have fit neatly into a corner of their building—with plenty of room to spare.

We arrived more than an hour before the program was scheduled to start, yet already a line of people waited in a line that circled halfway around the church parking lot. We made our way to the end, greeting folks we knew along the way. Soon after we'd found the end of the line, we were in the middle of it. Groups of people continued to arrive and filed in behind us, and the line grew and grew.

I knew Tony's preaching and ministry had touched many lives, yet each time I got a glimpse of the impact, I was overwhelmed. Tony Evans was Bernice's sister Esther's, son. Our nephew. He, his wife, and a few friends had started a little church in Dallas, Texas, years ago.

It didn't stay little, that's for sure, Now Tony was pastor of the 9,000 member Oak Cliff Bible Church. His preaching was broadcast on 500 radio stations and heard in 40 different countries around the world. He'd written stacks of books. Nevertheless, there was something about seeing the individual faces of people waiting to hear him preach. Hundreds upon hundreds of people coming to hear the boy I'd had the privilege of watching grow into a godly man. It was a humbling and proud moment for this old uncle.

Related or not, we had to wait our turn in line. Finally, the large glass doors opened. Irv, Peggy, Leslie, Bernice, and I filed in.

"Follow me!" Bernice said. "I know the way."

The massive, modern sanctuary held row after row of cushioned pews on the main floor and the balcony above—seating for 1,800 people. There was a stage up front, and a fancy sound and light system. It was quite an operation. But I was most impressed that, twenty minutes before the service would begin, almost every seat was full.

Bernice pointed to the first few rows of seats in front of the stage. "There's Esther and Carl. Yoo-hoo! Esther!" She grabbed my hand. "Stick with me!" We zigged and zagged our way through the crowded aisles toward Tony's parents, our friends following close behind. It had been weeks since we'd seen Carl and Esther, let alone all the rest of the family. Tony's aunts, uncles, cousins, sister, and local friends filled up the first several rows of the sanctuary. That boy sure knew how to get the family together.

We exchanged hugs and greetings with Esther and Carl. They knew Peggy and Irv, but they'd never met Leslie.

Bernice turned to make the introductions. "Where are they?" Her eyes widened.

"Who?" I asked.

"The Basils! Why aren't they behind you?"

"I thought they were." I turned and looked. No Basils.

Bernice laughed and explained to Esther and Carl, "We don't usually lose our friends."

We scanned the crowd and found them quite a ways back, halfway up the aisle. Irv was waving his hands over his head trying to get our attention over the loud buzz of the full sanctuary.

"Bernice! Smitty! *Help!*"

His expression was a mix of amusement and bewilderment, like a boy in trouble. Peggy and Leslie stood behind him, peeking over his shoulder as they were pressed in by the crowd. I tried to figure out what the problem was when Irv shrugged his shoulders and held up both hands, palms toward the sky. It looked like he didn't know what to do.

And no wonder—an usher the size of a professional football quarterback blocked their way. He was using his muscular body and outstretched arms to keep our friends from walking down the aisle. Bernice and I walked back toward them, realizing on the way what the problem was.

Irv pointed to us while talking to the young usher. "But I keep telling you, we're with *them*."

The twenty-something year old shook his braided head, unconvinced. "I'm sorry, sir, but this section is only for family, the Evans *family*."

This struck me so funny I could barely keep my composure. Not so long ago, it was black folks who had to sit in the back of the theater. Now here was my best friend getting a taste of how things used to be.

Even though that usher was just doing his job, I felt sorry for him as Bernice stepped forward. She smiled at the young man, but it was one of her school principal smiles.

She tapped him on one of his broad shoulders, then used her authoritative principal voice when he turned around. "Young man, these people *are* family. They are with us. I'm Tony's aunt. This is his uncle, and these three friends are family to us."

That poor usher's eyes widened as he mumbled his apologies.

Satisfied, Bernice gave a single nod to the young man. "Now please, let them through."

That poor guy looked more than embarrassed. He hung his head and shook it, so his long braids swung back and forth. Then he stepped aside so the white folks could walk to the front of the sanctuary.

I leaned close to Irv. "About time something like that happened."

Irv's big shoulders shook in laughter. By the time we

sat side by side in our seats, we both had to pull out our handkerchiefs and wipe our eyes.

Tony began the service by asking his parents to stand up so he could introduce them to the congregation. His brothers could not be there, but his sister was. He asked her to stand as well. Finally, he smiled his great, big smile and said, "Why doesn't *all* my family stand up?"

I wasn't sure, but I thought I saw Tony do a double take as he scanned the first few rows and finally focused on our three white friends in the middle of all our dark skinned family.

As I stood with the rest of the family, Irv stood part way up alongside me. He looked at me with an impish smile, laughed, and sat back down. I got to giggling too. We were like two boys misbehaving in church.

It might have surprised Tony if Irving had stood up, but it would have been fine with me. I trusted him and loved him like a brother.

And he loved me the same.

CHAPTER TWENTY-NINE

August 2008

Smitty, 84-years old

Michael Phelps, U.S. swimmer from Baltimore,
wins his 8th Gold Medal at the Bejing Summer Olympics,
surpassing the record of seven won by Mark Spitz

As I tell the voice recorder about that time going to hear Tony preach, Leslie's smiles the whole time. "What a great night that was. Thanks so much for including me in the invitation. That was the first time I met Esther and Carl. She just wrapped me up in her love like I was a long lost family member."

"She's that way with everyone." Bernice nods and smiles. "But you are special to her."

"She took me by the hand after the service and led me to the book table to meet Tony. I was so honored to be with her, let alone meet Tony." Leslie's eyes twinkle. "But then, Esther grabbed a book off the book table, handed it to Tony and said, 'Sign this one for Leslie.' He did, and I felt like I'd been given a precious gift from a precious woman." Leslie acts out the story. "Then she reached out for another book.

'This is a good one. Tony, sign this too.' He didn't look quite as pleased, and no wonder. Each book cost money. By the fourth book she had him signing for me, he pleaded, 'Mama. *Please.*'"

Now I'm laughing with her. "Sounds just like Esther. No matter how big Tony gets, he's still her boy, and she's his mama." I'm weary and weepy. "Yes, that whole night was special. I love sharing my family with my friends, and I had no better friend than your father."

Young people today may not think much of my friendship with Irv. Today there's interracial dating and interracial marriages, and there are children born from those unions. But for Irv and me, it was different. We might've grown up in the same city, but we grew up in two different worlds.

When my Boy Scout troop was turned away from the Scout jamboree, the church was in the very same neighborhood where Irv lived.

When I was at Camp Linstead as a Boy Scout cleaning latrines and swim nets, Irv was a few miles away vacationing with his family at their summer cabin.

When I dropped out of high school and joined the military, Irv was getting an education at Baltimore's prestigious Polytechnic Institute School for Boys.

And as I struggled to keep my family fed working as a stock room keeper, Irv was an electrical engineer at Westinghouse Corporation.

The only advantage I ever had over Irving was that my daddy lived long after Irv's father had died. And that was a big advantage.

All those other differences—neighborhood, schooling, income and so many more—kept me in my black world. There was nothing wrong with being in the black world, except it prevented me from ever having white friends. On top of that, plenty of times as an adult and an old man, I experienced the pain of racism. Mean and hateful things done to me that I care not to talk about. I don't want to hold on to them.

All that put together did not make it easy for me to trust a white person, but Irv earned my trust. And he deserved every bit of it.

The older you get, the more you learn not to take friends for granted. You come to learn what a blessing it is to have friends. More than twenty years after we met, Irv and I were reminded of that in the worst way.

Chapter Thirty

2006

Smitty, 82-years old

*Coretta Scott King, widow of Civil Rights leader Martin
Luther King Jr., dies at age 78*

*The final home game is played at Yankee Stadium
against the Baltimore Orioles*

A gallon of gasoline costs $2.63

I shut the breezeway door behind me, slid off my hat and raincoat, and didn't care about the water dripping on to the kitchen floor. My aching bones reminded me I was in my eighties. Tonight, I felt even older.

Bernice welcomed me with a kiss. "How was traffic?"

"Same as always on a rainy, Friday night. Terrible. It was stop and go all through the city." My mood matched the weather, dark and dreary. I'd been to Johns Hopkins Hospital plenty of times in my life. This was the worst.

"How's Irv?"

It was hard to answer. "Hardly looks like himself, Bern." I eased my weary self onto a chair by the kitchen table.

She sat down opposite me. "Did he know you were

there?"

"Oh yes. He was awake. We talked a little, but mostly I sat by his bed." I rubbed my hands over my face, wiped away one tear. "Before I left he asked me to sing for him. He's asked me that every time I've sat with him."

"Did you?"

"Of course. Tapped my foot, too." I tried to smile and started to sing. "Come Thou Fount of every blessing, tune my heart to sing Thy grace..."

I went silent.

Bernice sat there with me, quiet.

The clock in the dining room chimed nine o'clock.

A dog barked outside.

I sighed.

"It's hard to sing about God's grace when your best friend has brain cancer."

"I'm sure it is, darling. I'm sure it is."

My heart was breaking inside me as I gripped the iron railing and walked up the cement steps to the Basil's front porch. "I don't know if I can do this."

We stopped at the top step. Bernice put her arms around me and gave me a squeeze. "You can do it. You've got to. He's your dearest friend. The Lord will give you strength."

She didn't sound so strong herself.

A few days before, Peggy had telephoned. Irv was home. There was nothing more the doctors could do.

No more treatments to offer, no more hope from medicine.

He wanted me to visit and serve his last Communion.

Peggy met us at the door as my stomach wrapped itself up in knots.

We followed her through the living room to their bedroom. I wanted to walk slower. Truth be told, I wanted to run away. Inside this old, experienced pastor beat the heart of a grieving little boy.

It took a moment for my eyes to adjust to the dimly lit bedroom. It smelled of hospital antiseptic, Lysol spray, and baby lotion. A sliver of light from the afternoon sun peeked under the tightly pulled window shades. The floorboards creaked as we tiptoed inside.

Lying in the rented hospital bed, my cherished friend looked like a shadow of himself. As the cancer had consumed his body, Irv's hefty frame had shrunk to a mere whisper. He was skeletal and frail, his cheeks so sunken, he looked like a photo from the Holocaust. The face that used to be tan from working in his garden was pasty gray with a mangy, white beard. How could whiskers dare grow on the face of a dying man?

His paper thin eyelids fluttered open.

He had no strength, but through the death vigil silence, he lovingly murmured, "Smitty. Brother."

He struggled with trembling fingers to lift off the bed sheets and take my hand. Gingerly, I reached out took hold of his bony fingers.

There wouldn't be any more bear hugs.

I fidgeted with the brim of my hat and circled it under my fingers. Irv and Peggy's three grown children, Leslie, Deborah, and John, were there.

We exchanged a few whispered words.

I didn't know how long I could endure it.

Bernice understood and unpacked the supplies for Holy Communion.

I broke the bread and repeated the familiar words recited through the centuries. "On the night in which Jesus gave himself up for us, He took bread, gave thanks, and gave it to his disciples, and said, 'Take, eat; this is my body which is given for you. Do this in remembrance of me.' "

Bernice and I passed the bread to Peggy, their three children, and the Jamaican nurse.

I tore off a tiny portion of bread. I didn't want Irv to choke.

He opened his mouth like a baby bird, and I placed the crumb on his tongue. Could anyone hear my heart sobbing?

Bernice and I poured the grape juice that represented Jesus' sacrificial blood into little medicine cups.

I repeated the words of Jesus. "Drink from this, all of you. This is my blood of the new covenant poured out for you and for many for the forgiveness of sins."

Cradling Irv's head in the crook of my arm, I lifted him and brought the swallow of juice to his lips.

He looked at me with dull, sunken eyes.

He whispered something I couldn't understand.

He winced. "These are..." He gathered his strength again. "My...last rites."

I could barely find air to breathe. I nodded, kissed him on the cheek, and laid him down.

Irv's sunken chest rose with great effort. He opened his hollow eyes and peered at me. "Sing?"

I tapped my foot for him and kept time as we sang his favorite hymn. "My hope is built on nothing less than Jesus' blood and righteousness..."

Somehow, I made it through the song, but I didn't think I could walk out of the house before breaking down.

Peggy followed us to the front door. The world outside mocked me with sunshine. On the porch Bernice hugged and kissed Peggy. I did the same, but she wouldn't let go of my arm.

"Smitty, will you preach Irv's funeral?"

How could I say no? He was my best friend.

And yet, how could I say yes?

◆

Cool, crisp October mornings in Baltimore can be so lovely. That Saturday in 2006 was one of those mornings. Absolutely exquisite.

Except I was going to my best friend's funeral.

The sanctuary of Irv and Peggy's home church of more than fifty years was full. They'd always worshipped at Milford Mill United Methodist Church when Irv was not preaching. A couple hundred folks sat on beautifully polished wooden pews to share their love and respect for my friend. Sunlight beamed through the sanctuary's tall windows illuminating the pale blue walls. A large, stately white cross hung at the front of the sanctuary, dramatically displayed against a background of crimson cloth.

I sat on one of those hard pews next to Bernice and let her hold my hand. We grieved together through the opening music, prayers, and Scripture readings. I mostly looked at the beige tiled floor to avoid looking up at the flag-draped casket. Even so, I couldn't avoid the scent of lilies and other flowers that reminded me why we were there.

I checked the bulletin to see where we were at in the service and slipped my hand out from Bernice's. She understood.

Had to pray, just the Lord Jesus and me.

Silently, I poured out my heart despite the numbness

that had set in over the past week.

When it was my turn to speak, I felt every day of my eighty-two years. Slowly, I stood. With each step, the sound of my finest dress shoes against the tile floor echoed under the high ceiling. I made my way up the three finely polished marble steps and stood behind the white wooden pulpit. My fingers traced the edge of the pulpit's fine wooden rim. It was cool to the touch, smoothed to perfection.

I shifted my weight, trying to get my body balanced on my aching hips and knees.

I reached in the breast pocket of my suit pulled out my notes, and placed the paper on the pulpit. I didn't need it, probably wouldn't even look at it, but my hands methodically smoothed out the wrinkles while I took time to look at Peggy. Then at Irv and Peggy's family. Children. Grandchildren. Irv's sister. Nieces and nephews. Loved ones I didn't know.

I kept on smoothing the paper while I studied the crowd to see who else was in Irv's final congregation. There were two hundred people before me, and all but a few were white. Bernice's dark face gazed up at me along with four or five black neighbors of Irv's. People I'd never met before and would never see again.

How was I to preach to this unfamiliar crowd? Would my words minister grace and comfort? Would the Lord be honored? I bowed my head and silently prayed.

When I began, my voice was a mere whisper.

"Often we hear words from others who did not attend a funeral service. They want to know, 'Who preached the funeral?'"

I cleared my throat and swallowed.

"I say no one can preach the funeral of anyone else. You do as Irv did. Irv preached his own funeral by the way that he lived."

One by one the congregation came into focus. Individual faces twisted in grief, some tired and worn. Some young and curious. Others had glazed over expressions, going through the motions of another funeral. One woman in the back had a slight smile, and her eyes were closed.

I paused and savored the pain of honoring my friend.

"Nowhere in my dreams..." My voice caught. Tears swelled. My throat thickened.

I coughed and cleared my emotions.

I tried again. "Nowhere in my dreams did I ever expect I would be a part of eulogizing my closest friend, Irv Basil."

Stoic expressions changed ever so slightly. Aging eyes squinted, sharpening their focus on me. They tilted their heads to get a better look.

I shared stories of Irv's passions in life, his love for family and the outdoors. I watched as sad expressions hinted at smiles as they remembered. They knew Farmer Basil. Some had eaten his tomatoes, string beans, and kale. I mentioned trips we took occasionally and phone calls we shared almost daily. Gradually, my stories gave way to preaching.

The life my friend had lived made it easy to preach, and I felt the familiar rhythms of my black soul begin to stir.

"Irv had a great desire to see the Kingdom of God. He desired that everyone would be saved. Oh, *saved* is a bad word in some places, but Irv wanted everyone to know God for themselves."

My voice grew stronger. And my hips hurt a little less.

I swayed slightly, not because my knees hurt, but because I was preaching.

It didn't matter what color the congregation was. I would proclaim the truth as I'd always done.

"As we come eulogizing Irv, we should be concerned about ourselves. Wonder who will be next? It could be any one of us. Will it be you?"

"Is your heart right with God? Do you know God for yourself? Your mother may have known Him. Your father may have known Him. But do *you* know Him?"

My voice rose and fell, the volume and pitch varied, every syllable packed with love and gratefulness for a friendship given to me by Father God.

"Irving brought heaven into his home, and as a result, his children know the Lord. His wife loves the Lord. His grandchildren are being nurtured to love the Lord."

I felt strong surges of love stir my soul, and I heard the power in my voice.

I didn't need my notes.

Words flowed effortlessly.

"We come celebrating the passing of this man from life into Eternity. Some folks say he is dead, but Irv is not dead. He is very much alive!"

My heart hammered, and beads of perspiration trickled down my forehead.

I focused on the hope.

Swelling up within me was the inexplicable reassurance the loved ones who'd gone on before me were very much alive with the Lord.

One day I would see clearly for myself. My heart hammered in anticipation.

"I am reminded of when I was a boy. I grew up in the 1400 block of Mount Street. We had an old crystal set radio, the kind you needed ear phones to listen to."

Energy surged through my body, and I had all the vigor I needed to keep me preaching to the end.

"We had two wood stoves, one in the dining room, and

one in the living room. And sometimes, I would sit for a long time in the dining room near the wood stove and listen to that radio. After a while, I'd get sleepy. I'd lay my head on the dining table and go to sleep."

"And upstairs, my father would miss me. He would come down and take me in his strong arms and carry me upstairs."

My voice echoed off the high ceiling as it rose.

"This is what happened to Irv. The other day, he fell asleep in his home, and his Father God came down. Took Irv in His arms! And carried Irving upstairs!"

Some of those dear white folks probably weren't used to shouting from the pulpit, but I could not hold back. I *would not* hold back.

"This is where Irving is. He's upstairs!"

I was warm and perspiring, clinging to the pulpit's wooden rim.

I looked up toward heaven. As tears trickled down the side of my face, I talked to my dearest friend.

I did not care that others listened.

My voice rolled and fluctuated like the black preacher I'd always been, but my words were for my best friend.

"I don't know how long my life will last, nor what the future holds for me!

"But this I know, that when I fall asleep down here, Father God is going to do the same for me as He did for you!"

"He's going to take me in His strong arms, And He's going to carry me upstairs!"

I was breathless, wearing down.

"And Irv, I'll see you in that beautiful morning upstairs."

It wasn't a eulogy.

It wasn't a sermon.

It was a promise between best friends.

I steadied myself against the pulpit, caught my breath,

and let my racing heart calm down. With a slow, measured voice, I concluded.

"May God bless each and every one of you. And Heaven fix His love upon you. Amen."

As my weary legs led me away from the pulpit and down the steps, I reached out and leaned on the casket to steady myself. My best friend gave me strength and support one last time.

CHAPTER THIRTY-ONE

November 2008

Smitty, 84-years old

Barack Obama, an African-American, is elected 44th President of the United States

Gallon of gasoline, $3.39

"How are you feeling since your surgery, Mr. Smith?" Leslie asks.

"I feel great, ready to go!" It's been a while since we worked on the book, and a month after surgery, I'm ready to work.

"That surgery gave us a miracle!" Bernice grabs Leslie's arm "God is so good!" Bernice glows. "Since the surgery, Smitty has been up and around, better than ever!" She glances at me with those eyes and keeps talking. "Do you know what he did yesterday? He went marketing! Drove the truck, went to the store, and carried in the bags. Oh, I protested, but I was thrilled he was able to do it."

Women make the biggest fuss over the littlest things. A few months ago, I told the story how as a child, I hauled marketing with my wagon. And now they act all surprised

I can do it when I'm an adult.

Like every other visit we've had for working on my book, we're laughing already. I enjoy these times together. It refreshes me, reminiscing with my bride and sharing my story. I want to leave behind words of hope. I don't want to leave them behind any time soon, mind you, but I like to plan ahead.

It's hard to believe Irv has already been gone two years. Lately, I miss him more than ever. I don't know why but just thinking about him makes me weep.

I clear my throat. "Leslie, I understand you enjoyed some fellowship while I was in surgery."

"I had a wonderful time meeting more of your family. So many people were there for you, we took up half the waiting room. I felt sorry for patients who had only one or two people waiting."

"That hospital took good care of me. I have no complaints."

Bernice quickly challenges me. "You complained enough at the time."

"Me? Complain? Naw...."

"Don't you remember?" She smiles in the way that lights up my world. "You fussed because you didn't want to take your teeth out."

"Of course not." I turn to Leslie. "They told me to take out my dentures before rolling me down the hallway to surgery. I wasn't about to do that." I drum my fingers on the kitchen table. "Suppose we ran into someone I knew? How would that look? Me, a respected preacher, without any teeth?"

Bernice laughs. "And do you know, he *did* see someone he knew!"

We fill the kitchen with that liquid sunshine kind of

laughter that reminds me of Mama.

"Yes sir, as they were pushing me around on the gurney, we ran into some folks from one of my former churches." I turn to Bernice to make my point. "Sure was glad I had my teeth in. I hadn't seen them in years. They told me how handsome I was looking, too."

I'm quiet for a moment, that story took some energy. I'm not feeling as rested as I thought I was. Guess I'm still recovering.

"Isn't it time we get working on the book?" I pull my sweater closer to my body. I'm so skinny these days, it's hard to stay warm. "Can't wait to see my name on a book cover. Now that I'm an author I'll have to wear cardigan sweaters and smoke cigars."

We still have so much to do.

I need to get my story down before my time is up.

———————◆———————

I am sleeping more.

Or I sit.

Several times, we had to cancel our interview sessions with Leslie because I've not been up to it. Other times, I've felt well enough to enjoy our time together. But the truth is, the energy of life is rapidly leaving me. The pain is increasing.

I don't have too much longer.

I don't say it to others, but I know it in my deepest part.

Often I lie on our white sofa and gaze at the photo of Uncle Charlie, remembering the man who loved me as his own son. Sometimes, I still wonder why he didn't tell me from the beginning that I wasn't his own seed. Even though

I'm an old man finishing my life, that question still gets me down.

For too many years, the truth about my birth and background caused a painful storm of emotions. But when the swirling winds inside my soul started to settle, I saw Uncle Charlie's love more clearly.

Uncle Charlie took me in, a helpless little baby, when no one else wanted me. He gave me food for my body and a roof over my head. In all kinds of weather, Uncle Charlie subjected his body to hard physical labor so he could provide for me. The heavy labor of his work shaped his strong, lean body as much as his love shaped my life.

During Uncle Charlie's free time, he took me to church, got me into Boy Scouts, and walked with me to Druid Hill Park. He shared his wisdom, laughed with me, counseled me, and guided me through life.

And when I thought he was sleeping, he was on his knees praying for me. Even through those years when I tried to run away from his love, he loved me with all he had.

He faithfully prayed for me, just like a daddy is called to do. He didn't have to do all that. He chose to.

I hope I've been half as good a father to my girls as Uncle Charlie was to me.

The doorbell rings. Bernice goes to answer it as I ease myself up off the couch. It's time for another book interview. I'm tired, but determined.

Bernice and Leslie get things set up in the kitchen.

"Leslie, I've got something I want to show you. Wait here." I shuffle my way to the bedroom. It requires more time and effort to get around, but I can still do it.

When I reach my bedroom I see what I want propped up in the corner of the room.

As I enter the kitchen again, the ladies' heads turn in my direction because they hear it—the tap-tap-tap of Uncle Charlie's cane against the floor.

"This is it." I speak in a reverent tone. "This is Uncle Charlie's cane."

We're silent while I hold up the white, wooden cane in my hand. It's still strong and slender like the man who used it so many decades ago.

Tears well up in my eyes. Seems lately, all my emotions are so close to the surface. "I wish every little boy and girl had an Uncle Charlie in their life."

The ladies nod in agreement.

"Amen." Bernice murmurs.

"Imagine if every little child knew they were somebody special, that God loved them more than they could possibly imagine." The preacher in me awakens. "Think of the teenagers who try to run away from His love like I tried to do. They can't out run God."

"That's right."

"My hope and prayer is the Lord will remind them they are loved. Every person has a purpose. God's counting on them to find their purpose and live it out with his blessing."

I pause remembering Uncle Charlie's dream visit to me. I never knew why God chose to get through to me that way, but I'm grateful he did. Grateful he showed me my purpose.

The ladies look at me and wait for more.

"Each and every one of us is a somebody loved by the God of the Universe. It's *impossible* to be a nobody when you know the Lord's love. Being his child is the best kind of somebody any one can be!"

My congregation of two nod their heads and smile.

"God bless the child who knows for himself that God is his Father. Amen!" I conclude.

"Amen!" The ladies reply.

Humming a happy tune, I tap my way back down the hallway to the bedroom. There, I lean Uncle Charlie's cane in the corner of my room for the very last time.

CHAPTER THIRTY-TWO

The hardest part about dying is no one can tell you how to do it. No one has ever died, then come back to explain things.

No one except Jesus.

So he's the one I talk to, the one I pray to, the one I cling to in these difficult days. After all I've been through, I'm surprised that these days are the hardest I've ever known.

My energy is gone, but my heart keeps on beating. I don't talk much. I weep often.

These past few weeks, the days and nights are all the same to me. I don't leave my bed. I sleep a lot, and I'm grateful for the escape, because sometimes when I'm awake, the pain is overwhelming.

Bernice comes into the room. "Carl and Esther are here, darling. They came to pray for you."

Okay, I blink. There's no energy for words.

"Leslie's here too," Bernice adds.

Carl, Esther, Bernice, and Leslie gather round my bed. My eyelids flutter open to see Leslie's white hand holding my own.

How I miss her father. I'll see him soon.

Carl prays with passion and love. His voice is so deep and beautiful, full of wisdom and grace. He can pray like no one else I know. He's a mighty man of God. No wonder Tony has such a ministry with a daddy like Carl.

I'm in and out as he prays.

My heart's desire is in between worlds.

Yet I remain painfully anchored to this groaning body.

I look forward to leaving my worn out shell behind, but not the people.

My children.

My Bernice.

"...*In Jesus' name, Amen.*"

I hold on to Leslie's hand. I don't let go. "Do we...?"

That's all I have.

She understands. "We have enough for the book."

I try to smile.

She holds my hand with both of her own as her eyes glisten with tears.

I wonder if she also sees the angels surrounding us.

Leslie's voice is tender and determined. "I'll finish the book. I'll do all I can to get your story out, I promise."

"I know you will. You're Irv's girl."

She leans over and kisses me on the cheek.

Bernice comes up beside me, tucks in and smoothes out my blankets. She strokes my forehead, kisses my lips, and then whispers in my ear. "Carl's going to play the piano for you, Darling. I'll leave the door open so you can hear."

She kisses me again.

Sleep pulls me away.

Every time I wake, I hear Carl playing the piano. I love when he plays. He's so talented. So beautiful. He sings too.

I wish I could sing along. I can't even tap my foot.

But my heart listens, and the music soothes my soul. The music enlarges, expanding to a style I've never heard before.

An orchestra joins in.

And a choir.

The music broadens and builds.

Like a gentle breeze, it refreshes and invigorates.

Soon, several choirs sing. Some sing in different languages, making the music even more magnificent. I don't know the languages, but I understand it all, praising the Heavenly Father, the Son, and the Holy Spirit. The voices weave together seamlessly in the most splendid music and praise I have ever known.

I stir in my sleep, warm and content.

My bedroom brightens.

Luminescent.

Intense.

Dazzling.

And then there is a voice.

"Smitty, son, it's time to wake up. Time to come upstairs."

These are the most wonderful words of life my soul has ever heard.

Strong, everlasting arms wrap around me.

I'm embraced in perfect love.

Gratefully, I surrender and am carried upstairs.

My heart leaps within me and pounds with excitement as I look way off to the horizon. In the distance is a spectacular city, gleaming, shining and radiant.

It isn't like New York City or Baltimore.

It takes my breath away.

I want to study it more, but my attention is drawn to something between me and the city.

Coming from the brightness, a multitude of people approaches me and calls my name. At first, it's an indistinct crowd, like when a cruise ship is pulling away for a journey, and hundreds of people are gathered below on the pier to wave it off. But as this crowd draws closer, and I'm able to focus on their faces. Every single person is a loved one of mine.

Folks I knew so long ago in my life's journey.

They're here.

Greeting me.

Waving and calling to me.

All of them vibrant and alive, welcoming me home.

As they surround me, the radiance of their love overwhelms me. I've never felt such pleasure. Everywhere I look, people love me. And I love them back. Never in all of my days could I imagine such a wonderful feeling. I feel such joy, so alive and strong.

Wave upon wave of wonder and delight washes over me as individuals from all parts of my life greet me.

Boy Scouts.

Church members.

Neighbors.

Classmates.

Merchant Marines.

Coworkers.

Family.

Friends.

I know and love each and every one. They wrap me in their love as well as their arms, these witnesses to my life.

"So glad you're here, Smitty!"

"Hello, Smitty!"

"Welcome home!"

A group of folks from the very first church where I was pastor greets me. One by one, they smile and hug me. With each reunion, I feel more alive than I've ever felt before.

"Welcome to the best part of your life!" I hear a hearty voice as someone laughs and slaps me on my back.

I turn.

It's Abraham. We haven't seen each other since Boy Scouts, but I know it's him. The warm glow of his love mingles with mine, and the crowd rejoices at our sweet reunion.

From somewhere deeper in the radiance of the multitude, out steps Mr. Ames, our Scout leader. He comes forward, pulls me to his barrel chest, and hugs me with his strong arms.

"'Bout time you got here! We've been looking forward to your arrival."

I feel like a kid on Christmas morning.

Mr. Ames smile reveals perfect white teeth. His chipped teeth and secret cave are no more. Only a perfect Mr. Ames.

As I enjoy more greetings and hugs in this great reunion, the crowd envelopes me with love and radiance. Yet even as we stand together, I'm aware we are moving toward an even brighter light. Instead of squinting to protect my eyes from the brightness, my eyes adjust to the light and search for more.

Steadily, we come near a pair of spectacular gates. Each gate has been crafted from one massive shining pearl. It is the most glorious sight I have ever seen. We are close enough to see the gates, yet far enough away to see how enormous they are, sparkling with luminescent light coming from within. They shimmer like the sound of delicate wind chimes.

Around us and at the same time beyond the gates is a sunrise, a morning more magnificent than has ever been before. All the colors I knew on earth along with a kaleidoscope of countless more. All of my senses feel so alive, as if I am finally waking up after eighty-four years of living in a fog.

Music, more majestic and awesome than I've ever heard, meets my ears as loved ones continue to greet me.

My happiness soars as I go from one greeting to another. I don't tire of the reunions. I have never been so satisfied. My joy is beyond words. I don't know how long the welcome continues. It might have lasted minutes, it might have been years. I don't know, and it doesn't matter. There is a moment's pause in the reception, and I take a deep breath of sweet, celestial air.

Someone yells. "Smitty!"

Out from of the throng beside the gate steps a tall, handsome man.

"Uncle Charlie!"

People in the crowd step aside and open a path for me. They cheer and applaud as I run through the crowd toward my dear uncle. He flings his arms wide open and runs toward me. My beloved uncle has all the energy and strength of a young man. He pulls me into a hug, lifts me off my feet, and spins me around as if I'm his little boy again.

"I've been waiting for you, son. Welcome Home!" He stands me back up on my feet.

All I can do is smile as I gaze at his handsome, radiant face.

A softer voice comes from the crowd and catches my attention. She steps out from behind Uncle Charlie.

"Aunt Ola!"

It has been so long since I've seen her.

She looks more beautiful than ever. Perfect.

The composition of music coming from inside the gates continues as I hold Aunt Ola's hands and kiss her round, coffee-colored face. She wraps her arms around me, pulls me into her softness, and rocks me.

I have never known such happiness.

When I thought there could be no more, a familiar voice adds to my joy. "Hello, Brother!"

I turn and see Irv.

Tall, broad, and smiling, he has all the health and vitality heaven offers. His radiance joins with Aunt Ola's and Uncle Charlie's, and I'm surrounded by their love.

"Oh, Irv, how I've missed you!"

He pulls me into a powerful bear hug. When we finally pull away, through his radiant light, I gaze at his face and see he has a gardener's tan.

"This is amazing."

Uncle Charlie laughs. "This is heaven."

Irv puts his hand on my shoulder, "Uncle Charlie, Aunt Ola, and I have been helping prepare your mansion, Smitty. You're going to love it!"

Before I can question I remember Jesus' words, "*In my Father's house there are many mansions. If it were not so, I would have told you.*"

Irv claps his hands together and rubs them back and forth with enthusiasm. "Wait until you try the collards I've grown for you. You're going to love them. But first, you must come with me."

Everyone in the crowd murmurs and smiles as if they understand when Irv leads me away, off to the distance.

"Where are we going?"

"I was instructed we are to look beyond the Veil."

"Look beyond the Veil?"

"Yes, brother. We're going to get a glimpse of your final congregation."

———————◆———————

The Veil pulls back slowly. I don't understand how it works, but like everything else, it brings new pleasure to my soul.

My eyes begin to focus, and I croon. "Well, look at that."

"There's your final congregation, brother." Irv drapes his arm around my shoulder.

"It's all angels!"

Irv laughs that hearty laugh I've missed so much, but now it's even more full of life. "Wait a moment more for your eyes to adjust. The angels are surrounding those gathered at your service. Focus on the center."

Slowly, as I concentrate, an earthly scene comes into view.

In the pews of Mt. Olive Church, folks sit shoulder to shoulder while others are seated in folding chairs set up behind the sanctuary. Five hundred, maybe six hundred people. It's hard to tell how many are there, but there's not room for one more.

Some folks stand in the aisles so others can sit.

Old men with bad hips, young babies nestling in their grandmother's laps. Women are dressed in their finest Sunday clothes, many wearing decorative hats. Men wear suits, fancy ties, and their finest shoes.

They're almost all black, but I pick out Peggy sitting between her two daughters, her two sons-in-law beside them.

The organ thunders gracefully, filling the large sanctuary with the melody of *"Guide Me Thou O Great Jehovah."*

"Oh I love that song." I whisper to Irv as I start to tap my foot.

He nods.

The fifteen member church choir files up the long aisle. They are dressed in white flowing robes, and the hems of their garments sway with each step.

Behind the choir comes a procession of clergy members, pastors and bishops of the Methodist Church, more than forty people. They are dressed in their finest robes, which are used only on the most formal of occasions. It takes ten earthly minutes for them all to file down the long aisle to the front of the church.

"Is all this for me?" It's too much.

Irv understands. "You touched their lives, brother, more than you ever knew on earth. You made a difference for so many. They want to honor you one last time."

A closed casket is pushed down the center aisle.

My Bernice follows.

Our daughters, Carolyn, Sherry, and Yvonne, walk with her.

There are grandsons and granddaughters, son-in-laws, nieces, and nephews.

They sit in the first few pews at the front of the sanctuary.

Irv turns to me. "Now remember, the grief and sorrow of your death has scarcely begun for those you left behind. They've never even come close to experiencing all you have since your body died."

I'm consumed by an intense love for everyone in that church. So many of them live their lives in faithful brokenness. They try their best to follow Jesus despite earth's sin and sorrow. Some of the people don't know him yet, but they know and love me. In me, they saw Jesus. One day, God-willing they will see him for themselves.

"Look at my Bernice. She is absolutely radiant." My voice is soft with wonder. "She looks more beautiful than I've ever seen her."

"Yes." Irv agrees. "Her body is weary, but we're spared seeing her grief. Her soul is gold. She's living in simple faith that the Lord will take care of her now that you're gone."

"Gone?"

"You died." He gives me a side look, his little frown saying it all. "Remember?"

"I'm just messing with you, Irv." I laugh, more alive than ever before.

We refocus our attention beyond the Veil and watch as the congregation listens to the Twenty-Third Psalm.

Official proclamations of condolences are read to my family, letters of sympathy from bishops, the Governor of Maryland, Lieutenant Governor of Maryland, and the Mayor of Baltimore City. "*A great leader and friend to the people of the state of Maryland had been lost.*"

Other folks stand behind the pulpit and give testimony of my life, they share their hearts.

Amen's are called out.

"*Hallelujah,*" someone shouts.

The pianist's hands dance over the piano keys. The music sounds like the fragrance of Easter morning lilies, hopeful and alive. The notes blend and become the melody of one of my favorite hymns. Anyone in the congregation who really knew me knows that much.

One voice starts to sing.

"*Come, thou Fount of every blessing*"

And then another.

"Tune my heart to sing thy grace"

All the voices raised in song grow into a beautiful crescendo.

"Streams of mercy never ceasing,
call for songs of loudest praise."

Worship sweeps over the congregation.

Arms are lifted in praise.

Hearts tune closer and closer to the music of heaven.

One by one the congregation stands to sing.

A weary grandma rises to her feet despite her bad knees. Beside her, a young boy stands on the pew and happily sways. The church overflows with music, praise and song, lyrics of hope and mercy in their noisy, hectic world.

"Here I raise my Ebenezer;
Hither by thy help I'm come;
And I hope, by thy good pleasure,
Safely to arrive at home."

Irv and I stand tall with the strength of youth and watch the worshipping mourners. We are close to the Veil, yet safely Home.

Together we join in song with the congregation and raise our arms. We join hands, one dark, one light, united in praise to our Mighty God.

Every soul in heaven sings along.

"Jesus sought me when a stranger,
Wandering from the fold of God;
He, to rescue me from danger,
Interposed his precious blood."

Such amazing joy, joy beyond words, joy inexpressible.

The people who arrived too late to get a seat inside the church respectfully stand outside on the sidewalk, pulling their coats a little closer to their bodies, trying to keep out the cold December air.

As they hear the singing from inside the church, they also join in the beautiful song.

And then the Veil gently closes.

I feel refreshed, if it's possible to feel that way when I already feel better than I have ever known.

Irv and I walk on.

Uncle Charlie meets up with us. "Before you tend to other things, the Father wants you to see something."

Suddenly Irv is gone, and it's just me and Uncle Charlie.

He touches my elbow and gently turns me to see two angels. They are massive, like football linebackers. One is fair and has long, golden hair tumbling down his broad shoulders. The other is dark and wears neatly twisted dreadlocks. They are both stunning images of strength and beauty. Between them they carry a large scroll. The wooden spindle of the scroll is ornately decorated with exquisite mother-of-pearl that shimmers and shines.

Uncle Charlie turns to the angels and nods his head.

They set the scroll down to rest, as if on an invisible table. Together they unroll a small portion, then, with all their angelic might, push the scroll open. It unrolls again and again leaving a path of white parchment that continues into the distance for as far as we can see.

I am intrigued by the stunning display.

Uncle Charlie understands I'm still adjusting to this new life. "Start reading, son."

I look down at the flowing script and read the names of my wife and children, *"Bernice, Carolyn, Sherry, Yvonne..."*

Uncle Charlie explains. "This scroll lists the names of people whose lives were impacted by yours."

The long portion of names that follow are all somehow

related to me and Bernice.

"*Melinda Smith, Beverly Smith, Jessie Williams, Maurice Blount, Trisha Blount, Roscoe Evans....*"

The list of family names takes quite a long while to read through, but I have the time and energy.

Beyond the family relations, the list continues.

"*Irving Basil, Peggy Basil, their children John, Deborah, Leslie, Irv's sister Lillian.*" I touched their lives, but they also changed mine in a most unexpected way.

We continue traveling alongside the scroll reading the names of those who were in churches where I'd served. People who I dearly loved then and love even more now. There are also names of some people who I found harder to love when I was on planet earth, but now my heart overflows for them.

"*Ralph Jacobs, Ruby Taylor, Mary Johnson, Linda Parker, Alfreda Long, Carlton Smith, Delores King, Faye Morgan, Samuel Norris, Michael Jones...*"

The list seems endless.

I am amazed at the innumerable lives the Lord allowed me to impact.

For so long. I thought I was a nobody, but God used me as an ambassador of his love to more people than I had ever known.

The list continues. "*Tamika Bowman, Henrietta Goodson, John Morgan, Stanley Yeager....*"

I read the names. Love wells up inside me even as I struggle to recall the faces that go with each name. I see only profiles, so I ask Uncle Charlie to explain.

Uncle Charlie's eyes twinkle with glee. "These are the names of all the people you prayed for at traffic lights. Your prayers made a difference in their lives."

He pauses to let me remember and ponder.

"Up until now, the names have been of people you encountered throughout your life. Farther down the scroll, the names are of people who were not in your first line of contact. The list includes names of those you didn't know, yet you prayed for them. Farther still are the names of those you never knew but touched through your influence on your family and friends. Do you understand?"

"I think so."

He pointed and walked to a new section of names. "These are the names of the shut-ins Carolyn loves to visit. Down there are the people in Sherry's life touched by her enthusiastic love for life. And over there starts the names of those changed by Yvonne's pastoral ministry and counsel. Your scrolls also lists the people they will touch, but haven't even met yet."

We read as we walk for a long way toward a new section of names. "There are names from Tony's ministry at the Urban Alternative, those who go to his church and listen to him on the radio. You were used in Tony's life and he passes it on to others."

Uncle Charlie lets out a laugh. "Right here is the name of the grocery store cashier you used to chat with."

I remember the young girl with sad eyes.

"One day you told her you would pray for her, and you did. As a result, she went on and blessed someone else that day. Here's the name of the one she blessed because of you."

He points to a name that at the moment is more radiant than the others. "There's the name of the man you prayed for on March 12, 1979 at the intersection of Northern Parkway and Reisterstown Road. The results of that prayer went on to change the life of his daughter. There is her name followed by the names of her four children."

It is too much for me to absorb.

My traffic light prayers made a difference, a life changing difference.

Words of kindness and prayers I gave for the cashier lived on in her and others.

Uncle Charlie and I move on alongside the unending scroll. "Every Sunday you preached so faithfully. The people in your congregations left church and shared the Lord's love with their neighbors and coworkers. This section is the congregants' names. And further down there are the names of those neighbors and coworkers. After that is the section showing the names of the people those neighbors and coworkers went on to impact. Do you understand this roll better now, Smitty?"

"I think so." I still feel overwhelmed. Amazed.

"Son, when you were a child, you were hurt and confused. You thought you were a nobody."

"That's right." I can remember the fact, but I no longer feel the pain.

"Nothing could have been further from the truth. Every soul on earth is created with the purpose of knowing God personally and sharing His love. Sadly, not everyone accepts that calling." He places his hand on my shoulder and looks at me with perfect love. "You accepted the Lord's call on your life, sharing his love with the world one person at a time."

As I try to absorb what all this means, my eyes suddenly sharpen with new vision. Surprised and delighted, I look around in admiration of unending beauty. Uncle Charlie chuckles as I begin to see things he has been seeing all along. We are standing by a lake, a gorgeous body of sapphire-blue water mixed with other colors I don't yet know the names for.

"Now watch." Uncle Charlie reaches down and picks up a small pebble of glistening gold and tosses it in the lake.

"When you throw a pebble in a lake, the ripples extend out far from that little stone."

The ripples of shimmering sapphire spread out far beyond where the piece of gold fell in to the lake.

"In the same way, Smitty, your life touched the people you saw and had contact with in your everyday life. But you also had an impact that rippled out through those people to other folks you never met on earth. You will have the joy of meeting them here in heaven."

I nod, overwhelmed the Lord would use someone like me. "I thought I was a nobody. I figured out I was somebody simply because God loved me. I prayed he would use me."

"He did. Just look." Uncle Charlie points to the scroll, and we gaze at its unending path.

"When I came here, you were the first name on my list." Uncle Charlie smiles.

I swallow the lump in my throat. "I'm grateful. Thankful for your love and influence. I guess every name on my list is really the result of your life on mine."

"That's right. My love in raising you was blessed." Uncle Charlie smiles in a way that stirs my soul in its deepest part. "You in turn touched others, who went on to bless even more people. And so it goes, changing the world one person at a time."

We stand in silence and gaze at the list. Never in my wildest dreams did I ever think the Lord could use me like this. Yet I have a deep awareness this is only one of many surprises in store for me.

"Well, son, I think we could enjoy some nourishment before we continue reading your list."

"We get to eat here?"

"Not just eat, we feast." Uncle Charlie laughs as he drapes his arm over my shoulder. "Let's you and me go share a meal with Irving."

"Don't mind if I do."

As we walk along, my new eyesight sharpens to our surroundings. Each view is more stunning than the last and my joy grows even more.

Uncle Charlie looks at me. "You won't believe the greens Irv grows, best tasting greens I ever did eat."

"That's what I used to say on earth."

"Up here, everything is better, even Irv's greens. And no matter how long we pray around the table, the food never gets cold." Uncle Charlie laughs with gusto and I join in, alive and free.

Together we journey down a golden road.

Uncle and nephew.

Father and son.

I am finally home.

I had been and always would be a child of the King.

Dear Reader,

Thank you so much for taking time to read Smitty's story, I hope it was an encouragement. If you enjoyed *The Legacy of Nobody Smith*, please be sure to tell a friend, write an honest online review, or share about it via social media. Since the book is independently published your word of mouth advertising is what will increase the money earned for The Helping Up Mission of Baltimore and The Urban Alternative. Thank you so much for your support.

Grace & Peace,
Leslie Basil Payne

DISCUSSION QUESTIONS
for *The Legacy of Nobody Smith*

HISTORY

1. Do you relate in any way to Smitty's experiences as a boy growing up in Baltimore?

2. How do you think the relationship between blacks and whites in America has changed since Smitty's childhood?

3. Smitty and Irv's friendship was unique because it was unlikely they would've been friends as children, yet as grown men they were best friends. Do you enjoy friendships with people of other cultures, races and backgrounds? If not, why not?

4. There is little told about Irv's childhood years. How do you imagine his childhood would've been different from Smitty's? How might it have been similar?

5. Smitty and Irv's life experiences may have caused them to have different perspectives on issues as adults. How would that have challenged their friendship? How might it have enhanced their friendship?

FAMILY & FATHERHOOD

1. What do you think was God's purpose when creating the family unit?

2. How is a family made? How would you define "family"?

3. Imagine you were fifteen-years old and found out similar news the same way Smitty learned about his background. How do you think it would've affected you?

4. Why do you think Uncle Charlie didn't tell Smitty the truth about his birth?

5. How do you think fatherhood is regarded in America today? Consider what you see in movies, television and other forms of the media.

6. Suppose someone doesn't know or has a difficult relationship with their father. How might that affect their view or relationship with God the Heavenly Father?

FAITH & LEGACY

1. Have you ever thought about what you want to leave behind when you depart this earth? Who would you want to have influenced?

2. Think of someone who has already died who influenced your life. What did they leave you?

3. Do you think heaven is a comforting story or a real place?

4. In the New Testament Jesus says, "*In My Father's house are many dwelling places; if it were not so, I would have told you; for I go to prepare a place for you.*" *(John 14:2)* Your view of Jesus influences how you hear his words. So what do you think about Jesus? What do you think about his statement?

5. Consider the book title *The Legacy of Nobody Smith.* Who do you think is the nobody? Smitty? Uncle Charlie? Or someone else?

ACKNOWLEDGMENTS

Writing this book has been an amazing – and a long – adventure. I never would have completed it without the help of so many, but most especially my wonderful husband. He was the first to introduce me as "a writer." This book is one of many dreams he's helped fulfill. Darling, you forever have all my love and respect.

For everyone else who ever encouraged me, thank you! Below are a few of the people who come to mind.

Thank you...

Connie Almony – Thank you for always being a click away. What an encouragement you have been!

Jane Basil – You picked the best man ever to be my dad. Your lifetime of support, love and laughter are my heart's treasures.

The Birthday Club – Vicki Duncan, Kater Leatherman, and Tecla Murphey – Your inspiration, laughter, and love of writing are the best thing in town. Who do we celebrate next?

The Black Writers' Guild of Baltimore – It's been too long since I've been able to be with you, but I'll always hold dear your warm welcome. There are so many stories that need to be told.

Janelle Brown – You gave delightful insight and critique. Beautiful Niece, you're the most determined and faithful young woman I know. Don't ever stop being you.

Lori Brown – My first friend, my sister. Thank you for always cheering me on even through these recent sojourning years. You are my hero.

Kathy Brazby – Before we even met in Colorado, you were a friend to Janelle and me. Thank you for sharing your heart, family, and knowledge of sheep.

Julie Coleman – You faithfully pushed me when I was weary and ignored my laments. Let's meet for coffee!

The Evans & Smith Family – You welcomed me whenever our paths crossed in family members' homes, hospital waiting rooms, and at funerals. It has been an honor.

Tony Evans – Your years of teaching over the airwaves have deeply impacted my life. Thank you for honoring your Mama and your Aunt's request for a foreword.

Karen Fitzgerald – Your reading, support, and understanding hugs when my body hurts are deeply appreciated.

Fowler United Methodist Church – You welcomed me with smiles and open arms. It's been too long since I've been able to worship with you and I miss you.

Jeannie Malkiewicz – My very first reader, I'll meet you for coffee anytime, anywhere!

Meghan McKnight – Your insights and encouragement were on a completely different version of this story so long ago. Thanks for believing in me way back when.

Robin Patchen – Your red pen was a magic wand for my writing, and made my Cinderella efforts ready for the ball. Thank you for your professional insight, editing, and encouragement.

Emily Rodgers – You read, taught me to knit, and prayed at stoplights. You are forever my sister.

Louise Smith – You shared your dear husband with me during his last months on planet earth. Our times around the kitchen table were an honor I will never forget.

Heavenly Father, thank you for helping me keep my promise. Do with it what you will. Amen.

For more information on Jesus
or the ministry of Dr. Tony Evans
go to www.TonyEvans.org

For more information on the author
go to www.Leslie Basil Payne.com